THE BASEMENT ANGEL

LeeAnn McChristian

Inscript

The Basement Angel

To my precious mother, Helen "Janie" Ash
You have always been my inspiration.

FOREWORD

Hello fellow readers,

If you are like me, when you first crack open a book, you are eager to get right into the story. But may I encourage you… do not skip over the prologue! It is a concise and sound treatise on angels. As she rightly points out, they are not who our culture often portrays them to be.

In the pages that follow, you will discover not only what sound doctrine looks like, but a touching story of grace, love, and redemption. Knowing LeeAnn as I do, it does not surprise me in the least that she would meld together such a beautiful story with such endearing truth.

I have had the privilege of knowing LeeAnn for, well, longer than either of us would care to disclose. And my life is richer for having her in it. We worked together side-by-side for many years building people up in their faith and loving them where they are. I am glad she finally answered the call to write this book and acquiesced to the persistent nudges of several friends to finish it. It has been been several years in the making, but the wait was worth it!

This book is for everyone – young or old, male or female, Christian or skeptic. You will find yourself in here, and you will find God in here. Blessings await.

So get comfortable. And I sure hope you don't have anything else scheduled soon, because you won't want to put this book down!

Hospitably,

Jon Sherman

Executive Coach

Former Senior Pastor, Trinity Bible Church

ACKNOWLEDGMENTS

*Y*ears ago, God placed this story of redemption on my heart. I shared the idea with a handful of people, hoping someone else might bring it to life, but they encouraged me to embrace it myself, since it was entrusted to me. At first, the task seemed daunting, but as I pressed on, God unveiled new layers of the story in ways that surprised and inspired me. There were moments when I questioned my ability and wondered if I was truly meant to write this book. Yet, time and again, God gently guided me back, reminding me that this story was always His.

I have been surrounded by many supportive "angels" who cheered me on, lifted my spirits, and covered me in prayer throughout this journey. Thank you, Mom, for your loving encouragement and wise advice on what makes for a good story. Janet Crain, your unwavering belief in me from the very first page gave me the courage to keep writing, and I am deeply grateful. To my "Friend for Christ," Liz Juarez, your steadfast support and faith in me—especially when mine faltered—has been a priceless blessing. And to my daughter, Megan

Parker, your gentle honesty and heartfelt encouragement have meant everything to me.

I am also deeply grateful to Val Woodward, Sarah Eggleston, Gloria Ray, Leslie Webster, and Carolyn Johnson for reading my early manuscript. Your enthusiasm and thoughtful feedback have been a lasting source of encouragement.

Finally, I want to thank my pastor, Jon Sherman. The way you dove into my book and wrote a foreword in just a couple of weeks speaks volumes about your generous spirit and steadfast friendship. I treasure the memories we built together in ministry and thank God for every moment spent serving alongside you. Your graciousness and support continue to inspire and guide me as I move forward.

My hope is that readers will discover through this book that no matter how deep their struggle, God's redeeming love can reach anyone and bring them into His glorious light.

For I am convinced that neither death nor life, neither angels nor demons, neither the present nor the future, nor any powers, neither height nor depth, nor anything else in all creation, will be able to separate us from the love of God that is in Christ Jesus our Lord. Romans 8:38-39

PROLOGUE

Angels are real. They are not glorified human beings. People do not die and become angels, complete with a halo and wings. Neither are they cute, chubby babies floating on soft, white clouds while strumming a golden harp. Angels do not marry, and they do not reproduce. Unlike the Lord Jesus, they are not omnipotent, omniscient, or omnipresent. God created them for Himself.

So, who are they? First, angels serve as God's messengers, communicating His will to humanity. In addition, they are ministering spirits sent out by God to give aid for the sake of those who will inherit salvation. They serve at the Lord's discretion to protect, provide, deliver, strengthen, and encourage humankind.

Few people have seen an angel, but they are all around us, whether we believe in them or not. Although they are spirits, they can take human form when the occasion demands. And, when the occasion demands, God can send an angel in a completely different form *and* in a completely unique way.

It is just a matter of perception.

CHAPTER 1

Wednesday, December 31, 2008

The predicted cold front furiously roars across the Red River from Oklahoma into North Texas, smashing against the man's house just before midnight. Each blast of frigid wind hammers the old house, rattling its weary bones and snatching the man from a deep, uneasy sleep. In the blue-tinged twilight glow of the television, he raises his head, blinking away sleep. He glances at the clock, its hands barely visible in the darkness. Not only is a new day approaching, but also a new year. He slumps back against the chair, a low curse escaping his lips. Now wide awake, he knows another long night looms ahead. Another sleepless night wrestling with the relentless grip of the past. The storm raging outside mirrors his own turmoil within. The past holds him in its cruel embrace, a constant, echoing voice that reminds him there is no escape.

Covered under a mound of quilts, he brushes his hands over the surface in a desperate hunt for the television remote. Television is his escape, his only defense against the storm of his own internal thoughts. Impatience flares. "Where is that damn remote?" he snarls, patting his lap furiously. Changing the channel will shield him from the torment of watching the superficial, smiling faces of revelers celebrating a new year, a celebration he finds meaningless. Too late. A deafening cheer erupts from the screen, "5...4...3...2...1... HAPPY NEW YEAR!" followed at once by a chorus of drunken voices singing "Auld Lang Syne."

The camera slowly pans the crowd of happy people, stopping to focus on the proverbial lovers sharing a kiss in anticipation of their new year together. Their happiness is a stark contrast to his solitary existence. He raises an empty hand in a phantom toast. "Happy New Year," he whispers, his voice dry and hollow. Then, raising his arm higher, he adds, "And to hell with all of you." Bitter sarcasm is an automatic defense, a shield against the pain, but it offers no warmth in the empty room. "Now, where's that stupid remote?" he mutters, fingers still blindly searching. Finally, he finds it buried under layers of quilts. With the same cold precision usually reserved for his Colt 45 when at the gun range, he aims the remote across his arm at the television screen. His final act of defiance. "And that's a good night to all of you," he whispers. A simple click extinguishes the dim glow of the television, plunging the room into total darkness. The chill is immediate, a tangible presence that seeps through the walls with each gust of wind. He rubs his arms against the chill, pulling the top quilt closer to his chin. Powerless to stop the encroaching cold, he sinks deeper into the recliner.

The gruffness of his voice reflects his despair. "I may know a lot about carpentry, but an old broken-down gas furnace," his voice trails off, "not so much. And those damn repairmen are expensive, too. Hell, everything's expensive when you're broke." He shivers, despite the heavy layers of warmth, as the familiar voice continues its assault, holding him captive, reminding him that there is no escape.

Attempting to stop the onslaught of self-pity rarely occurs to him any longer. After all, the past year had been brutal, especially for carpenters such as himself. Now, the current mortgage crisis has given little hope that 2009 would be any better. People no longer enjoyed luxuries such as building or remodeling, and, if they did, they were cautious of a failing economy. Large jobs were gone, leaving only minor ones, few and far between. He has every right to curse his luck. His face hardens as bitter thoughts swirl through his mind. "They can keep sending me bills month after month," he growls, "and I'll keep ignoring them. You can't get blood from a turnip."

Unopened envelopes lie scattered across the kitchen table, a rising tide of demands he refuses to acknowledge. He knows their contents: the electric company, the gas company, the phone company, the mortgage company; everyone wanted their share of what he did not have—money. His bank account is a barren wasteland, with only a few dollars as its occupants. He does not have a credit card. "Never believed in 'em. I pay as I go," he often proudly declared as though that fact made him a little better than the average person.

Truthfully, he hated having debt, but what can he do? After all, it is not his fault, but the damn economy, or so he tells himself.

Among the unopened bills, the remains of several half-eaten meals sit like forgotten dreams. Sniffing the air, he lightly pinches his nose. The rancid smell of rotten food is more noticeable in the dark. *This place stinks just like my life stinks.* He is unable to remember the last time his home was thoroughly cleaned. *Probably not in the last fourteen years,* he guesses. *And, probably not in the next fourteen years.* He is not about to clean on New Year's Day, not with football games on all day. He is an expert at excuses, not just for cleaning but for whatever he does not want to do. Sarcasm, blaming others, and excusing his actions help him justify his pitiful life.

Desperately yearning to sleep, he squeezes his eyes shut, trying to clear his mind, but it is useless. He cracks one eye open. The blinking red light of the answering machine pulses incessantly, reminding him of the encroaching disaster. The mortgage lender calls daily now. "Eighteen years of faithful payment," he mumbles to the silence. "Now, I miss a few months, and they're threatening foreclosure? Fine, let them take this crumbling shell. It ain't worth much anyway." Complaining was useless. To them, he was just an account number in their ledger, not a person.

The passage of time has taken its toll on his little house, making it unsellable in the current downturned market. A long, shaky breath fills his lungs with the cold air. "I should've sold," he sighs, the words heavy with a regret that was unfamiliar, unwelcome. He saw again the faces of the young family next door, their earnest request, his own self-serving refusal to budge on the price. His pride and greed had driven them to another house a block away. He pushes the memory aside, a familiar defense mechanism kicking in. "No one takes advantage of me," he declares to the empty room, "not then and not now." His words are only an attempt to drown out the voice of his conscience.

The night air offers no comfort, leaving him chasing sleep in vain. His thoughts, unwelcome guests, turn inevitably to Mandy. He fights to keep them at bay, but tonight, the memories flood his mind. This was the year she would have stepped across the stage as a young woman of eighteen and accepted her high school diploma. But her face at that age is a ghost, a blur of his mind's eye. Only glimpses of the four-year-old remained—sharp, vivid details. She had long, soft brown hair and the sweetest little gummy smile. She had her mother's smile. The bigger she grinned, the more gum you saw rather than teeth. His little girl had a precocious sense of humor, too. Strange how a four-year-old could deliver a punch line with the finesse of a professional, but she could. And then, a memory, a sudden burst of laughter, of a joke told, and she was before him, vibrant and real, as if the years had not passed, as if she had not been gone.

"Knock, knock, Daddy." Mandy's eyes gleamed with anticipation.

"Who's there?" He always played along, even with a familiar joke.

"Mandy." Her lips twitched, trying to hide a mischievous smile.

He had not heard this little joke before. "Mandy who?" Dutifully, he answered as expected.

Putting her hands on her hips, she rolled her eyes, pretending to be indignant. "Duh, you're my Daddy! Shouldn't you know my last name?" Unable to keep a straight face any longer, she fell to the floor in a fit of giggles. "I got you, Daddy!"

She got him, all right. Got him right in the heart!

Memories of his little girl flood his mind, a bittersweet tide. His life as a carpenter, chasing jobs wherever they led, had meant long stretches away, and Mandy hated it. He could still feel the small, firm grip of her hand on his, hear her voice, earnest and demanding, "Promise you won't be gone so long next time, Daddy. You have to pinkie swear!" she exclaimed, holding up her chubby, pink finger.

He drew a deep breath and exhaled slowly. "Mandy, sweetie, I can't make that promise. You know I must work hard because a man takes care of his family." He gave her a pleading look, but Mandy's stubborn persistence showed no signs of backing down. "Sometimes that means I must go out of town. Just remember, I only do it because I love you and Mommy so much."

"I know, I know, Daddy. Mommy said the same thing." Hands on tiny hips, she stuck out her jaw in defiance. "But that doesn't mean I have to like it!" She ended her last statement with a slight stamp of her tiny foot for emphasis.

He could not help but laugh. "Good! I don't want you to ever like it when I'm gone. You know, Mandy, I'm in big trouble the day you and Mommy stop fussing at me for being gone!"

Mandy wagged her tiny finger at him. "I'm not gonna ever stop fussin' at you, Daddy. Mommy says it's our job."

He continued to grin. "And you both are good at your job!"

People referred to Mandy as a "daddy's girl," and it was true. Of course, she adored her mother, but whenever she needed comfort, she came to him first. At times, he worried Liz might be jealous, but she was quick to give reassurance.

"Little girls need strong relationships with their daddies," Liz often reminded him. "I have a great relationship with my dad, and look how good I turned out!"

A heavy sigh escapes him as he closes his eyes, the memories crashing in like waves. The thought of Mandy brought sorrow, but Liz…Liz was a different kind of pain, a profound, lingering emptiness. Liz was right, though. She was more than good. She was perfect.

He had married later than some, but, for him, he had found Liz exactly when he was meant to. That moment arrived on a beautiful spring day in 1989, when a captivating young woman asked to sit beside him on a park bench.

"Not my bench." He did not mean to sound so brusque—especially upon seeing how pretty she was, so he quickly softened his tone. "You can sit wherever you like."

"Oh, it is your bench...your butt's on it, so it must be yours."

Her warm smile, along with the sparkle in her big brown eyes, instantly impressed him. Reluctantly, he gave a shrug, then moved over. "Fine then. Have a seat."

Sitting side by side, they both silently stared off into the distance. He was a quiet man, not necessarily shy, but quiet. Thoughtful conversation in a small group was fine, but idle chit-chat was something he detested. Usually, he said what needed to be told and not much more, but now, he found himself trying to think of something to say to the beautiful woman sitting next to him. Thankfully, she was the one who finally broke the awkward silence.

"So, what do you think about the Rangers bringing on Nolan Ryan?" She stared in the distance, a slight smile playing on her lips.

"Can't hurt and possibly could help. I suppose he still has a few good years left in him." He could not believe she was talking about sports, especially baseball!

"I don't know about that," she said, turning towards him, cocking her head. "Seems to me, forty-two is a little too old for a pitcher in the major leagues. I know he's the strike-out king, but his arm can't last forever. I think the Rangers should have gone after younger blood. Someone with a longer career ahead of them rather than a guy who's on his way out."

"Oh, so you think forty-two is old?" A smile began to form on his lips, his eyes gleaming.

"It's certainly not young! I mean, for a pitcher, you gotta admit, it's pretty old."

"Maybe so. Come October, we will see what 'old man Ryan' has done for the team. Could be the shot in the arm the Rangers desperately need." He paused, then added casually, "I'm forty-three myself and not even close to being on my way out."

She smiled lamely, giving him a sideways glance. "Oops! You don't look that old...not that forty-three is old..."

He grinned broadly, thoroughly enjoying her frantic backtrack as she tried to convince him of what she really meant.

"Of course, I was speaking in the context of baseball. I never meant to imply an ordinary man in his forties was old...not that you are ordinary...I just meant, for baseball, forty-two is old...but it's not really old when you're a man like Nolan Ryan...not that you're not a man like Nolan Ryan..." The more she talked, the more flustered she became, finally giving him a pleading look. "Please, help me out of this hole I'm digging for myself!"

Unable to contain his amusement, he began to laugh. "It's okay. I knew what you meant. But you must admit, you set yourself up for that one."

"Yeah, open mouth, insert foot." Rolling her eyes upwards, she exhaled deeply. "This may surprise you, but that's not the first time I've done so."

He chuckled. "I have a feeling you're a gal full of surprises."

"Maybe I am!" She stuck out her hand. "By the way, my name is Elizabeth, and, since I know how old you are…you should know I'm twenty-eight. Obviously, a very young and stupid twenty-eight."

His rough hand engulfed hers. Delicate and warm, he held on a little longer than intended. "Young, yes… stupid, no," he assured her. "Nice to meet you, Elizabeth. You wouldn't have any opinions about the Cowboys, would you?"

Raising her eyebrows, she looked at him questioningly. "Do you really want to know, or are you just hoping I'll make a fool of myself again?"

He liked this girl. "I really want to know."

Time passed quickly that afternoon. Lunch, work, errands—all became unimportant the longer they talked. Mostly, Elizabeth did the talking. She accomplished what most people found extremely difficult with him—holding a conversation. And much to his surprise, he enjoyed it. This young woman had depth and maturity equal to his own. In addition, the twinkle in her eyes was mesmerizing.

"You seem like the strong, silent type," she observed through the course of their discussion. "Me, well, I'm the strong, talkative type! My dad always said I could talk the ears off a stalk of corn."

He agreed with her father's observation, yet every word from her lips held him captive. Usually, talkative people annoyed him. Their chatter was simply filling empty air in his estimation, but Elizabeth was different. She was genuinely eager to know more about him. Being quiet, he was often overlooked by women and rarely went on dates. However, by most people's standards, he was considered a handsome man. Chatty women seemed foolish to him, and as for quiet women—well, there rarely was enough conversation to even start a relationship. This time, the beautiful woman sitting next to him seemingly possessed every quality for which he had searched. Interestingly, he had not known he was searching.

"So, what makes you happy?" she asked, tilting her head slightly. Such a personal question surprised him, yet he did not mind.

"I don't know. Never really thought about it."

"Well then, let me rephrase my question. What do you do for fun?"

He shrugged his shoulders. "I like to go to the shooting range and fish a little now and then, but mostly, I just work. I suppose my work makes me happy, if you want to call it that. It certainly leaves me feeling satisfied."

Her face lit up. "Work makes me happy, too. I am a schoolteacher. Fourth grade. What do you do?"

"I'm a carpenter. I mainly do remodels, but I've built a few houses, too, from the ground up."

"You must be quite creative," she said, smiling. "I like people who enjoy working with their hands."

"I don't know how creative I am, but I do like to take a piece of wood and make something useful out of it. My father was a carpenter and taught me all I know. He took me to work with him from the time I was five years old. I guess you could say it's in my blood."

"There must be other things you like to do?" Her persistence amused him.

"I like sports, but you've probably figured that out. I am more of a spectator these days, but, once, in my younger days..." He paused and glanced in her direction. Did she get the joke?

She smiled. "You aren't going to let me forget how foolish I was, are you?"

"Nope." He returned her smile with a wink. "As I was saying, in my younger days, I was quite an athlete. Growing up in a small town, I played a variety of sports, including football, baseball, and basketball. But baseball has always been my favorite. I even coached a Little League team for a few years. What about you? Play any sports?"

"Nothing conventional. I rode horses. I dreamed of being a professional barrel racer when I was a little girl, but God had different plans for me."

"How could you know that?" He was genuinely curious. How could she really know?

"I prayed and asked Him what He wanted me to do with my life. I left it up to God to close or open the doors He wanted me to go through. The barrel racing door closed, and the teaching door opened." She gave a little shrug. "So here I am!"

"And teaching little kids makes you happy?"

"Why, yes, it does," she replied in earnest. "I love my students. Sometimes, I learn more from them than they learn from me. But I love lots of other things as well."

"Such as?" he asked innocently, not knowing how long the list would be.

"Of course, I love my family. We are all close, but my sister, Leslie, is my best friend. Let's see...I love horses, obviously, but then, I love all animals. I love Texas and being from Texas. The bluebonnets this spring are amazing. So, where are you from?"

"Texas! Born and raised. Wouldn't want to live any other place." Good to know they shared the same passion for their beloved state. "Is that the end of your list?"

She laughed. "I'm just getting started! How much time do you have?"

"Go on. I'm listening." He suddenly had all the time in the world.

"Let's see…I love country music. I prefer the older stuff, like Waylon and Willie, more than what you hear on the radio today." She took a quick breath, then continued. "Oh, and I love going out to Lake Texoma. My dad brings his boat up here every summer, and we spend all day water skiing, fishing, and exploring the coves. I love Mexican food, and I love ice cream. Chocolate mint is my favorite!" She paused, turning serious. "My list could go on and on, but there is one thing I love more than anything else."

"And, what's that?" Her list was already extensive; what more could she possibly love?

She took a deep breath. "I love God. I love Him above and beyond anyone or anything else."

Her declaration was unexpected, leaving him unsure how to respond. Clergymen might feel like this, or maybe a nun, but ordinary people? How do you love someone you can't see or touch? It was a mystery to him, but he did not care. All he knew by the end of the day was how desperately he wanted to be on her Love List.

Bachelorhood had offered a comfortable simplicity. He did as he pleased when he pleased, responsible only for himself. But his world shifted the day he married Elizabeth, just six months after their chance meeting in the park. On their wedding day, a new kind of responsibility began, one he embraced wholeheartedly. Love, he discovered, was never as complete or fulfilling until it meant caring for another. He loved Elizabeth fiercely, loved their life together. He knew his place was not first, but he was happy to be on her Love List, a list where God held the top spot. He understood that her love for him was deeply rooted in her faith, and if that meant God was part of the equation, he gladly accepted the whole package.

But now, he did not think much about God. At least not since Elizabeth and Mandy were gone. Elizabeth's lifelong faith contrasted sharply with his own fragmented experience. Occasionally, his mother had taken him and his brother to the local Baptist church when they were children, but his father had refused to attend.

"That place is full of hypocrites." It was always the same old excuse from his father. "Besides, the good Lord and I have an understanding. I can worship Him just as well from my fishing boat as I can sittin' in a pew."

It had been hard to argue with his dad's logic, and eventually even his mother stopped trying. Occasionally, he had attended Vacation Bible School, but only to be with friends. One summer, his best friend invited him to a revival. He was not sure what a "revival" was, but his mother encouraged him to attend. At the end of the week, all the kids "walked the aisle," including him. The pastor declared they were all saved, but, truthfully, he never quite understood the significance. Not much changed after that, but his mother was happy, and that was important.

Elizabeth's deep reliance on God had always intrigued and baffled him. His upbringing had preached independence. "Seems a good man takes care of him and his," a statement he often proudly quoted. Sure, he believed in something, a Higher Power, but daily prayer? Regular interaction? That was not part of his world of self-reliance. Even in a tight spot, he was not likely to ask for God's help. "The good Lord helps those who help themselves. I got myself in this mess; I can get myself out. God has more important things to deal with than my problems." A mantra he often quoted. His stubborn principles had never changed throughout the years.

Fifteen months into their marriage, Amanda Joy burst into their world. She instantly stole their hearts, securing a permanent spot on both of their "Love Lists." Though a brief period of colic challenged them, she blossomed into a perfect little girl—bright, energetic, beautiful, and completely adored by him. He eagerly tracked her growth, cherishing every milestone: her first tooth, the wobbly sits, triumphant first steps, the joyful pedaling of her tricycle, and that poignant first day of preschool. In hindsight, he wished he had slowed down, allowing those precious moments to linger instead of rushing to the next achievement. For, as the saying goes, hindsight is truly 20/20.

During the early nineties, his skills as a master carpenter kept him busy, in high demand for projects both grand and small. Bachelorhood faded into a distant memory, replaced by the profound pride of being a family man devoted to his young wife and cherished daughter. Their days were predictable yet filled with happiness. As a teacher, Liz relished the summer months spent at home with Mandy, a time she deeply desired. Through careful saving and sacrifice, they bought a modest house south of Sherman, with dreams of transforming it into a testament to his carpentry talents. Their life was not without its challenges, but it was good—wonderfully good.

A fleeting moment of peace comes with thoughts of Elizabeth and Mandy. The cozy cocoon of blankets finally warms his chilled body, allowing his eyelids to grow heavy with much-needed sleep. Drowsiness is a welcome relief. Eventually, he relaxes, and his chin falls to his chest, only to be snapped back up by a familiar, venomous voice.

"Yeah, but memories are not reality," it hisses. It is the same discouraging voice he hears almost every day. "You have enough trouble without dredging up the past. When was the last time you put your arms around a memory? They were the only people who truly cared about you, and now they're gone, never to return. You're all alone in this world, so what's the use in trying anymore?"

Fully awake again, he tries to push the voice out of his head, but it is useless. The voice is right. The voice tells the truth, and there is nothing he can do about it. God had cruelly taken his girls, leaving him alone for the rest of his life, but it is hardly a life. He might go through the motions of life, but he is not truly alive. Even his home is just the shell of a house. Photographs, toys, candles, jewelry, clothes, Liz's trinkets—all were given away. He wants no reminders of what he has lost. Erasing their memory might help erase his hurt. But it was no use; the ache remains. Elizabeth would be horrified by his neglect: the peeling paint, the leaking roof, the rot, the failing systems. But her potential disapproval does not penetrate the wall of his apathy. The house he had dreamed of transforming into a home became just "a wooden building" fourteen years ago, offering only inadequate shelter from the elements: cold in winter, hot in summer.

The night drags on as his thoughts race from one subject to another. Sleep is not going to happen tonight. The last time he slept through the entire night without periods of wakefulness was nothing more than a dim memory. It had not always been that way. His ability to fall asleep easily, even in the middle of an argument, had once been a source of frustration to Elizabeth.

"How can you sleep when we haven't settled this issue?" Liz would sit up in bed, prop a pillow behind her back, thus indicating she was settling in for a long talk.

"Because we don't have to resolve everything tonight." He made no attempt to hide his irritation.

"Please, Lizzie, let's talk tomorrow. I must get some sleep. I have an early day tomorrow."

"Well, I can't sleep knowing..." Too tired to keep his eyes open, he never heard the end of her sentence.

Things are certainly different now. Most nights, he attempted to sleep in his old recliner. Although held together with duct tape, it was the one thing he had not parted with after Liz had left. A poor substitute for a bed, it was not necessarily comfortable, but it was comforting. It had been a gift from Elizabeth on their first anniversary.

"I need you to take a stroll with me," Liz told him early that Saturday morning.

"Now?" he asked. "I need to call the dealership and find out what time my truck will be ready."

"Okay, but hurry because I want to show you something, and we need to get back here before the Longhorns play this afternoon." Her eyes sparkled, telling him that whatever she had planned must have something to do with their anniversary.

He left the room while she waited patiently for him to make the call. After a few minutes, he came back, brows furrowed, frustration written on his face.

"We can take that walk now. My truck won't be ready until Monday. I guess I'll have to call and get someone to pick me up for work." He hated depending on others, even for something as simple as a ride to work.

"Maybe you'll cheer up when you see my surprise. Come on." She took him by the hand and led him a few blocks down the street to a house with numerous items for sale in the front yard.

"It's over here." She guided him to the front porch, where a large, ugly, olive green and dirty yellow-striped recliner sat. "Well, what do you think?" Her eyes beamed brightly. She could barely contain her excitement.

"Uh...you want the truth?" he asked, scratching his jaw. Liz eagerly nodded. "That's about the ugliest piece of furniture I've ever seen." The words had barely left his mouth before he instantly regretted his honesty. The disappointment and hurt on Liz's face was heartbreaking. There were times the truth was not necessary, and this was one of those times. "I mean, it may be ugly, but it certainly appears comfortable." He walked to the recliner and sat down. It was an ill attempt to rectify his tactlessness, something his mother had warned him about long ago. Words, once spoken, may be forgiven, but not soon forgotten.

Liz gave him a long, thoughtful look. "It's okay," she said calmly. "I thought you would enjoy a recliner to sit in while watching ball games. My dad always had one, so I thought you needed one too. I'll talk to the owner and see if I can get my money back." Her earlier excitement had dissipated faster than a puff of smoke in the wind.

He quickly stood up, grabbing her hand. "No, Lizzie, please don't do that. I'm sorry. I spoke without thinking. You know I have no taste when it comes to furniture." With a sheepish grin, he knelt on one knee. "I would love to have this fine piece of furniture from which to watch ballgames. My dad had one too, and I've always wanted one. It is an extremely thoughtful anniversary gift. Thank you, Babe."

"Are you sure?" she asked tentatively, eyeing him with suspicion

"I am absolutely positive!" He replied enthusiastically. He genuinely did not want to hurt her feelings.

"As soon as we get a little extra money, I promise I'll get the recliner recovered. In the meantime, I can clean the upholstery," Liz said, cheerfully optimistic once again.

"OK, done!" His smile quickly faded. "But how will we get it home since my truck is still in the shop?"

Liz looked down the street and then back at him. "Well, we could carry it home. It's not all that far."

Off they went, carrying that heavy recliner home between the two of them, arriving just in time for the Texas Longhorn game that afternoon, which he enjoyed sitting in his new recliner. That game was just the first of many he would watch from the old recliner over the years. Too many to count, but hundreds, he supposed. Now, he rarely leaves it except to grab something to eat or use the toilet. Funny thing, they never recovered it and, more than likely, he never would. It was old, worn, and tattered — just like him.

Like a train jumping the tracks, his memories jump to the night his perfectly created world came crashing down. He did not remember much about that night, and he did not want to remember. Squirming uneasily in the recliner, beads of sweat begin to form on his brow. It has been fourteen years, but the sickening feeling in his stomach is the same. Time heals all wounds? Not in his case. It seems like time stopped that night and never started again.

September 1995 was typically hot. Autumn did not arrive in Texas until November, so September was simply another month of summer. Elizabeth and Mandy had traveled down to the Hill Country to visit her parents for a long weekend. Too busy on a job to accompany them on the trip, he encouraged them to go anyway. The phone rang around four in the afternoon they were to return, waking him from a nap. It was Liz.

"Hey, Babe, hate to tell you, but we haven't left Mom and Dad's yet."

"You should be halfway home by now. What happened?" he asked, trying to hide his disappointment at this unexpected news. "Are you staying another night?"

"No...no, we're leaving in the next hour. Mandy's had such a wonderful time and begged me to let Dad take her fishing one last time this afternoon. They just got home, so we'll leave as soon as I wash the 'fish' smell off Mandy. Want to say hi to her before we leave?" He heard the muffled sound of the phone being passed to Mandy.

"Hi, Daddy. I caught a fish!" Mandy proudly exclaimed before he could even say hello.

"You did? That's great! What kind of fish did you catch?"

"It was a kitty fish, and it was really ugly, with whiskers. Papa took it off the hook for me and threw it back in the water. We used old bread rolled up in a little ball to catch it. Did you know kitty fish like bread? Papa said the fish was too small for Nana to cook. I don't like fish. Not even the fish that Nana cooks. Have you ever seen a kitty fish before, Daddy? I think..." He hated to interrupt, but he also knew Mandy could talk without taking a breath—much like her mother.

"Whoa, little lady, I can only answer one question at a time. First, do you mean catfish instead of kitty fish?"

Mandy giggled. "Uh, yeah, I think Papa said catfish. But it didn't look like a cat!"

"I've caught several catfish before, and I've even caught a few with your papa. Have you had a fun time with your grandparents?"

"I've had the best time, Daddy. We went out on the boat, and the water was still warm enough to swim. Then, Papa made a big fire in the fire pit, and Mommy let me cook my own hot dog, and Nana let me make 'some mores'!" Her voice, full of excitement, made him smile.

"'Some more what?" he teased.

"You know, Daddy!" She didn't miss a beat. "Those things you like with graham crackers, chocolate, and marshmallows. 'Member, you always say, 'I want some mores.'"

"I know what they are, honey. I was just teasing. I'm glad you've had a fun time, but I'm ready for my girls to come home. This old house has been lonely without your giggles." Mandy giggled in response. "Now, go get cleaned up and hurry home. Tell Nana and Papa 'hi' from me and put your mother back on the phone."

"Hey," Elizabeth said. "If we leave by five, then we should be home before ten. Hopefully, Mandy will sleep most of the way. That little girl is worn out from her busy weekend. Don't feel like you need to wait up for us."

"Oh yeah, like that's gonna happen. Of course, I'll wait up. I can't wait to see my girls. Please be careful, and get some coffee if you get sleepy."

"We'll be fine. Don't worry," she reassured him. "I can't wait to sleep in my own bed tonight next to you."

"Same here," he replied with a sigh. "See you soon. Bye, Babe." He brought the receiver down from his ear, then quickly back up. "Wait…wait!" he said, breathlessly.

"I'm still here. What is it?" she asked.

"I love you." Those three words, spoken often between them, were his last words to Elizabeth.

She chuckled lightly, "I love you too, honey. Bye." Her last words to him.

He waited, counting the seconds on the clock, each tick echoing the emptiness that had already begun to settle in. The drone of the nightly news faded as his eyelids grew heavy. He soon sank deep into the recliner, his eyes falling shut despite his best efforts. A jarring ring around midnight shattered the quiet, yanking him from a restless sleep. Panic, cold and sharp, seized his chest the instant he saw the late hour. Elizabeth was not home.

"Hello?" His voice trembled with fear. He longed to hear his wife's sweet voice on the other end of the line, but a man's deep tones answered instead.

The call was brief but chilling, lasting only a few minutes. He hung up and stumbled across the room, collapsing to the floor, his mind in disbelief of the officer's sorrowful news. This cannot be real; it had to be a nightmare. "Oh my God!" He choked out the words. "This… can't…be…happening!" He huddled there on the floor for several minutes, unable to grasp the officer's words: drunk driver, head-on, both died upon impact. The phrases became a broken record in his throbbing head. His voice grew louder. "This… can't…be…happening!" His words escalated into a tormented wail of despair. "NO—NO—NO!" Fist clenched, he pounded his skull. The room began to spin with the rush of blood to his head. A wave of nausea doubled him over. Retching violently, he emptied his stomach until his body was empty of everything but the grief. He lay his head on the tile floor, hoping the coolness would soothe his burning skin. Tears began to flow. Hesitant at first, they became a torrent, turning into a tidal wave of anguish. Sorrow and grief devoured his heart, leaving him bereft of any feelings. In a sense, he died that day as well.

Following the accident, the days blurred into one another. Liz's parents and her sister arrived in the early morning hours, taking over the sad preparation of the funeral for the two people he loved most in the world. His parents had passed on years earlier, and he had not seen his estranged brother, Gabe, since high school. As a result, he found no comfort from his side of the family.

He stood in line with Liz's family, greeting the attendees at the memorial service. Above his mumbled "thanks," he could hear the hushed whispers of "lovely service," but to him, it was anything but. What was "lovely" about burying Liz and Mandy? They had barely lived, and now they were gone. He could not recall the pastor's sermon, except for a snippet: Liz's words about having no fear of death, believing God had a purpose for her, that life wasn't random, but full of "God-cidents." That was so like her, always so sure. But what about him? They might be with God, but he was left here, a hollow shell where a husband and father used to be.

He shivers, despite the rising heat in his face. Fourteen years of buried rage and frustration rise to the surface, like scum on a pond. Anger, bitterness, and resentment gnaw at him, just as cancer consumes a body, and the blame is clear…in fact, it has never been clearer. God. God is to blame for his misery. If this is how God loves, then he wants no part. How could anyone believe in—let alone love—a God so merciless, so vengeful, so selfish? A sneer twists his lips, his face resolute. "Not me." The words were a raw whisper. "No, sir, not me!"

Chapter 2

Thursday, January 1, 2009

The next day mirrors his mood—gray and bleak, a typical wintry Texas day. Easing himself out of the recliner, he stands and stretches, rubbing his forehead. A dull throb behind his eyes is a reminder of the long, sleepless night he suffered. Shuffling down the hallway to the bathroom, he swallows a couple of aspirins, hoping for a little relief. Turning, he glimpses himself in the vanity mirror, barely recognizing the disheveled old man glaring back. Running his hand over his face, he feels the stubble of a beard. "You need a shave, mister. You look eighty-three, not sixty-three." Turning sideways, he pokes his soft stomach. "And you better do something about that paunch. You're looking a little round." The silence of the reflection is deafening. "Oh? You don't care?" he challenges. "Fine. Neither do I."

Grabbing a beer from the almost-empty fridge, he settles back in his recliner for a marathon of classic New Year's Day football games. Watching football games had once been a passion, but now, it is more of a habit. Often, Liz and he took Mandy to the Sherman High School football games. Liz found a little Bearcat cheerleader uniform, which Mandy proudly wore to each game. She saw no difference between the home team and the opposition, but she cheered for every team, along with every player. Picturing her with pigtails flying while waving pompoms brings a soft smile to his face, but only briefly. Darkness always returned. The voice of hopelessness countered every positive thought. "That was then, this is now. You have nothing to live for any longer. No one cares about you. Your life is a waste." He cannot deny it; the emptiness has become his constant companion, and he is too tired to argue.

The Texas wind, fierce and unrelenting, seems determined to tear the little house apart. It howls and blusters all day, while he remains seated in his recliner, oblivious to the storm's fury, until the phone rings in the late afternoon.

"Hello," he abruptly declares, irritated at being disturbed just before the Rose Bowl kick-off.

The woman's voice on the other end of the line is hesitant. "Oh, sorry to bother you. I thought I would get an answering machine since it's New Year's Day."

"Well, you didn't. What can I do for you?" he gruffly replies. Immediately, he regrets the rough tone of his voice.

"Uh, well, your name was given to me by a friend for whom you did some carpentry work a few years ago. And, well, I wondered if you could come to my house and give me a quote on a small project?"

"I think I can work you in tomorrow, if that's okay?" His voice is lighter, trying to sound a little friendlier.

"Yes, tomorrow will be great. Say around three p.m.? I live in Denison. Sorry, forgot to tell you that."

"Denison, huh? Well, Denison isn't too far away. I can be there at three. So, what's your name and address?"

He knows the area where she lives. It is near the old downtown area and about forty minutes from his house. Although Denison, Texas, is a sister city to Sherman, he rarely went there. Not much is going on in sleepy old Denison these days, and, in fact, not much has gone on there for quite some time. Denison's only claim to fame is that it is the birthplace of President Dwight D. Eisenhower. Once, he had taken Mandy up to see the old house where the president had been born. Still, she was much too young to appreciate the historical significance. Much more exciting was the promised ice cream cone that was to follow their so-called history lesson. Like her mother, Mandy loved chocolate mint ice cream, or "green ice cream," as she liked to call it. Bringing it home as a treat for his girls would prompt a slight groan from Elizabeth.

"You know, you're the reason I can't stay on a diet!" she would say with a scowl, pretending irritation, all the while taking the bowl of ice cream he offered.

"Oh, hush, you don't need to diet. I love you the way you are, perfect in every way. Ice cream is meant to be enjoyed, so have at it!"

Her brows furrowed. "You say that now, but will you still love me when I am old, fat, and gray?"

What a preposterous question! His love for her was unconditional, and it did not matter how old, how fat, or even if she were purple! "Haven't you figured out by now that I love who you are. What you look like will never change my love. Besides, I am the one who will be old, fat, and gray long before you will."

Her demeanor promptly changed. "Will be? Who's to say you aren't already that way?" She poked him in the stomach and snickered. "Remember when I thought forty-two was old?"

"Yeah, and look what Nolan Ryan did for the Rangers. Three years later, and he's still the strike-out king."

"And three years later, I'm still the happiest girl in the world," she sighed. "Okay, I'll enjoy my ice cream... since you insist."

Her laughter, her happiness, and their shared joy were the foundation of his happiness. Now, without Liz and Mandy, his world was flat, devoid of color and light. God had stolen his happiness. God had robbed him of love.

Hanging up, a brief lightness lifts his spirits. *Time to get out of this house for a bit,* he thought, *a change of scenery will be good, and maybe this will be enough to keep the lights on another month.* But the glimmer of hope is fleeting, a dying ember in a cold hearth. Once again, the gloomy inner voice reminds him of reality, and if anything, he is a realist. Liz was the one with endless optimism in their family, a characteristic that had occasionally annoyed him.

"I swear, Lizzie! If the house were burning down, you would have a wiener roast!" he jokingly complained.

Smiling sweetly, she was quick to correct him. "Stop swearing! I would not have a wiener roast—it would be s'mores!"

"Yeah, yeah, always the optimist. Sometimes I think you live in La-la Land." That statement was sure to get under her skin.

"Well, at least I am not a pessimist—like some people I know." Her lips tightened, a signal that she was trying to restrain her frustration. "Why do you always think of the glass as half-empty instead of half-full?" Conclusive terms like "always" or "never" got under his skin, something she knew well.

"I'm not always a pessimist." He gave her a look of disdain. "I'm a realist. I just call it like I see it, and the glass usually looks half empty to me. You know I don't sugar-coat any situation."

She rolled her eyes. "That's an understatement!"

He continued, ignoring her remark. "I haven't gotten this far in life by keeping my head in the clouds. I have both feet planted firmly on the ground. My brother was like you, and look how that worked out for him."

"What do you mean by that?" By the tone of her voice, he knew she was offended. Being compared to his brother was not a compliment.

"Sorry, Liz," he quickly apologized. "I did not mean that in a negative way. I just meant he was an optimist, like you. Gabe was always looking for something better."

Liz interrupted with a laugh. "Always?"

This time, he rolled his eyes. "Yes, always, Miss Smarty Pants. Gabe was a dreamer who lived his life up in the clouds, refusing to face reality. While our father's grip tightened, Gabe yearned only to escape, for a life of boundless fun. He turned his back on our family—on me—in pursuit of that fantasy, leaving all of us behind."

"I'm sorry, Babe," her voice softened. "I know you miss your brother. Sometimes I even forget you have a brother. I'm sorry to say that I've neglected to pray for Gabe, but I assure you, I will from now on."

"Don't waste your breath, Lizzie. Sometimes, people are too far gone, even for God."

"That's not true. If Gabe is still alive, then it is never too late. And I can truly use the word never!" She reached out to hug him. "We are a good match, mister. You keep my feet on the ground, and I help you have a little fun now and then up in the clouds."

Right now, he would give anything to have a little of her optimism and encouragement. "But, she's not here and never will be again," the voice reminds him. "Never" is the sad truth.

USC's Rose Bowl victory was predictable, at least for him. Since childhood, he has possessed an almost eerie ability to call football games, a skill born not of luck but of diligently analyzing details and stats others overlooked. Gabe quickly recognized the potential, turning it into a lucrative betting operation. Every Bowl season, he would carefully consider the outcome of each game and give Gabe a list of his predictions. Not all of them were right, but enough were to ensure a tidy sum of money at the end of the season. Of course, Gabe took most of the money for himself, claiming he did all the work. Still, there was usually enough for something special— a new fishing rod or baseball glove. Sure, Gabe exploited his unique abilities, but it meant Gabe paid attention to him, and that meant more than money could buy.

"You know, kid...one day you and I will have it all." Gabe had promised. "We'll leave this town behind and head out for the big city like Dallas or Fort Worth. We won't answer to anyone but ourselves. We will live by our own rules. I've got big plans for the future, and you're coming with me."

That promise never came to fruition. Gabe left, vanished without a trace, taking his "big plans" with him, leaving his little brother behind. This was the one thing he could not predict—abandonment.

Chapter 3

Friday, January 2, 2009

Another sleepless night tossing and turning in bed finally drives him to the recliner as exhaustion claims him. Breakfast the next morning is simple: cold cereal along with a piece of slightly burnt toast. Making his way to the bathroom, he flips on the light only to see the same old disreputable man in the mirror from the day before. Turning his face from side to side, he critically examines his reflection. "You might look presentable with a good shave," he mutters, "But that gut is not going anywhere." Lack of work led to a lack of exercise, creating a vicious cycle. "Ya know, cowboy, in the words of our friend, Garth, 'you're much too young to feel this damn old!'"

He turns on the shower, and his image quickly fades as steam begins to fog the mirror. He steps under the spray, the warmth a welcome relief from the chill that seems to have settled in his bones. Just as the tension in his back begins to ease, the tiny bathroom goes dark.

"What the hell?" Feeling for the towel, he steps out of the shower and hastily wraps it around himself. "That better be a burnt bulb," he angrily mutters, walking down the hallway while leaving a trail of wet footprints behind. He rounds the corner to the living room only to find the entire house dark. No lights, no television, no blinking red light on the answering machine; everything is dark. A string of profanities erupts. "That stupid electric company did not waste one single minute gettin' back to work after the holidays. I bet they could not wait to shut off my power! Just wait 'til they hear from me!" He slams his fist against the wall, each step back to the darkened bathroom echoing his frustration. His tirade continues, "This is insane. They'd better fix this fast, or they will be dealing with a very angry man!"

Still damp from his disrupted shower, he yanks on his jeans and marches back to the living room. "Where's the number for that damn electric company?" he snarls, jabbing at the phone buttons with furious force. The usual pre-recorded maze of options feels like a deliberate insult this morning. When a woman's voice finally comes on the line, he launches into his complaint. Her attempts at reassurance mean nothing to him.

"Of course, sir, we understand how frustrating a power disruption can be. We can reinstate the service as soon as we receive $600.00, which includes your current and past due amounts. Oh, and there is a $50.00 reconnection fee, which you must pay as well. I am happy to take a credit card number over the phone and get your power restored at once."

"Look, ma'am, I don't think you understand. I don't have much money right now, and I don't have a credit card, but I do have a new job starting next week. I can pay the full amount then. Right now, though, it's freezing outside, and I need my power back on. I can go ahead and pay the fifty to reconnect if that would help." He can only hope there is at least fifty dollars still in his account.

"I am sorry, sir, but we have sent you notice after notice. I am afraid the grace period is over, and you will need to remit the full amount."

His face flushes with anger. "Did you hear anything I just told you, lady? I do not have that much money right now!" he shouts in frustration.

"I heard everything you told me, Sir," she calmly replies. "But you will need to remit the full amount…."

He slams the phone down, interrupting the representative. "Just as expected," he spat the words laced with venom. "They don't give a damn about anyone, especially me."

The Denison job is now his only hope; without it, he faces serious trouble. *Surely this day can't get any worse,* he thinks to himself. *Finding a way out of this mess is not going to be easy.*

He has only one thing of any real value, his Colt 45. Selling it could be a way out. A fair price was likely for the WW1 relic that had been his grandfather's, then given to him by his father on his eighteenth birthday. The thought sends a jolt of pain through him. It is not truly his to sell; it should have gone to Gabe, but Gabe had not been around to claim it for his own eighteenth birthday.

Memories of his family are painful, ones he usually shoves deep down. But the mention of the Colt 45 has brought them surging back. A massive heart attack at the age of seventy-two had claimed his father's life, barely a decade older than he is now. He can still feel the scorching summer heat, the dampness of sweat soaking their clothes as they worked side by side on that remodel job the day it happened. The memory is as sharp and clear as if it were yesterday.

"I gotta take a break and get a drink of water. This heat is about to do me in!" his dad had said.

"All right. I'll join you as soon as I finish nailing this header in place." He had an odd feeling watching his father disappear around the corner of the house. It was unusual for his dad to be the first one to recommend a break. In hindsight, he should have followed him. Maybe he could have done something. A few minutes passed, and still no sign of his father. "Hey, Dad! Bring me a bottle of water when you come back." He listened for a response, but there was only silence. He called again—still no response. A knot tightened in his gut; something was terribly wrong. Dropping his hammer, he sprinted around the corner of the house.

The sight that awaited him stole the air from his lungs: his father, slumped lifelessly beneath the shade tree, the water bottle still clutched in his hand. It was an image burned into his memory; one he would never forget.

He had grown up believing his father was invincible, a "man's man" respected throughout the community for his skill and integrity. Stern and stoic, his father rarely showed emotion even to his sons. To say his dad was opinionated was an understatement. Most people found his father abrasive and shied away from arguments with him. All except his older brother. Gabe had always been a rebel, even as a child. Gabe pushed the boundaries with their father, prompting his father's exasperated remarks like, "I give you an inch, son, and you take a mile!"

He and Gabe had been close, only two and a half years apart. Popular with everyone, Gabe was known as the "fun" brother of the two. He was the golden boy—smarter, better looking, funnier, braver, and more athletic than almost everyone else. Though a twinge of intimidation always lingered, he looked up to his older brother. They shared a mutual fear and respect for their father's authority, at least initially. High school brought a shift. Gabe began to pull away, a chasm growing between him and his parents. By graduation, Gabe was a stranger who rarely appeared at home. His friend and ally was gone, replaced by a distance that made it hard to even acknowledge him as a brother.

"Where're you going, Gabe?" It was only six p.m., but Gabe was already heading out for the evening.

"None of your business, Bro." Scarcely seventeen, Gabe had bought himself an old Chevy pickup. Where the money had come from was a mystery. He suspected his brother had obtained it less than honorably.

"Can I come with you, Gabe? I don't want to be stuck here by myself all evening." He knew the answer but asked anyway.

"Nah, Bro, you don't need to hang around with me. I've got important things to do tonight. Besides, one of us should keep the old man happy, but it ain't gonna be me!"

"Aw, Gabe, you could make Dad happy too," he pleaded in earnest. "Just stay home once in a while and try talking to Dad instead of constantly arguing, for a change." Attempting to persuade his brother to make the first move was useless.

"If Dad wants to talk, then he can come to me. He's the father, and it should be his job!" Gabe reached out for a fist bump. "Hey, Bro, I'm not mad at you. Man, I just can't stay in this house much longer. I've got my life to live. Once I turn eighteen… I'm outta here!" Gabe strode out the door, leaving a trail of disappointment behind.

Drugs were suspected, a silent intruder in their home, but neither mother nor father dared to name it. Instead, their father chose to challenge the behavior rather than the reason behind it, resulting in loud, lengthy arguments followed by prolonged periods of icy silence. Gabe, as unyielding as his father, transformed their once peaceful home into a battleground with no winners. As promised, Gabe left the family home the day he turned eighteen. No one had seen him since. A desperate search for Gabe after their father died led nowhere. Each lead was a dead-end. He could only assume the worst: Gabe was either dead or in prison.

Five years later, their mother lost her battle with breast cancer and, once again, Gabe was absent. There was no one to share the burden of burying a parent, no one to share in the grief, no one to unlock shared memories. For the first time, he understood the true meaning of abandonment, a crushing isolation that left him utterly alone.

Duty bound him, shaping him into the man his father had wanted: a "man's man," adhering to an unspoken code of stoicism, sternness, and relentless resolve. He was a man of his word, unwavering and predictable, yet opinionated enough to drive most people away.

Only Liz and Mandy were able to penetrate his tough exterior. Their love reshaped him in ways he thought impossible. After their deaths, he withdrew, diving deep into the familiar abyss of solitude, a fortress against his raw and profound grief. Gradually, he withdrew from Elizabeth's family, as well as the few friends he had, until he was entirely alone, adrift in a sea of his own making. He had allowed love to redefine him once, a mistake he would not repeat. Better to be alone than to chance having his heart ripped to shreds for a second time. For fourteen years, he had not truly lived; he had merely existed.

Nope, selling the gun is not an option. Come hell or high water, he will find a way to get the money, although it won't be easy; he has nothing else of value. The job in Denison is his only hope. *With any luck, I can make enough to get the power back on*, he reasons. *I can take having a cold house, but no lights or television*, he shakes his head, *that's where I draw the line.*

The wind continues its relentless assault throughout the morning, a mournful howl that matches the deepening gray of the sky. The forecast paints a grim picture: freezing rain transitioning to sleet by late afternoon. He tries calling the woman, hoping to reschedule or move up their appointment, but the phone goes unanswered. The last thing he wants is to be trapped in Denison during a notorious North Texas ice storm. But he is a man of his word, and that promise holds him to the trip, regardless of the worsening conditions.

A memory he has almost forgotten surfaces, December 1989. He and Liz had awakened to a similar forecast. Still, back then, they were newlyweds, the promise of a snow-day a delightful, unexpected gift, an excuse to linger in bed. The phone's ring shattered the quiet morning just after seven, and the immediate slump in Liz's shoulders spoke volumes. Her school was not closing. The day of stolen intimacy, of shared warmth against the winter chill, was gone.

"I'm sorry you have to teach today while I stay here under these warm blankets." It was not a suitable time for a joke, but he tried.

"Yeah, you're sorry, alright!" Picking up a pillow, she flung it across the room, hitting him squarely in the head. "I can't believe you are going to let a little rain and ice keep you from working on poor Mrs. Turner's roof. What kind of man are you?"

"I'm a man who loves his wife! Now, get back over here, and let me warm those cold toes of yours." Hopefully, he could entice her to stay home.

She gave a quick laugh. "My toes will just have to suffer because, right now, I'd better jump in the shower and head to school. I doubt there will be many kids today, but even if there is only one, I still need to be there." She left the room, heading for the shower.

"Good Lord! What a rare woman I have," he remembered thinking. "Not only is she beautiful, but she's a great teacher. No doubt she will be a wonderful mother someday, too."

The drive to Liz's school was only twenty minutes long, but suddenly, an ominous feeling overwhelmed him as she walked out the door. "Hey, Babe, I do not like the look of those clouds. Why don't you let me drive you to school? My big ol' truck can handle icy roads better than your car." Liz stopped in her tracks, slowly turning, defiance clearly written on her face, but he continued anyway. "Or…if the weather gets worse and they decide to close the schools, then call me, and I'll come pick you up. Otherwise, I'll be waiting for you at four, the usual time."

Liz simply waved him off, turned, and kept walking. "I'll be fine. A little ice doesn't scare me. Besides, it is unlikely to do anything but rain. You know how inaccurate these weather forecasts can be." It was no use arguing with her once she had made up her mind.

"Okay, but if you aren't home by 4:30, then I'm gonna come lookin' for ya!"

She turned before opening the door, flashing him a quick smile. "Have a mug of hot chocolate waiting for me, Mister, and I'll let you warm my toes all you want." She ran out the door and was gone before he could think of a quick comeback.

He spent the morning working on the list of "honey-dos" Liz had taped on the refrigerator door. Around noon, the wind renewed its fury, and the rain hammered down, growing heavier with each passing minute. Soon, he heard the familiar tinkling of freezing sleet hitting the windowpanes. At one o'clock, the announcement finally came—schools would close early due to severe weather. *Liz should be home by two*, he thought. A flicker of warmth passed through his body. *Better get the hot chocolate ready. Maybe this day won't be a complete washout after all.* Two o'clock came and went without any sign of Liz. By three, a knot of worry tightened in his gut. He called her school, but the phone rang unanswered in the empty building. Outside, a thick layer of sleet now covered the roads, making driving extremely hazardous for anyone, even a careful driver like Liz. Without further thought, he grabbed his keys and jumped into his truck to begin the treacherous drive to find her. Following her usual route to school, he cautiously drove down the slick highway, his heart pounding with each careful turn. Numerous cars and trucks had slid off the icy roads, a testament to the perilous conditions, but her car was nowhere to be found.

He reached the school parking lot only to find it empty. "Where could she be?" he whispered under his breath, a frantic edge to his voice. If she had hitched a ride home, then her car would still be here. "Never should have let her drive to school alone," he muttered while carefully turning his truck around. His only choice was to drive home, trusting she had, somehow, managed to get back home safely.

He inched the truck forward, retracing his route, but the roads had become an impassable mess. His knuckles were white on the steering wheel as he fought for control. The old truck slid and skidded on the frozen roads, almost dumping him in a ditch along with everyone else. His stomach churned at the thought of Liz driving under such adverse conditions. Only a few miles remained between him and home, and still no sign of her. He passed a side road, remembering it was a shortcut Liz sometimes used when in a hurry. "Oh, good grief," he groaned, dismissing the thought. "She would not take that road today. She is probably home by now."

"Turn around," a small voice urged in his head. "Go down the shortcut."

"Nah, she wouldn't have taken that road today," he argued with himself. "She's probably home."

Traveling another quarter of a mile, the voice returned, louder this time. "Turn around. Go down the shortcut road."

Unable to ignore the urgency of the voice, he flipped on his blinker, making a U-turn on the highway. Driving at a snail's pace, he left the main road, the deserted side road barely visible through his frosted windshield. After a couple of miles, he lost hope. He could not risk getting stuck himself. As he shifted in reverse, a flash of light pierced the darkness. Squinting, he peered through the ice-coated glass. Another flash. Ignoring the icy road, he sped ahead, skidding to a sliding stop when he spotted her car, backwards, firmly planted in a ditch. He bolted out of the truck, running as fast as possible, even though the road was as slick as an ice-skating rink. Flinging open the car door, a wave of fear washed over him. But there in the driver's seat sat Liz, a calm smile on her face.

"It's about time you got here, mister!" she playfully scolded.

"Lizzie!" he exclaimed. Relief flooded his face. "Are you alright, Babe?"

She gave him a wide smile. "I'm fine, but my toes are freezing!"

Right away, he wrapped his arms around her and eased her out of the solidly stuck car. Careful of the slippery conditions, they walked back to his truck—the sound of crunching ice breaking the silence of the dark afternoon. Once she was safe, it was his turn to scold her.

"How can you be so calm? What if I had not found you?" Trying to hide the worry and strain of the past hours was of no use. His face clearly reflected the anguish he had endured.

"Well, I guess it would have been a long, chilly night," she answered calmly. "But I knew you would find me." Her confidence momentarily annoyed him.

"Well, I wouldn't have...except something, some kind of voice, told me to turn down this road."

"It wasn't something...it was someone," she said quietly. "I prayed and asked the Lord to show you where I was, and He did."

Unsure how to respond, he hugged her even more tightly. "Whatever or whoever it was doesn't matter to me. I'm just glad you're okay. Now let's get home and do something about those cold toes."

"Sounds good to me!" she replied. "Let's go home."

The truck rumbled to life, and they began the slow, cautious journey home. That night, long after Liz had slipped into sleep, he lay awake, the day's near-tragedy replaying in his mind. *Could she be right?* he wondered. *Had some unseen force truly guided me to her?* They had only been married for a few months, but the thought of life without Liz was a terrifying void. Overwhelmed by a wave of gratitude to whatever entity had orchestrated their meeting, he looked heavenward and whispered, "Thank you."

The ticking of the clock brings him back to the present. After an agonizingly long wait, sitting alone in a cold, empty house, it is time to head north to Denison. Stepping to the window, he peers through the frosted panes. "I'll be lucky to make it back before this weather gets worse," he supposes, the gray sky offering no promise of change. He grabs his keys, leather jacket, and, at the last moment, a knit cap off the coat rack. "This may come in handy later." A blast of freezing wind greets him upon opening the door. He ducks his head against the wind, quickly trotting to his truck. "She may be old, but she's got one hell of a heater," he reassures himself, knowing the long drive would warm him.

Thankfully, the predicted sleet holds off, granting him an uneventful forty-minute drive. Or so it seems, until he glances at the gas gauge. "Runnin' on fumes," he groans, a wave of panic rising. He scans the seat next to him, searching for his cell phone to call the woman, but it is not there. A quick check of his coat pocket confirms his fear—no cell phone! "Damn phone," he curses, hitting the steering wheel. "Left it on the table. Just my luck. If the power had not gone out…" He attributes his forgetfulness to the morning's chaos. "Guess I'll have to chance it." He knows his choice is reckless, but he cannot bear to be late. *If she hires me, I'll ask for cash up front*, he thinks with a flicker of optimism. *Then I can fill the tank and maybe even get the power back on.* Confident, he presses on, reaching Denison just before three in the afternoon.

The lady's house is a few blocks off Main Street. The older neighborhood is typical of Denison—small, neatly kept homes interspersed with those that are less tidy. He finds the address with no trouble. Luckily, it is one of the nicer homes on the street, and right away, he feels encouraged. "Looks like these people have money," he reckons, feeling another surge of hope. He takes a deep breath. "Here goes nothing." The biting north wind continues to blow with gale force. Pulling the knit cap low over his forehead, he thrusts his hands deep into his pockets and heads for the front door. Before he can ring the doorbell, a woman slightly older than he is opens the door. Instantly, he extends his hand—a gesture she does not bother to return.

"Oh dear, I am so very sorry you came all the way up here for nothing!" she exclaims, taking him by surprise. "After my husband and I talked, we decided this just isn't a good time to embark on a remodel project. Lord knows what's gonna happen with this economy! I tried to call your cell but never got an answer. Again, I am so sorry." She shrugs, smiling weakly.

"I don't quite understand what you're sayin', ma'am. It was just yesterday that you called." Removing his cap, he pleads earnestly. "I guarantee my quote will be reasonable. In fact, I will give you an even better deal. I have several references to assure you of the quality of my work." The woman looks uneasily back towards her husband, standing a few feet behind. "I'll be honest, ma'am," he peeks around the woman, "… sir, I could really use a little work right now. You're right, this economy has been tough for all of us. Hiring me would do both of us a favor. You get a good deal for excellent service, and I get to turn my lights back on." He smiles warmly, hoping it will thaw their icy coolness towards him.

"No...no," the woman shakes her head before continuing, "we really can't do a project right now. But thank you so much for coming. I hope you have a safe trip back." She glances upward, frowning. "This weather's turning nasty. You best be gettin' back home before the roads ice over."

With her last statement, she turns, firmly shutting the door behind her. He stands there debating whether to leave or ring the doorbell again and give her a piece of his mind. How dare she lure him up here in such awful weather and then change her mind? Just by looking at their house, it is clear these people don't have money issues, unlike him. A storm of fury builds inside. Unable to contain it, he shouts angrily through the closed door.

"Really, lady? You could, at the very least, let me bid the job!" The curtains in the window flutter slightly. He is sure they heard him, and either are too afraid to open the door or just don't care. Clenching his jaw, he hisses, "Aw, hell! This weather ain't the only thing turning nasty. And I thought this day couldn't get any worse!" Turning furiously, he stomps back down the sidewalk as the gray sky gives way to icy rain. Things are going from bad…to worse.

Without that job, he has little hope of getting his power restored. The thought of selling his gun resurfaces, but that dismal thought must wait until later. The empty gas tank is his priority. He remembers passing a gas station on Main Street. If not, then it will be a long, cold walk. The few blocks back to Main feel like miles, but it is still another quarter mile to the gas station. "Made it!" he confidently exclaims, relief washing over him as he turns into the station's lot, only to have the old truck cough and jerk to a halt just shy of the pump. A strange mix of gratitude and anger surged through him. He hops out and pushes the vehicle the few remaining feet to the pump. His fingers, numb and clumsy from the cold, fumbled with his wallet. "Please," he whispers, sliding the debit card into the pump. "Please let there be enough." He holds his breath, waiting for the verdict.

AUTHORIZATION DENIED. PLEASE SEE ATTENDANT.

"Hell no! I'm not going to see the attendant," he mumbles angrily under his breath. He slides the card once again, only to receive the same infuriating message: Card Declined. Now what? Groaning, he climbs back into the warmth of his truck, a meager shield against the miserable weather. The freezing rain has soaked his jacket, leaving him chilled to the bone. He sits there, at his wits' end, trying to make sense of his options. He is a self-sufficient man, trained to handle adversity. There must be a way out of this mess.

Most people have someone they can rely upon when facing difficulty, but he has no one, a consequence of his own making. Offers to help had been plentiful, but his stubborn pride kept everyone at bay. Liz's parents, along with her sister, had tried to stay in contact during the years following the accident. Although suffering their own grief, they had repeatedly offered to pray for him, but it was a waste of time. Cards with comforting scripture references went straight to the trash. He did not need reminders of what he had lost. He had no need for a God who took wives and babies whenever He felt like it, with no regard for those left behind. And then there was the unexpected visit from Liz's pastor, an encounter he would rather have avoided.

"Hey there. Just wanted to check on you. Are you doing okay?" Frankly, he liked the pastor, but he wasn't sure how to graciously answer such an absurd question. He would never be okay!

"I'm okay," he flatly replied, no emotion whatsoever in his voice.

"Are you really okay?" asked the pastor. His skepticism was evident. "Elizabeth's sister is worried you aren't coping very well."

His jaw tightened. Trying to keep his voice under control, he replied, "Coping? Tell me, Pastor, how does one cope after suffering the kind of loss I did? I don't think a man can lose his wife and little daughter and simply cope with it!"

"Of course not," said the pastor in earnest, "I certainly didn't mean to diminish your loss. We all loved Elizabeth and Mandy very much. I just meant..."

He interrupted the pastor before he could go any further." Granted, you may have loved my wife and daughter, but their death didn't change your life like it changed mine. You still have a home. You are still a husband, and you are still a father. You know what? I am nothing now. I'm not a husband or a father. In addition, I don't even have a home, just a house. I don't think anyone, especially Liz's sister, can judge whether I'm coping or not!" Dismissing the pastor, he attempted to shut the door, but the pastor inserted his foot at the last moment.

"Wait a minute!" the pastor exclaimed. "Yes, you're right. I can't even begin to understand what you're going through, but some people can. We have a grief support group at our church, and they will welcome you with open arms. They meet every Wednesday evening around 6:30 at the church. I could have the leader of the group give you a call if you are interested."

"Not interested," he said, his voice reflecting the same monotone as before.

"Excuse me?" the pastor questioned, surprised by his cold reply.

"I am not interested in your little support group," he said, bluntly. Tact had never been his strong suit.

"I think Elizabeth would want you to get some help. She loved you so much. She would be the first person to encourage you to get on with your life." The pastor continued his heartfelt plea." Let me have someone give you a call. Everyone in the group has suffered a loss. They will understand what you're going through and can help you through these stages of grief."

"Look, Pastor. I appreciate your concern—I really do. But I don't need anyone's help. I'll deal with my grief in my own way." He didn't want to be rude, but the conversation was over. There was nothing further to say.

A look of helplessness crossed the pastor's face. "Well, here's my card. Please…give me a call…anytime. I'll be praying for you."

"Save your breath, Pastor. I'm not worth the effort." He gave the pastor a wry, knowing smile.

Vigorously shaking his head from side to side, the pastor was quick to answer. "You're wrong about that. God thinks you were worth dying for. I'm sure Liz had several Bibles. Pull one out sometime and read John 3:16. In fact, read the whole book of John in the New Testament. You'll discover just how much God loves you. Why don't you and I get together for a cup of coffee and talk about it?" The pastor forced a smile and gave him a hopeful look. "I'm free next Wednesday."

Despite the pastor's persistence, he remained steadfast. "Like I said, Pastor, you're wasting your time on me. My soul doesn't need saving. Now then, you have a good day. Goodbye." He quickly shut the door. That pastor would never get a foot in his door again, and he sure wasn't going to call anyone from a grief support group. His mantra remained the same. "A man handles his own problems—I don't need anyone's help."

But, sitting there helpless at the gas pump, his arrogance finally catches up to him. He had gone to great lengths to distance himself from everyone who once cared for him. "Even if you did call someone for help, no one would bother to come." The voice is always right and, this time, he agrees.

After half an hour of agonizing over his situation, his indecision persists. The trip to Denison solved none of his problems, only made them worse. It is getting late, and he must decide on a plan. Through the icy windshield, he spots a bank a few blocks away, a glimmer of hope in the deepening gloom. "This station may not take checks," he grumbles, pulling out his checkbook, "but a bank will." He clings to the faint hope of having at least five to ten dollars in his account, enough for a small amount of gas to make it back home. Home might be cold and dark, not idyllic, but a welcome alternative to spending a miserable night in his truck. If the bank refuses his check, however, then he is out of options.

Like most carpenters, he has a battered old truck that is home to all sorts of tools and random wood scraps. Among them are several short half-inch dowel rods, forgotten remnants from an earlier job. Lost in thought, he stares at the dowel rods, insignificant pieces of wood, but essential when used by a carpenter to join and connect. Now, they seem to mock his own state of disconnect and despair. Like a stuck record, the insidious whispers of despondency clearly speak the same repeated, relentless message. "You deserve more. Life is unfair. No one cares about you. You are alone." With every passing moment, the voice grows louder, amplifying the torment of his thoughts. He is weary. Weary of arguing, weary of countering his own negativity, weary of…life. Reaching down, he picks up one of the dowel rods. It is smooth, perfectly round, and about six inches in length. He observes it for a few minutes, his thoughts racing. *The voice is undeniably right. I deserve more than this cold, bleak existence, and life has been horribly unfair.* A chilling realization crosses his mind. *There is not a single soul in the world who cares whether I live or die. I am and will always be totally alone.* Embarking on an unknown path, he slips the dowel in his pocket, opens the door of his truck, steps out into the cold, and walks towards the bank, driven by a desperation that can make a man do funny, and sometimes tragic, things.

The rain turns to heavy sleet, relentlessly pelting his face with every step. Zipping the leather jacket up to his chin, he pulls the knit cap low over his forehead. Barely able to see, he marches on, pounding the pavement with each step, voicing curses under his breath. "Damn this weather! If there's bad luck around…it's gonna find me. I'm sick of people. I'm sick of losing, and I'm sick of life!" Growing even more irate with each step, he continues his tirade. "No one else must put up with this kind of crap. Hell, can't I ever get a break? I deserve more." With each despondent negative thought, he takes another step down the ladder into the abyss of self-pity. This dark pit is familiar, a place where he has often resided over the past fourteen years. He knows the only way out is to feel nothing, to have no emotions. Life can become bearable, but only if it is mechanical.

By the time he arrives at the bank, his anger and resentment have reached a boiling point, and he is seething. The small branch bank is still open, but quitting time is obviously close at hand. Taking a deep breath, he pushes the door open and enters the deserted lobby. The squeak of the closing door draws the lone teller's attention. She rises from her desk below the window. The plump, middle-aged woman wears thick glasses, her smile genuine and warm.

"Quite a storm out there, isn't it?" she asks cheerfully. Her voice has a typical, thick Texas accent. "What can I do for you today, sir?

Her smile and friendliness annoyed him. At that moment, everything about her only serves as another reminder of his hopeless plight. He glares at her for a moment, trying to ignore the insistent nagging voice in his head. She stares back at him, eyes wide with expectancy.

"Sir, is there somethin' I can help you with?" she patiently repeats her earlier sentence.

His hands remain plunged deep in his coat pockets. In the right pocket, he feels his checkbook, a last, flimsy hope. In the left, the six-inch dowel rod, a symbol now twisted into a weapon. An eerie stillness settles over him. With no emotion and devoid of any rational thoughts, he shifts the dowel within his pocket, pushing it against the fabric until a rounded impression appears, aimed squarely at the woman behind the counter. The teller's gaze glances from his face to the vague bulge in his pocket, a flicker of uncertainty crossing her features before returning to his eyes.

"Yes, ma'am, you can give me all the cash in your drawer," a low, quiet voice emerges, the words sound foreign and ridiculous.

The teller's warm smile disappears, replaced by a puzzled stare and furrowed brow. She obviously wonders, *is he joking or serious?*

Raising the "gun" a little higher, he hoarsely whispers, "Now, please."

Keeping her eyes glued to his face, without a word, she opens her drawer. She stuffs a bundle of bills into an envelope, then slowly slides it under the window. He hesitates before grabbing the bundle, thrusting it into his pocket. His breath catches. "Thank you," he whispers, his voice thick with fear that threatens to choke him. He turns and walks out the same way he came in, not looking back.

The woman, staring after him in disbelief, not fear, whispers under her breath, "Well, I'll be!" Then, she triggers the alarm.

Fearing someone had seen him abandoning his truck or walking to the bank, he does not return to his pickup. His leg muscles coil tight, a powerful urge to run coursing through him. He glances quickly up and down the street, then walks in the opposite direction. Dusk has fallen early under the heavy clouds. Fortunately, the sidewalks are deserted, and people are tucked snug inside their homes due to the nasty weather. He instinctively pulls off the knit cap that was surely part of the teller's description and stuffs the money envelope and dowel rod inside, tucking it up under his jacket. Main Street, with its potential for witnesses, must be avoided. He veers right at the first cross street, walking two more blocks before turning again. This part of town, older and quieter, offers a brief respite from the bustle of Main Street. Brightly lit houses line the street, but their beckoning warmth feels more threatening than reassuring.

His life, already surreal, has plunged into the bizarre. The bank teller's eyes confirmed her doubt about his makeshift dowel rod pistol, yet she had complied. If the whole scenario were not so dangerously foolish, he might have laughed, but the knot of dread in his stomach reminds him there is nothing comical about his plight. Now, though, he has only one concern—get off the icy sidewalk before someone spots him. He stops walking, scanning the street. At the end of the lane sits a dark, lonely house much smaller than the surrounding homes. *No lights, no threat*, he reasons, a fleeting hope sparking within. Perhaps, if it is truly empty, the backyard might offer temporary refuge, a desperately needed moment to think, away from the street's glaring exposure. But it is too late! Headlights slice through the darkness, bright lights shining in his eyes, temporarily blinding him as a patrol car turns onto the street just ahead. His pulse quickens. Without a second thought, he pivots and strolls down the sidewalk towards the unlit house as if it were his own. The old wooden front porch creaks and moans under his weight, but he keeps up the pretense. Feigning a search for a house key, he casually glances over his shoulder as the city police car idles slowly past. Confident his ploy has worked, he watches from the dark recess of the porch as the cruiser continues for another block.

A flash of red causes his heart to skip a beat. Abruptly, the patrol car stops, then begins to execute a slow, deliberate U-turn. There is no time to think. He scrambles off the porch, then darts around the corner of the old house and hastily crawls under a row of evergreen bushes. Crouching next to the wall, he feels the indentation of a basement window low to the ground. Frantically, his fingers trace the panes of the window, looking for an entry. A jagged hole, big enough to slip a hand through, greets him. The edges are sharp, threatening to slice the skin with every movement, but the desperate need for escape drives him forward. Reaching inside, his fingers fumble for the latch. It is tightly stuck. The patrol car pulls to a stop in front of the house, and a car door quietly opens and closes. *This is it*, he thinks, a hollow resignation settling over him. *Guess I deserve to get caught.* With one final desperate push, the rusty latch breaks free. Carefully sliding his arm out of the hole, he waits breathlessly, his heart pounding so loud he fears it will betray his hiding place.

The soft beam from the officer's flashlight passes over and around the surrounding trees. If the beam sweeps over him, then all hope will be lost. Moments pass before the glow disappears. A brief sliver of hope ignites. *The officer must have circled around the house.* He gently pushes the basement window inward. Then, with a desperate lunge, he flattens himself against the ground, slides in feet-first, and drops onto the cold, damp floor below with a soft thud.

The acrid smell of the musty basement fills his nostrils. He promptly rises and secures the window as the beam from the officer's flashlight approaches. He is being pursued. His hands pat the wall and floor next to him, looking for something, anything, to cover the window before the police officer has a chance to peer inside. Finding a small piece of plywood, he lifts it above his head and presses it against the window. His arms tremble, growing numb under the strain as he stands, breath held, for what feels like an agonizing eternity. He braces himself for the blare of sirens, the shouts through a bullhorn to come out, but only an unnerving silence follows. Still, he waits.

As his arms reach their limit, a dull ache spreads through his shoulders, and he tentatively lowers the plywood. His arms tingle with relief as the blood rushes back in. Peering out the dirty window, he can only see the outline of the bushes. There are no flashing patrol lights, but only the soft glow from a nearby street lamp. He slumps to the cold, hard floor, relief washing over him. He is safe, for now.

His eyes, accustomed now to the darkness, begin to pick out the details of the basement room. Several kinds of machinery line the walls, along with a large wooden table in the center of the room. He runs his hands over one of the machines. Right away, it feels familiar—a drill press. Moving along the wall, he feels each piece with the same familiarity: band saw, router, table saw, scroll saw. This is no vacant house, no forgotten space. But, for now, the owners are thankfully absent, and with a bit of luck, they will remain that way through the coming night.

Outside, the frigid wind and freezing rain rage, a stark contrast to the relative warmth and stillness of the basement. A grim reality hit him by now: a fleet of patrol cars would be searching for the bank robber, and he could not risk going back out on the street. Spending the night in the basement offers a temporary reprieve, a chance to gather his thoughts, to plan his next move.

Safe for now, he continues exploring the room. The long table in the center of the room is littered with an assortment of tools and hardware. Curiously, a doll's cradle sits among them. "Alright, a flashlight!" he exclaims, picking it up from the table. Its weak, dingy beam cut through the darkness, revealing a well-equipped workshop. Clearly, this person shares his passion for woodworking. Fine tools, neatly stacked lumber—plywood, 2x4s, 2x6s, even drywall—spoke of ambitious renovation plans. Yet, a thick layer of dusk coats everything, suggesting neglect. "What a waste!" he mutters, the sight of expensive, unused tools irritating him.

He turns, the flashlight beam flickering, revealing steep, narrow steps leading to what was once a doorway. Now, a thick sheet of plywood seals the opening. Lying next to the staircase, on the basement floor, is a shattered handrail. No other entry exists. Before he can unravel the mystery of the silent workshop, a violent tremor shakes the house above, the resounding thuds echoing like a stampede of horses.

***

Ten-year-old Janie's gaze lingers on her mother. The lines around her mother's eyes seemed deeper, her shoulders in a subtle droop that was not there this morning. Janie can almost see the weight of the day pressing down, a weariness that Momma tries—and fails—to completely hide. She understands the unspoken toll the long drive and her brothers' squabbling have taken. Their bickering and whining have even tested Janie's patience in the final hour. But now, they are finally home, and the familiar comfort of their house welcomed relief. The cold, empty house springs to life as the family of five bursts through the front door. Backpacks hit the floor with dull thuds, wet coats find their hooks on the hall tree, and muddy boots are flung, with practiced aim, under the bench.

"Janie, help the kids get their suitcases to the bedroom, and then get everyone to the table so we can eat before baths and bed." Her mother's voice, though filled with weariness, had the familiar request for help. Janie nods her head, always ready to help, especially after her daddy had left two years earlier. She often overheard people quietly comment to her mother how brave and strong her daughter was. She certainly did not feel brave or strong; she simply did what was needed. Things are different now. Once her daddy had been the one to help her mother, now it is up to her. Even now, she misses him; she will never, ever stop missing him. Remembering the day he left still gives her a tummy ache. It should have been a perfectly wonderful day, her eighth birthday.

Daddy was going to be home all day, and Momma had let her help make the cake—chocolate with chocolate icing—because it was her birthday, and she loved chocolate. Her father had spent the morning in his basement workshop. The occasional whine of the saw or the steady hum of the sander came through the floorboards, along with the smell of fresh-cut wood. Janie was not sure, but she suspected her father was busy crafting her birthday gift that morning. Each time he came up the stairs, he would grin and tell her, "Stay out of the workshop, young lady. Surprises are not fun if they aren't a surprise."

She loved surprises, especially if they involved her daddy. She tried to imagine what he was making, picturing a cradle for her doll, though she would cherish anything her father made. He often made wooden toys, which she proudly showed off to her friends.

"My daddy is a carpenter," she would announce with pride, "just like Jesus." Ashley, her friend, had been skeptical, as usual. She always questioned Janie's imagination.

"If your Daddy is a carpenter, then why is your house falling down?" she said with an air of superiority.

"It's not falling down!" Janie replied indignantly. "It just needs some…TLC."

"Okay, what's TLC then?" Ashley's smugness was irritating. Some friend she was!

"Tender…loving…care. That's all. My daddy is going to fix it up, and he is going to build a new bedroom in the basement for him and Momma so I can have their old bedroom for myself someday!" She was not positively sure about her last statement. Still, Ashley seemed impressed and no longer questioned her father's profession as a carpenter.

Janie often heard her parents discussing plans for their little old ramshackle house. Her father was careful to set aside money from each paycheck to buy tools and supplies. He wanted to have everything needed to begin his project, as running out of money halfway through was not an option. Her daddy was that kind of man, always finishing what he started. Sometimes, though, it took a long time for him to start. Momma called it procrastination. Seeing her mother's exasperation, a mischievous gleam would appear in her father's eyes. "I'll have you know," he would tease, "you are talking to the leader of the largest nation on earth!"

"And just what nation is that?" Momma asked, trying to hide a smile. She knew full well what came next.

Janie and her father both answered in perfect unison." Procrasti—nation!" Her father's ability to change a potential argument into an opportunity for laughter, much to her mother's annoyance, was something Janie loved and missed.

Instead of a large birthday party, Momma had invited a few of Janie's friends to come over around four that afternoon for cake and ice cream. After lunch, Momma tucked Hannah and the boys into their beds for naps, but she was now eight and exempt from such childish rituals. Besides, it was her birthday! Her father, after finishing his last bite of sandwich, rose and gathered a stack of boxes destined for the basement. As he passed, he gave Janie a quick, conspiratorial wink, a silent promise of the surprise waiting below.

"I have just a little more work to do in the basement, then it will be party time. Help your mom clean up this lunch mess, will you, Janie?"

She nodded enthusiastically. "Sure, Daddy. I'll do it," she said, her voice bright with eagerness. She began putting the bread and lunch meat away, a familiar routine she enjoyed.

Suddenly, a sharp, loud crack ripped through the silence, followed by a heavy, sickening thud. Janie's first thought was that one of their large trees had fallen on the roof. Only, the sound had not come from above. It came from below, from the basement. Her heart leaped into her throat. Janie ran to the open basement door and stared down the shadowy stairs. Something was wrong. Terribly wrong. The handrail, once sturdy, hung in jagged splinters. Taking a tentative step down, then another, she peered over the edge. There, among the scattered boxes and pieces of wood, lay her daddy, a crumpled heap, not moving in the slightest. A silent scream tore through her, but caught somewhere in her chest. Her mother was there instantly, flying by Janie and down the steps. She remembered her mother's desperate cries, screaming for her father to wake up. Over and over, she screamed for him to wake up, but Janie knew her daddy would never wake up again.

The rest of that day was a dim blur of memories: the arrival of many people, their hushed voices and somber faces filling their tiny home. They were not there for a birthday party. The chocolate cake sat untouched on the counter, the balloons slowly deflated, and a sudden emptiness descended upon their lives. The silence where Daddy's laughter should have been.

It had taken a long time before Janie stopped hearing the screaming. Sometimes, it was her mother's screams she heard, and sometimes, her own. She suspected the awful noise was just in her head because no one else seemed to notice. The screams surfaced mainly at night, just after her whispered prayers. Momma, sensing her struggle, told her to "Sing to Jesus when it starts." And Janie did, her voice rising loudly to fill the dark space, drowning out the unwanted sounds.

"Mommy, tell Janie to stop singing so loud. It hurts our ears!" her brothers would complain. But Janie kept singing until all she heard was the sound of her own voice and nothing else.

Her mother's voice interrupts Janie's thoughts, bringing her back to the present. "Caleb—Benjamin—Hannah—Janie. Go wash your hands and come to the table. Your grilled cheese sandwiches are ready." They are just settling into their chairs, hands clasped, heads bowed, when the doorbell rings. Her mother's brow furrows slightly as she peers through the lace curtain before unlatching the door. Janie strains to hear the muffled conversation, but only her mother's anxious voice carries into the dining room.

"Oh goodness! Thank you for letting us know." Momma's face visibly pales. "Yes, sir, we will lock all our doors." Her gaze goes to the table, and a shadow crosses her eyes. "Of course, we will contact the station if we see anything unusual. Good night, officers."

"What's wrong, Momma? Is everything okay?" The worried look on her mother's face was unusual.

"Everything's fine. Don't worry, honey. God always protects us. Remember what Daddy used to say, 'If God is for us, who can be against us?' Okay, who's hungry for some grilled cheese?" The abrupt change of subject and the forced enthusiasm for dinner speak volumes. Janie understands and turns her attention to the plates before them.

***

The rhythmic creak of floorboards above freezes the man in his tracks! The noise can only mean one thing: they are home. Fear grips his heart as he darts back towards the basement window. He jumps up, but with no ledge to grasp, it is impossible to get himself high enough to slip out the window. A furious thought echoes in his mind, *Hell! It was easier to get in than out.* The darkness of the basement suddenly presses in, intensifying his panic. Frantically, he sweeps his hands across the floor, looking for anything to stand on. A couple of small plastic buckets are within easy reach, but one alone isn't enough. Foolishly, he stacks one bucket atop the first. Lifting his leg, he steps on the unstable perch, the precarious tower swaying under his weight. He teeters as the buckets wobble. Pushing the window open, he hoists one leg up, leaving the buckets completely unstable beneath him. In that instant, his makeshift platform gives way with a loud crash. A sharp stabbing pain shoots through his right ankle, causing him to gasp. "Oh crap!" he groans in agony. "What was I thinking?" Halfway expecting someone to burst through the boarded doorway, he lies still and rigid, not daring to move despite the throbbing ankle. A broken ankle is the last thing he needs.

Time stretches, but eventually the searing pain in his ankle dulls to a persistent throb. Muffled voices drift through the wood floor above him, indistinguishable sentences, bursts of occasional laughter, and the rapid pitter-patter of tiny feet scampering overhead. The ruckus above confirms they did not hear his disastrous fall. Slowly, he turns over, pushing himself up on hands and knees. Using one of the buckets for support, he attempts to stand, but a bolt of fire shoots up his leg, sending a wave of nausea through him. He grimaces and sinks back onto the bucket, his breath catching. He unlaces the boot, gently pulling it off. His foot is already beginning to swell. Broken or sprained is irrelevant. He isn't going anywhere tonight.

The absurd bank robbery seems like a lifetime ago, an act by a stranger, certainly not him. Adding to his list of crimes is breaking and entering into a house not his own. Then an ill-fated attempt at escape leaves him stuck in a basement with a severely sprained or broken ankle. All of this unfolds as the family upstairs goes about their evening, blissfully unaware that a wanted criminal is hiding beneath their feet. The word echoes in his head: *criminal. I am a criminal.* Even if he escaped, what would he do? Where would he go? Was his truck still sitting empty at the gas station, or had the police impounded it? Had they traced it back to him? Were they watching his house, hoping he might try to return? Had the woman at the bank identified him? The endless questions confirm what he already knows to be true. He has no choice. He is not going anywhere tonight.

A loner by nature and by choice, he usually relishes solitude. Tonight, however, an unfamiliar loneliness settles over him, far deeper than anything he felt before. Deeper than when Gabe left, or when his parents died, even deeper than when Liz and Mandy died. There is no pleasure or satisfaction in this isolation, only stark fear. Hungry, tired, and scared, he feels lost and helpless. Exhaustion threatens to overtake his body. Moving off the bucket, he pulls off his other boot, then stretches out onto the cold cement floor. Drawing his arms inside his coat and using his hat, stuffed with the stack of bills as a pillow, he closes his eyes. The old wood floor above him creaks and groans in rhythm to the sound of children laughing and light-hearted chatter. The controlled chaos of a family he has never met lulls him into sleep, deep and undisturbed, a sleep he has not experienced in years.

Chapter 4

Saturday, January 3, 2009

Janie rolls over in bed, her eyelids still heavy with sleep. She catches a groggy glance at the digital clock: 6:30. Time to face another week of school. Stretching and yawning, she struggles to become fully conscious. A sluggish confusion clouds her mind. Where is the usual morning bustle? Usually, Momma would have awakened her by now. Still, no light shines under the bedroom door, nor any other sign of Momma. Silence hangs heavily in the air. Then, as she pushes herself into a sitting position, a wave of joyous realization hits her. Saturday. Two more days of Christmas vacation stretched ahead, two glorious days to enjoy the treasures Santa had tucked under the tree during their holiday visit with Grandma and Grandpa.

Christmas at her grandparents' home was a much-loved family tradition. The familiar scent of freshly baked cookies and cinnamon rolls greeted her family the minute the door opened. Hugs and kisses quickly followed. Soon, Grandpa would gather the children, his eyes twinkling with excitement, and lead them out to the woods on their annual quest for the perfect Christmas tree. Year after year, Grandma's stern warning followed them out the door. "Now Ross, don't go gettin' a tree too big like you did last year. A smaller one will do just fine!" Grandpa nodded his head in mock agreement, a sly grin on his lips, only to return hours later with the largest tree he could find. The rest of the day was filled with decorating the tree while Christmas carols softly played in the background.

A few days later, they would attend Christmas Eve services at her grandparents' church. Janie's heart swelled with anticipation as the pastor called all the children to the front of the church. There they would listen, captivated, as he read the Christmas story. The tale of Mary, Joseph, baby Jesus, the shepherds, and the wise men never lost its magic for Janie. Her father had instilled in her the true meaning of Christmas, the profound love of God to all mankind. Afterwards, the entire congregation would rise and sing "Silent Night." Each child would light their individual candle from the Advent Candle, then slowly carry their flickering candle back to their family. The flames would pass from person to person until the whole room was ablaze with the warm glow of candles and the smiling faces of the congregation. After the service, they would return to Grandma's house for steaming mugs of hot chocolate and warm apple cider. A sweet end to a sacred evening. Finally, tucked in bed, Janie's mind was filled with visions of sugarplums dancing. Janie wasn't even sure what a sugarplum was, but it danced in her head regardless.

Janie squeezes her eyes shut, trying to stop the tears. She loved Christmas, but it wasn't the same without her daddy. Too late, a single tear escapes and trickles down the side of her head, landing just inside her ear. A soft giggle escapes. Remembering Daddy's "wet willies" always made her smile. Licking his pinky finger, Daddy would chase her around the house, threatening to insert his wet finger into her ear. Her brothers would inevitably join the pursuit, escalating the chaos, prompting Momma's usual intervention. "Y'all need to settle down before someone gets hurt." At this point, Momma became the target of Daddy's wet finger, leading to even more laughter and screams. Those were good memories. Momma told her to focus on the good times when the sadness of missing her daddy became overwhelming. Keeping her eyes closed, Janie's thoughts drift back to their last Christmas with him.

The weeks leading up to Christmas were always a whirlwind of activity, but Janie's favorite tradition was the annual Downtown Denison Christmas Parade. Every year, her family bundled up in coats and hats, filled a thermos with steaming hot chocolate, and walked the few blocks to the parade route. Main Street, usually dark and quiet at night, transformed into a vibrant spectacle of floats, costumes, and colorful lights. The grand finale was always the horse-drawn wagon carrying Santa, along with a group of adults and children dressed as elves. The crowd buzzed with anticipation, craning their necks, waiting for the clip-clop of the faithful old horse that pulled the ornately decorated wagon.

As the wagon approached, Janie noticed her mother frantically scanning the crowd. "Oh my gosh, John, where's Benjamin?" her mother exclaimed, her voice strained despite her attempt at calmness.

"I don't know," her father replied, his own voice tinged with alarm. "He was just here. Janie, did you see where Ben might have wandered?"

Janie, the eldest, usually kept a watchful eye on her younger siblings. But tonight, the vibrant spectacle, the music, and the swirling lights had stolen her attention. "I…I wasn't watching," she stammered, a hot flush creeping up her neck. "I'm so sorry, Daddy. I'll find him!" Without a second thought, she plunged into the dense crowd, ignoring her father's desperate shouts to come. *Please God, please help me find my little brother*, she silently but fervently prayed.

Despite her small size, Janie pushed her way to the front of the crowd. From there, she could see up and down Main Street. Worried that Benjamin might be in the path of Santa's wagon, she began to call his name. "Benjamin! Benjamin! Where are you?" Her desperate cries were lost in the joyful roar of the crowd. Taking a deep breath, she yelled with all her might, "BEN—JA—MIN!"

Santa's wagon was nearly upon Janie when a faint, familiar sound cut through the parade's cheerful din. "Sissy!" It was Benjamin's voice, startlingly close, yet he remained hidden somewhere among the laughing elves. "Sissy! Look over here!" he called again, a little louder this time.

Janie's head whipped around, eyes wide, desperately scanning the wagon. Benjamin was nowhere to be seen. "I don't see you, Ben!" she shrieked, her voice swallowed by the rhythmic clip-clop of the horse's hooves.

The wagon rolled directly in front of her. She heard it again—the sweet, unmistakable sound of Benjamin's giggle. "I'm right here, silly!"

Her jaw dropped. There, perched triumphantly on Santa's lap, was her missing brother. He was completely absorbed in the joy of the moment, oblivious to the frantic search he'd caused. He tossed candy into the crowd, a wide grin plastered across his face. Her parents pushed through the throng and arrived just in time to witness Benjamin's beaming face as the wagon rumbled past.

Her mother moved to retrieve their adventurous son from Santa's lap. Janie's father gently placed a restraining hand on her arm. "Let him have his fun for now. We can talk about it later," he said, a smile finally breaking through his earlier worry. "We may not have known where Ben was, but the Lord did!" His voice boomed the last sentence, carried above the crowd, followed by a hearty, "Merry Christmas, everybody!" A few minutes later, Benjamin, still nestled on Santa's lap of honor, disappeared around the corner, leaving Janie with a memory she would never forget.

It worked! Sweet memories of her father chased away the sadness. Janie, with dry eyes and a smile, climbs out of the warm bed she shares with her sister. Across the room, her brothers sleep soundly in their bunk beds. Sometimes, she wishes for her own room, or at least a "girls-only" room. Her father's words instantly came to mind: "If wishes were horses, beggars would ride. So, turn your wishes into prayers, Janie. God promises He will supply all our needs according to His riches. Just remember, though, there is a difference between what we need and what we want. You can always trust God to know the difference." She suspects God will not see a room of her own as a need. However, she whispers the wish in her morning prayers, not asking outright, just mentioning how nice it would be. A familiar sadness threatens her cheerfulness. Without her daddy, having her own room seems unlikely, even for God.

Janie's bare feet pad softly down the hallway to the kitchen. She usually closes her eyes when passing the basement door, but not today. Today, she stops and gazes at the door—this is where she last saw Daddy.

The day after her father died, Momma had called Uncle Larry. Janie remembered the sharp finality in her mother's voice. "I need you to come over and seal up that doorway. I don't want to take any chances on anyone falling down those stairs again."

Uncle Larry came at once but made the mistake of arguing with Momma. "It's not going to look good, Beth," he said. "You don't want to walk down this hall and see an ugly sheet of plywood over the door. Let me just put a lock on instead."

Momma's head tilted, considering the idea, but only for a second. "No, I want it sealed. No one is going down there again as long as I live in this house." Her voice was a low, hard line of refusal. "Seal it from the inside of the door, then I can keep the door as it is."

Uncle Larry sighed. It was pointless to argue with Momma once she made up her mind. "Fine, but we have one little problem."

"What's that?" Momma asked.

"How do I get out?"

Janie saw the slight upward curve of her mother's mouth—the hint of a smile. "Simple. Climb out the window."

Uncle Larry's eyes widened, then he chuckled. "Easy for you to say, sis. You're half the size of me."

"There's plenty of room, don't worry. I think there's a step stool by the wall," Momma said, smiling, but her eyes lacked their usual sparkle. "The kids and I will pull you out if we have to."

Janie stifled a giggle, a sudden picture in her mind of five small figures straining to hoist a protesting Uncle Larry.

"Right," he said, shaking his head. "Like you're strong enough to pull me." He stared at Momma before admitting defeat. "Okay, but first I'll make sure I fit through the window. If I do, I'll seal the doorway like you want. Why do you always win?"

Momma's smile remained thin and tight. "Practice… that's how."

Janie remembered watching, noticing a real grin on her mother's face this time, as Uncle Larry squeezed through the narrow opening. It was tight, but he fit. Just as Momma knew he would.

Her smile quickly vanishes, replaced by a heaviness she couldn't ignore. Behind that unmoving door, down the stairs in her father's workshop, was the birthday gift. The gift that Daddy never had a chance to give her. Reminding her mother of the gift in the days following the accident seemed wrong. Back then, Momma's tears had flowed too easily, leaving Janie helpless and sad. She wanted to beg Uncle Larry to check on the surprise before he came out the window, but she couldn't. Taking a gift on a day that felt so wrong seemed like a betrayal.

Now, stealing a look through the dirty basement window is her only hope of seeing what her father had made. Several times, Janie had pressed her face against the basement window, straining to see beyond the darkness, but the filtered light had been too dim to see more than a few feet. Just last week, she tried another peek, but a new jagged hole in one of the windowpanes stopped her. She did not want to be blamed for a broken window!

Standing alone in the quiet hallway, her thoughts race. The broken pane could work to her advantage. If she could reach through the hole, she could unlock the window, push it open, and get a real look inside the basement. It is a risky idea, but the promise of that hidden treasure—a link to her father—makes it worth every risk. All she needs is the right moment and the courage to seize it.

Lost in thought, Janie rounds the corner into the kitchen. Her mother, already there, sips her first cup of coffee, eyes scanning the morning newspaper. "Good morning, Momma!" Janie forces a brightness she does not quite feel.

"Hey, baby," her mother replies, not looking up.

Janie stands in the doorway, hesitant to bring up the subject of Daddy's workshop. Probably not the ideal time, but she takes a deep breath and asks, "Momma, do you think we will ever open the doorway and go down to daddy's workshop again?"

Her mother slowly lowers the newspaper, a frown appearing. "What prompted that question this morning?"

"I don't know." She does know that the mysterious birthday gift weighs heavily on her mind, but shame prevents her from revealing the actual reason. "I was just wondering."

Her mother's gaze drifts, her expression shifting. "Actually, it's about time we sell some of your daddy's tools. Lord knows, we could use a little extra cash around here. Maybe I'll give Uncle Larry a call next weekend and have him open the doorway."

Janie, too young to understand her mother's financial difficulties, knows the standard answer to most requests is "We can't afford it." Many times, her mother said it was time to sell Daddy's tools, but Janie doubts that will ever happen. The tools represented her father more than anything else. Often, Daddy had reminded them of his priority list—God first, then Momma, followed by the children, and finally, his love for woodworking. He had spent many hours in his workshop, causing Momma to scold him when he became obsessive.

"Come up for air now and then," Momma would chide.

Lifting his head from his current project, he would grin and agree. "You're right, Bethany. This wood isn't going anywhere, but those babies of ours—well, they will all leave someday." Then, his safety goggles would come off, and her father would bound up the stairs in search of his family. After tucking them in at night, he would find his way back to the basement to finish his project. More than once, Janie had fallen asleep to the low hum of one of her father's power tools.

Janie's mother spoke candidly, her voice losing its cheerful tone. "Your daddy was a wonderful man, but I wish he'd left us with fewer bills and more money." She continues, a heavy sigh escaping. "This old house is falling apart. The pipes are leaking, the roof is in desperate need of repair, and these squeaky floors are driving me crazy!" With her last statement, Janie's mother suddenly stands up and begins hopping and dancing. The old wooden floorboards squeak and creak in tempo beneath her mother's bare feet. "See what I mean?" she exclaims breathlessly, collapsing back into her chair. "I suppose I could get a second job, but until your sister is in school full-time, I would spend more money on childcare than I could possibly earn. Selling your daddy's tools seems like our only choice right now."

Janie hugs her mother reassuringly. "It'll be okay, Momma," she said. "I think Daddy would want us to sell his tools. He once told me God said not to worry about anything, but instead to pray about everything. He also said God would take care of all our needs."

Nodding her head in agreement, her mother sighs again. "You're right, hon, although that's sometimes easier said than done. But you're right, and I appreciate the reminder. I'll give Uncle Larry a call soon." She hugs Janie tightly, resting her chin on Janie's head. "Out of the mouth of babes...out of the mouth of babes..." she whispers softly.

***

A thin stream of morning light invades the basement through the grimy, broken window. It rested on the man's face, forcing one eyelid open, then the other, pulling him from the deepest sleep he'd known in years. But, he is much too old and too tired to sleep on a hard cement floor another night. Wishing the previous day's events had been nothing more than a bad dream, the ache in every bone and muscle confirms it is, indeed, reality.

Rolling to his side, a low groan escapes him as he pushes himself to a sitting position. He reaches down, fingers gingerly probing the swollen mass that is his ankle. Much to his discouragement, it is still tender to the touch with shades of blue and purple bruising just beginning to appear. "Oh great," he mutters. "This doesn't look good." Standing is out of the question. He carefully maneuvers himself onto the now-righted bucket, the plastic creaking under his weight.

Above, the old floorboards creak under gentle footsteps announcing the early morning rising of at least one of the family members. His gaze lifts upwards, a professional assessment already forming. *A few carefully placed shims, screws, and a little shoring up of the low spots would certainly quiet down that old floor,* he thinks. *Maybe these guys need a handyman.* The thought brought a faint, almost imperceptible smile to his lips. Even in this absurd situation, his dry humor, thankfully, remains intact.

A low growl, then a louder rumble, comes from his empty stomach. Gnawing hunger pangs intensify. His meager breakfast from the day before has long since vanished, and he is starving. To make matters worse, the fragrance of freshly brewing coffee seeps through the floorboards, filling his nostrils with the delicious scent of morning. Going without breakfast is one thing, but going without coffee? That is a different kind of torture! He can only sit, a prisoner on his bucket, while someone else enjoys their cup of coffee directly above him.

Minutes later, more footsteps and muffled voices join the sounds above. Knowing how wood carries sound, he closes his eyes and listens intently, hoping to catch snippets of conversation. Although the voices are garbled, he is certain they are from a woman and a child—most likely a mother and young daughter. It is not a surprise; the previous night's ruckus hinted at a family, and a large one at that. A few clear sentences here and there confirm his suspicion: this young family has the same old money woes he does. "Well, join the club!" he mumbles sarcastically. "At least you have a roof over your head, and you're not stuck in someone else's basement!"

The conversation halts abruptly, replaced by what sounds like an Irish jig. The old floor creaks and groans as if in agony. He braces himself, imagining the entire floor collapsing down onto his head, showering him in splintered wood. Thankfully, the hopping and dancing soon stopped, and the tired old floor seemed to moan with relief. The conversation between the mother and daughter resumes, but the last few sentences are quite disconcerting to him. The little girl, bless her heart, is reassuring her mother about God, prayer, and all that fairytale nonsense. He shakes his head, a wry grin twisting his lips. "You're just a kid," he mumbles. "What do you know? Just wait until you have a few years under your belt, little gal. After you've been knocked down a few times, you'll see, God and prayer won't help." He is not being cynical, as Elizabeth would have accused. He is just speaking the truth, or that is what he tells himself.

A chorus of noisy commotion soon erupts above him. Surprisingly, he finds himself enjoying the exercise of deciphering the family's dynamics. Clearly, he hears a mother's voice, but no father's deeper tone. Harder to tell with the children's voices, but he distinguishes at least four or five voices, both boys and girls, perhaps two of each. This lively family, with its sound of laughter, playful teasing, and even childish arguing, helps him feel a little less alone.

The tantalizing smell of frying bacon soon begins its slow descent into the dimly lit basement. Once again, his stomach growls loudly, reminding him of his escalating hunger and his ridiculous predicament. The basement offers a safe hiding place, but it is only a temporary respite. He knows he should leave at once, but without ice, heat, or even a simple aspirin, walking would be impossible. The swelling could take days to subside.

The meager daylight filtering through the window is just enough to survey his surroundings. As he had noted the night before, only two entry points existed: the sealed doorway and the broken window. A rusty metal step stool, leaning against a wall, catches his eye. This is a much sturdier option for reaching the window than the flimsy plastic buckets. Getting out of the basement is not the challenge, though; the real problem lies in what happens next. Looking around the room, he spots the knit cap, his pillow from the night before. The money! He has completely forgotten the wad of bills still stuffed inside. A glimmer of hope, however dim, sparks within him. Depending on the amount, this could be the solution to his problems. He pulls the envelope out of the cap and begins to count. There are a few hundred-dollar bills, but most are smaller denominations. He counts, then recounts the bills, growing sicker to his stomach with each tally. The total amount is only $3,000. He had robbed a bank and ruined his life forever for a measly three thousand dollars—barely enough to cover his late mortgage payments.

Burying his face in his hands, he squeezes his eyes shut, picturing the worst. What would be the penalty for robbing a bank of only three thousand dollars? Even with no prior offenses and good behavior, the best he could hope for was a ten- to twenty-year prison sentence. Bank robbery is a felony! At sixty-three, spending twenty years in prison could mean the rest of his life. Breathing rapidly, his heart pounding, panic threatens to overwhelm him. The bleakness of his situation presses down, suffocating him, yet what alternative does he have? He desperately needs more time to think and more time for his ankle to heal. Staying in this oppressive basement dungeon, for now, is his only option. This is not just a bad dream; it is a living nightmare!

***

"Janie," her mother calls, "will you help me get the others dressed and ready? We need groceries. Old Mother Hubbard's cupboard is bare."

Janie would rather stay home and read, but her mother needs help again. She tries not to grumble, sometimes feeling her mother forgets she is merely a child herself. Dutifully, Janie complies. Soon they are all bundled and out the door.

The northerly winds begin to subside as the winter sun gradually peeks from behind the clouds. Grocery shopping with four children demands patience and time. Nearly two hours later, the family returns home and begins the task of unloading the car. As usual, her mother has meticulously counted every penny spent.

When her father was alive, he would "accidentally" slip cupcakes or candy into their cart when Momma turned her back. Putting his fingers to his lips, he would give Janie a wink—it was their little secret. At the register, Momma would sigh and frown at her father upon discovering the tasty treats but would always let Daddy keep them. Grocery shopping was fun back then… now, not so much.

After putting away the groceries and finishing lunch, Janie puts on her coat, taking her new Christmas doll and stroller outside. Tired of parading up and down the front sidewalk, Janie ventures around the side of the house to the backyard. Rounding the corner of the house, she glances at the row of evergreen bushes. Tucked behind them is the broken basement window. It has been a long time since she peeked through the cloudy window into Daddy's workshop. *A quick look won't hurt*, she thinks. Checking to make sure no one is watching, she carefully squeezes under the hedge, mindful not to tear or dirty her coat. *It's probably better Momma doesn't know what I'm doing,* she reasons with herself. *I don't want to make her cry again.*

Janie carefully crouches behind the hedge, facing the basement window. She leans forward, cupping her hands around her face, and peers through the dirty panes. A faint, earthy smell, thick with damp, seeps through the hole in the glass, a silent warning to proceed no further. She tries to see through the opening, but the dim light barely illuminates only a few feet inside. Time for her plan to unfold.

Taking a deep breath, Janie slowly reaches her arm through the broken glass, feeling for the window latch. The danger of the sharp glass never crosses her mind until her coat sleeves snag on the jagged edge. A frantic pull, then another, but the fabric holds, firmly stuck with no chance of saving her sleeve. Wiggling her arm back and forth only worsens the tear, but finally, it comes free. Horrified, she yanks her arm out and stares at the damage. What will Momma say? How can she possibly explain the torn sleeve? She is in serious trouble.

"Janie! Where are you?" Her mother's voice cuts through the air. Janie hastily scrambles from beneath the bushes, making her way around the side of the house. Pressing her hand tightly over the torn spot, she timidly climbs the steps towards her waiting mother.

"Janie Lynn!" Her mother's voice is stern. "Just what have you been doing, and why are you holding your arm like that?"

When Momma uses both her names, trouble is sure to follow. Janie looks up at her mother, eyes wide. Should she reveal the truth or what she wishes is the truth? "I…I," she stutters hesitantly, "I was going around back, but I got too close to the bushes, and… and a broken limb snagged my coat." Janie regrets the lie the minute it comes out of her mouth. A wave of nausea rolls through her stomach—she has no memory of ever lying to Momma before.

"Well, baby, you need to be more careful!" Her mother's tone softens. "Come inside and I'll see what I can do to mend it." Janie knows the situation will be bad if the real reason for the torn coat and the lie is revealed. She obediently follows her mother inside and slips off her jacket.

"That must have been a sharp branch," her mother remarks, her fingers tracing the edge of the tear. "You need to show me where that limb is so I can cut it off before it snags someone else."

Janie's cheeks burn, a sudden rush of heat, but her mother's attention remains fixed on the damaged fabric. "Is it okay if I wait until later?" she asks, her voice barely a whisper. "Right now, I need to study my Bible verse for next week."

"I suppose so. But please don't let me forget, Janie."

Janie nods vigorously, perhaps a little too much. "Yes, ma'am. I won't forget." She runs off to her room before her mother can ask more questions. The door clicks shut behind her. She sinks onto the bed, opening her Bible. Still, her gaze drifts past the pages, drawn to the memory of the murky basement window. She had not seen much this time, but with a flashlight, perhaps she could glimpse her gift. One thing is sure: the next exploration would have to happen without another lie to Momma.

"You barely touched your supper, Janie," her mother observes later that evening, her eyes scanning the plate of uneaten red beans, fried potatoes, and sweet cornbread. The familiar aroma, a comfort that once always sparked Janie's appetite, now sat heavy and ignored. Even the thought of this, her father's favorite meal, cannot tempt her. She remembers Daddy claiming to be an "easy keeper" whenever Momma asked what special meal he wanted for his birthday.

"Just beans, taters, and cornbread followed by coconut cake and I'll be a happy man," was his usual response. His words echo in her mind, offering a brief moment of warmth.

This memory prompts Janie to ask, "Momma, how old was Daddy when he died?"

Her mother's smile fades, replaced by an all-too-fa-miliar sadness. "He was only thirty-six. Why do you ask?"

"My Sunday School teacher said Jesus was about thirty-three when He died on the cross, so I just won-dered if he and Daddy are about the same age in heav-en." Janie has no doubt where her father went after he died. His often-repeated words of assurance flooded her memory.

"Janie, the only way to heaven is through Jesus," he would say, taking a deep breath. "You can try to be good—you can go to church every day—you can pray—you can read your Bible—you can give all your money to the poor, but none of those things will get you a ticket to heaven." Without taking another breath, he would continue. "Jesus said, 'No man comes to the Father except by Me.' All we must do is believe Jesus is God, who came to the earth as a tiny baby. He grew up to become a man who taught us about love. Some people refused to believe He was who He said He was, so they crucified Him on a cross. Jesus willingly gave Himself as a sacrifice for our sins so, by believing in Him, we might have eternal life." His eyes would gleam with his last statement. "The good news, Janie, is Jesus did not stay in the grave, but He rose again on the third day, and He lives forever!" She loved how excited her father became when he talked about Jesus, and she longed to feel that same excitement herself one day.

That day happened last summer during Vacation Bible School. The pastor led the older children into the sanctuary for a special talk. On the whiteboard, he drew two cliffs separated by a deep chasm. One side represented people, and the other side, God. The chasm, he explained, was sin, and the Bible says everyone has sinned and is separated from God. He went on to say that there was no way for us to bridge the gap on our own. People try to do good things, but our good works are like filthy rags compared to God's righteousness. The pastor continued to tell the children how God had given Jesus Christ as a gift to be the bridge over the chasm. When we believe in His sacrifice, we are no longer stranded but can cross over to have peace with God forever.

During the pastor's talk, Janie's heart began to beat rapidly within her chest. She finally understood! This was the missing piece, the truth her daddy had always talked about. She had always tried to be a good girl, but all her goodness would never be enough. She needed Jesus to be her bridge to God. That night, kneeling by her bed, Janie told God how sorry she was for trying to be the bridge instead of accepting Christ as the bridge. She thanked Jesus for taking the punishment for her sins and making her clean. She then asked Him to enter her heart and live there forever. Her prayer concluded with one small request. "Please, dear God, would you let my Daddy know that, just like him, I know where I'm going when I die."

***

The old house falls silent after the breakfast pandemonium. Through the broken window, the sound of car doors opening and closing drifts in. He positions the step stool and peers out, watching a vehicle back out of the driveway and disappear, leaving him alone with his increasing thirst and a rumbling stomach. With the energetic family's departure, a cautious wave of relief washes over him. Emboldened, he reaches for the light switch above the worktable, and with a simple click, the once dark basement floods with light. A wide sink in the back corner immediately catches his eye. Hobbling as quickly as his swollen ankle allows, he makes his way to the faucet. The cool water is more satisfying than any liquid he has ever tasted, even his favorite beer. He drinks deeply before stepping back to survey his now brightly lit surroundings.

Above the sink is a metal cabinet. He opens it, rummaging through its contents. A grin spreads across his face—pay dirt! Whoever loved woodworking also appreciated peanut butter-filled crackers. He has not eaten since his pitiful breakfast yesterday, a distant memory from before he became a stranger to himself. His life has changed dramatically in the last 24 hours, and not for the better. Right now, though, food is his sole focus. He rips open the package, joyfully biting into the small orange square. *A little stale, but not bad,* he thinks, despite having no idea how old the crackers are. He ravenously devours five crackers, saving the remaining unopened packages for another time.

Having his thirst quenched and his hunger pains temporarily satisfied, he surveys his surroundings more thoroughly. The room measures roughly 14 x 20 feet, not a full basement, but ideal for a carpenter's workshop. Along the far wall, cabinets hold meticulously organized nails and screws of every size and type, along with various drill bits, wrenches, and an array of other tools. He examines the carefully stacked building materials, ready for assembly. "This guy's gearing up for a big project," he muses, but the layer of dust covering everything is still a puzzling detail. Further exploration of the room leads his eyes to a large pile of old blankets and quilts, all neatly folded and stacked under the staircase. Finally, a little luck comes his way. If he must spend another night in the basement, at least it would not be on the cold, hard cement floor this time.

Feeling a bit more alive, he sits down to consider his next move. Turning himself in is out of the question—that much he knows. Spending time in a federal prison is not on his bucket list! Denison is only a few miles from the Texas-Oklahoma border—maybe he could make a run for it. But then what? His ankle, throbbing with a possible break, rules out most options. And three thousand dollars? A paltry sum that will not last nearly long enough. A tension headache begins to pound in his head. Crawling under the stairs, he burrows into soft blankets. With a sigh, he lies back, closing his eyes. There is no easy answer to his predicament, but given enough time, he will figure something out. He has no other choice.

After a few minutes, his eyes flicker open, fixating on the ceiling. The memory of the squeaky floorboard from earlier returns. A simple repair, an easy fix that any attentive homeowner would have tackled at once. If they were HIS floors, he would have silenced the first squeak. But who is he kidding? A bitter laugh escapes his lips. His floors? His own house was a testament to neglect, with every repair ignored since Liz's death. A crazy thought occurs to him. Suppose he is doomed to remain in the basement another night. Why not silence that obnoxious squeak before the family returned?

Guarding his tender ankle, he searches, finding all the tools needed to make the repairs. Some areas simply require a few carefully placed screws to reattach the subfloor to the upper wood planks, while others need gluing and inserting shims between the joist and subfloor. The worst spot, he suspects, is where he heard the little jig earlier. After blowing the dust off the table saw, he cuts several wood braces to reinforce the sagging floor, the clean scent of fresh-cut lumber gradually replacing the basement's musty smell.

The familiar hum of the saw, the focused precision of his work, begins to unravel the tension in his nerves. He almost forgets where he is and how he came to be there. For a short time, he is simply a skilled craftsman doing what he loves most. After tightening the last screw, he steps back, proudly admiring his work. "That ought to take care of 'em for the next 50 years," he concludes, and, for the first time in a very long while, he smiles.

Only moments later, fantasy turns into stark reality. The distinct thud of slamming car doors signifies the family's return from their excursion. He lunges for the light switch, flipping it off, allowing darkness to envelop the room once again. His smile quickly fades as he hears the rowdy group above him head for the kitchen. The sound of feet traipsing back and forth across the floor suggests groceries being hauled in from the car. After a few tense minutes, the thunderous thud of feet finally calms down, and a slow smile spreads across his face once again. He has not heard a single squeak.

The afternoon wears on. Lunch in the house above comes and goes, and the old house becomes peaceful once again after the children are down for their naps. Mandy, he recalls, hated taking naps. She was a tiny master manipulator, with a legendary repertoire of excuses for avoiding sleep. "She would have been a great lawyer," he chuckles to himself. He remembers one time when she came out of her room, tears streaming, claiming she had lost a crucial toy—suddenly essential for her to sleep. He had searched, finally giving up and demanding she get back into bed. Moving her pillow to one side as he was tucking her in, he found the missing toy.

"Mandy, did you hide the toy under your pillow?" he questioned, his voice betraying a hint of amusement.

Without skipping a beat, she continued, "But I forgot where I hid it, so I needed your help to find it." Her sweetly innocent grin softened his resolve, and he laughed, knowing it was just another stalling tactic.

It never took much to melt his heart when it came to his girls, and they knew this exceptionally well. He loved it when Mandy and her mother would hold up their pinky fingers while declaring in unison, "We've got you wrapped around our little fingers!" And they absolutely did.

The inviting stack of blankets beneath the stairs soon beckons. Like a mother bird preparing a nest, he unfolds, rolls, and refolds the bedding assortment. Satisfied with his "nest," his thoughts turn to the shattered handrail lying just beyond his reach. He can only assume some kind of accident occurred. Judging from the scattered boxes among the splintered wood, something, or someone, must have met an unfortunate fate. Could this be the reason for the boarded doorway? His mind begins to drift, contemplating these thoughts. His head nods, and soon, he dozes off, warmly tucked away in his improvised bed.

The nap, however, is a short one. He awakes to find the basement window darkened by a small face peering through the panes of glass. "Oh my gosh," he whispers, pressing himself further back into the dark recess under the stairs, slowly pulling the blanket to his chin. The hairs on his arms bristle as the eyes of a child become visible through the hole in the window. Not daring to breathe, he sits quietly as the child attempts to look around the dark basement. Visibility is poor, hopefully poor enough! The face retreats, then a small pink-clad arm slowly eases through the opening.

Fear, hot and sharp, flares within him—not for himself, but for the child. The memory of his own encounter with the hole's jagged edges is still fresh. He watches, frozen, as the arm explores the dark space, clearly searching for the window latch. He braces for the inevitable, for the end of his escapade, but his primary concern now is to avoid startling the little girl and causing her to cut herself. He feels certain she wants to enter the basement for some other reason than finding him. But what? He glances around the murky room, his eyes resting on the doll cradle seen earlier. The cradle's craftsmanship and meticulous detail are remarkable. Yet, they only serve to remind him of a similar one he had lovingly built for Mandy on her fourth and final birthday. He hopes the little girl's presence at the window is driven by mere curiosity, but could she be seeking to retrieve the cradle, mysteriously kept in the basement workshop?

The little pink arm starts to retreat, then abruptly pauses. Her coat sleeve catches on the jagged edges of the hole. She struggles momentarily, finally pulling free, but not before tearing the sleeve of her coat. The rustling of bushes outside the window accompanies her hasty departure, and a woman's voice calls, "Janie... Janie, where are you?" The sound of the front door slamming shut is followed by a heavy sigh of relief. He sits up, lowering the blanket. How foolish of him to think the basement is a safe haven. If the girl is indeed searching for the cradle, then she will undoubtedly return. Whatever her motive, she clearly desires entry into the forbidden basement, and next time, she might succeed.

It is a risky choice, but he decides to spend one more night in the basement. He will leave at the first opportunity the next day, not so much for his own safety, but to protect the young girl from the frightening trauma of discovering a man in her basement. Entangling anyone else in his chaotic life would be disastrous, especially for the family upstairs, and most especially for a little girl named Janie.

***

A heavy heart accompanies Janie to bed that night. Lying to her mother was both wrong and sinful; however, the urge to solve the mystery of the birthday gift overrode any feelings of regret. She was able to reach the latch, so unlocking the window would be easy. Slipping in without anyone seeing her is the challenge! Momma has an uncanny ability to always know her whereabouts, or her ever-watchful siblings might be around. She will have to wait for the right opportunity. That night, Janie falls asleep dreaming of her beloved daddy, though a part of her understands he would be saddened by her less-than-honest plans.

***

He spends the rest of Saturday afternoon sitting passively in the dimly lit basement, a prisoner, not only to this oppressive place, but also to his thoughts. The sight of the little pink arm rattled him, but his injured ankle leaves him with no choice but to stay. He tears open another package of crackers, but the dry crumbs seem to catch in his throat, and each swallow is a struggle. Nevertheless, he is grateful to have something in his aching stomach.

Throughout the afternoon, his thoughts centered on the family above. The clues are everywhere: the lack of a man's presence, the rundown house, the broken stair railing, the dusty workshop, and the boarded door. Each detail hints at a story as tragic as his own.

He imagines strangers wandering through his house; they would not need to be told how little he cared. His house contained only the barest necessities: a television, his old recliner, a lumpy, unmade bed, a dining table buried under paperwork, and a lonely coffee maker on the kitchen counter. There were no family pictures, no artwork, no warmth of any kind. Once, it had been a home filled with laughter and love, but now, it was just an old, dilapidated house, as empty as he felt inside.

His thoughts, uncontrollable, drift back to the dark days after the accident that took Elizabeth and his daughter. The drunk driver had survived, a bitter irony that fueled his rage even fourteen years later. That scumbag had lived, even walked away from the accident, while the two people he cherished most were gone. Unfair. Unjust. Unnecessary.

Elizabeth's older sister, Leslie, had called him one evening about a year after the accident. Usually, he avoided calls from Liz's family, but for some reason, he answered that night.

"Just wanted to see how you're doing," said Leslie. "I am surprised you answered the phone this time."

"Yeah, well, I'm surprised too." He answered Leslie's directness with his own.

"I know you hate chit-chat, but I thought you would like to know that the kid who hit Elizabeth has had a real change in his life since the accident."

"Oh?" he laughed sarcastically. "Well, good for him. Glad to help. I had a real change in my life, too." He bristled at the mere thought of the murderous kid.

"I know you're having an extremely tough time, but I thought it might help to know. God promises to bring good out of all things—even tragedies. I talked with the kid's parents, and they said he has committed his life to the Lord and plans to attend seminary and become a pastor."

"Like I said...good for him. His life is great, and my life is ruined. Tell me, Leslie, what good is God going to bring to me?" He was shouting into the phone by now, but he did not care. He was tired of her "Polly-anna" attitude.

"You know, you aren't the only person who loved Liz and Mandy." Leslie's voice quivered with anger. "We are all hurting, but with God's help, we've been able to forgive this young man. Maybe you should as well." She raised her voice right back at him.

"Forgive him? You gotta be kidding! Hell no, I won't ever forgive the person who took everything precious to me. My life was shattered in one night because of him. I hope he rots in hell!" Typically, his anger caused people to back off, but Leslie persisted.

"Hating that boy only hurts you. Forgiving him doesn't change or excuse what he did. Forgiveness changes you! It will free you from the painful burden you are carrying. Please...please ask God to help you forgive this boy...for your own sake." Her plea, deep and intense, failed to move him.

He remained silent for several minutes, unsure how to end the conversation. "You do what's best for you, Les, and I'll do what's best for me. Hatred is about the only thing that keeps me alive these days. If I don't feel hate, then I don't feel anything." He softened his tone. This was Liz's sister, after all. "Look, Leslie, I appreciate your call, but it's probably best if you and your family go on with your life, and I'll… I'll go on with mine. You don't need to call and check on me anymore. I'll be fine. Please tell your parents the same thing. Goodbye, Leslie."

"But…but…" He ignored Leslie's insistent plea and hung up the phone. She tried calling him back, but he never spoke with her again.

Short days and long nights, typical January days, allow darkness to slowly seep back into his basement hideout. Above, the house exhales its last noisy breath, settling into a deep quiet. He pulls the blankets tighter, grateful for their warmth, though sleep does not come as easily as it had the night before. Usually, his dreams vanished with the first light, but tonight, they stubbornly refuse to let go. Images of little girls in pink coats, rocking their dollies, singing sweet lullabies, spin in his head. Sometimes the little girl is Mandy, sometimes Janie. Neither girl will look at him directly, nor speak to him, yet he can feel their tremendous disappointment. Disappointment in him.

After the initial shock of finding out his girls were gone, he had not cried. He had learned young that men did not cry, that emotion was a sign of weakness. People had called it "stoicism," admiring his control, even though they thought it was "unusual and abnormal." Once, after a particularly wet spring, he had driven out to the Denison Dam to see the water from Lake Texoma as it overflowed the spillway. It was a rare sight for the locals, but the huge lake had held all she could and seemed to groan with relief as the rushing water poured forth from her swollen banks. Now, alone in his dark basement prison, the dam within him breaks. The water from his own swollen banks of emotions pours forth. The darkness of the basement consumes the uncontrolled sobs racking his body. He weeps for what he has done, for what he has become, for what he has lost. Tears flow for the little girl in the pink coat, knowing, like him, she has suffered terrible loss. It had to be her father who had tumbled down the stairs, broken the handrail, and met his death on the cold concrete floor. That sealed door stood as a memorial to her father's untimely passing. And, this workshop, his current refuge, was the space of a man now gone, a space he occupied as an unseen, unwanted presence. In his dreams, Janie and Mandy looked at him with disappointment, but no one's disappointment cuts deeper than his own.

CHAPTER 5

Janie stares at the open bible in her lap, unable to focus on the familiar words. Sundays are usually Janie's favorite, a day full of happiness and excitement. Today, though, the heaviness of yesterday's troubles followed her throughout the morning. The Sunday School room buzzes with childish chatter and giggles, but Janie sits quietly. When the teacher asked a question, half the class shot their arms into the air, but not Janie. Typically, she is the first one to wave her hand. Not today. The piano begins to play, the children stand, their voices rising in joyful worship, but today, Janie did not join the chorus of cheerful hymns. Ordinarily, singing lifts her spirits, no matter how down she is. Not today. She misses her father. Her throat tightens at the memory of her father's voice—warm, off-key, full of joy. He had loved singing as well, and he and Janie often broke into song at the most inappropriate times, prompting giggles and laughter.

The teacher's voice fades into the background as Janie's mind wanders to a special memory. Daddy had taken the whole family down to Arlington for a Texas Rangers baseball game. The day was a rare and exciting treat. Momma let them splurge and buy all the typical baseball game goodies: hot dogs, buttery popcorn, and pink cotton candy. But it was the Cracker Jacks, with their secret toy surprise inside, that Janie wanted more than anything else.

"Please, Momma, just one box," Janie pleaded, her voice soft. She tilted her head down slightly, her eyes wide and upturned, fixed on her mother's face. "I promise to share with the others."

Always practical, her mother refused. "You kids have had enough junk food for one day. Have some of your sister's cotton candy. She won't be able to eat it all by herself." Usually, Janie would have just agreed, but this time, disappointment showed clearly on her face as she sat down. Out of the corner of her eye, she saw her father watching the exchange.

With a wink and a wide grin, he suddenly stood up and began loudly singing, "TAKE ME OUT TO THE BALLGAME. TAKE ME OUT WITH THE CROWD."

Beaming from ear to ear, Janie was quick to stand up, joining her father's lively song. "BUY ME SOME PEANUTS AND CRACKERJACKS. I DON'T CARE IF WE EVER GET BACK."

By this time, the surrounding crowd began their accompaniment. "LET ME ROOT...ROOT...ROOT

FOR THE HOME TEAM, IF THEY DON'T WIN, IT'S A SHAME."

Finally, her mother, no longer able to resist the merriment, joined her voice with the boisterous crowd. "FOR IT'S ONE...TWO...THREE STRIKES YOU'RE OUT AT THE OLD...BALL....GAME!" Janie got her Crackerjacks that day!

Sunday afternoon stretches long and quiet with Janie playing in her bedroom. Unable to shake her curiosity, her mind wanders back to the forbidden, mysterious gift in the basement. It wasn't fair. Daddy meant the gift for her, so why not try to see it? A little peek won't hurt. She deserves better. The struggle between right and wrong troubles Janie throughout the afternoon.

Later, her mother's head pokes through the doorway. "Janie, are you feeling okay? You barely ate your lunch, and it's not like you to be this quiet."

"I'm fine, Momma. I'm just not very hungry this evening." Janie says, though she doesn't mean it. In truth, she's not fine at all.

Daddy once told her that Jesus had forgiven all her sins, even before she had done anything wrong. She didn't quite understand what that meant, but she finds some comfort remembering those words. Then, she remembers something else he'd said. "Even though God has already forgiven all our sins, He still wants us to confess our sins so we will feel better. When we do things that displease God, we lose His peace and don't feel good. But once we tell God what we've done, we feel better, and our peace returns. When a person becomes a believer, sin no longer has power over him.

Sin becomes a choice we make. We can choose to ask the Holy Spirit to help us resist the temptation to sin, or we can choose to give in to sin. Janie, no one makes us sin. The devil can't make us do anything! Likewise, no one makes us confess either. We choose to confess our sins and receive God's forgiveness and peace. It's all about the choices we make."

Janie yearns for that peace, for that feeling of lightness. But confessing her secret to Momma terrifies her. She knows she should eventually tell the truth about her coat, but not yet. Not until she has one last, quick glimpse into the basement to see the gift Daddy had made for her. After that, she would spill everything. But for now, right or wrong, she has made her choice.

***

The crew is up early the next morning, and soon they are gone. He remembers it is Sunday, and Sunday means church for most North Texas families. Liz had taken Mandy to church every Sunday since she was born. He would tag along for Christmas or Easter, but only to please Elizabeth. From time to time, Liz would ask him to attend with her, but she never pushed. No, it was Mandy who begged him every Sunday morning.

"Daddy, please go with us today. Carley's daddy comes with her every Sunday...why can't you?"

His answer was a well-worn record. "Honey, like I told you last week…and the week before, I need my sleep. You know how hard I work, and Sunday is the only day I can get a little extra shuteye."

"I know, Daddy, but I won't give up!" she would exclaim, hands on her hips. And she never did. Her persistence was just about to pay off when that fateful night changed his life forever. Now? He'd be damned if he ever set foot in a church again!

Feeling safe with the family's departure, he turns the light on again. The overhead glow instantly warms the concrete room. His ankle, still throbbing, feels less swollen than before. He slowly stands, trying to put a little weight on it. A sharp jolt of pain buckles his leg, sending him sprawling back down with a wince. Walking is out of the question. He knows he should leave, especially after yesterday's close call, but travel is impossible with his ankle in this state. Plus, his swollen foot would never squeeze into a boot. He sits for several minutes, racking his brain for an alternative to staying in the basement, but nothing comes to mind. He has burned too many bridges over the years to call anyone for help, not that he has a phone to call them with. *How preposterous can this be?* He shakes his head, unable to stop a wry chuckle. *What would Liz think of the mess I'm in? Of course, I wouldn't be in this dilemma if she were still alive.* That sad thought offers little consolation, though, because deep down, he knows the only person to blame is himself. He has no choice. He is stuck in the basement until his ankle heals enough to allow him to walk. Looking around the now brightly lit room, he takes heart; things could be worse. At least he is out of the nasty weather, has water and food—well, crackers—and a warm place to sleep. The only foreseeable problem is Janie. He is concerned she might come back, but for now, the family is gone, and he can move freely without worry.

Unable to resist his nature as a meticulous carpenter, he continues to repair a few more creaky floorboards, hoping for a distraction from the painful memories of his lost family. He steps back, admiring a job well done. A long-forgotten feeling begins to settle deep in his chest—a gentle warmth that spreads outwards—the quiet satisfaction of helping others. He glances around, a new energy stirring within him. *What else can I tackle next?* His eyes land on the jagged remains of the stair railing, a splintered mess hanging precariously, a hazard begging for attention. The flimsy construction, now laid bare, practically screams a violation of building codes. He walks to the lumber pile, his gaze sharp and focused, pulling out a sturdy piece of oak, precisely what the repairs need.

The workshop fills with the screech of the saw, the whine of the drill, and the rhythmic thump of the hammer. Often, he pauses, looking anxiously outside the window, fearing a curious passerby. But the sidewalk and street remain empty. Several times, he catches himself whistling as the time passes quickly. He stops himself at two hours, mindful of how long his family had typically spent at church on Sunday mornings. Just as he hammers the last nail and turns out the lights, the family returns, as if on cue. He scurries back to his bed, satisfied knowing the stair railing looks better than new.

Settling in for a long afternoon, he has time to think against the backdrop of muffled sounds from the family above. But only one word consumes his mind: food.

The workshop is directly below the kitchen and dining area, where most of the home's activities occur. The alluring aromas from the kitchen torment him. He tries to doze, but the gnawing pain in his stomach grows with each passing hour, making him feel increasingly uncomfortable. Unable to bear the hunger pangs any longer, he tears open the last package of crackers, devouring every crumb. Knowing that only a thin sheet of plywood separates him from the family's kitchen leads to wild and crazy thoughts. "Better eat a few more crackers," he mumbles to himself, "before I march up those stairs, knock on the door, and beg for food!" Considering how truly "crazy" his life has become, nothing would surprise him at this point.

The afternoon drags on until darkness finally fills the room. This is his third night in the basement, and the house's nightly rhythm has become as familiar as his own heartbeat. Supper, then baths, followed by what he can only guess are rituals much like those he once shared with Mandy.

Typically, Liz would cook supper while he gave Mandy her nightly bath. She would sit patiently while he bathed her and then washed her hair. Once finished, she'd pull out all her bath toys, disappearing into the imaginary world of her bathtub kingdom.

"Mandy, you have a vivid imagination for such a little girl," he would tease. "You must get it from your momma."

"Is a 'bibid' imagination a good thing or a bad thing to have?" Her innocence always amused him.

"It's a very good thing!" Liz chimed in, startling him. She had been standing behind him, unnoticed. She answered Mandy's question in a way that differed significantly from how he would have. "God gave us our imaginations so He can create beautiful things through us. You once told me you wanted to be an artist when you grew up, right?" Mandy nodded. "Well, it takes a vivid imagination to be an artist—or write a book—or be a good schoolteacher—or…"

"Or be a carpenter, like Daddy!" Mandy interrupted.

"Absolutely! Daddy may think he doesn't have much of an imagination, but we know he does." Liz winked at him. "If you let Daddy play with one of your mermaids, I think you can help him realize he has a vivid imagination, too."

"Thanks, Liz," he sarcastically replied. "Okay, little lady, shall I be the pink or the purple mermaid?"

Imaginative or not, getting out of this predicament will require every ounce of creativity he can muster. Looking back, he never dreamed it would involve such insidious deception.

After the house falls silent, he hears quiet footsteps enter the dining area. A chair gently scrapes against the floor as someone sits. A faint sound of crying follows—he worries it's Janie's mother.

Life must be incredibly hard for a young widow with four small children. Based on what he'd overheard earlier, she faced similar financial struggles as he did. The stark difference, though, was that she had four mouths to feed, versus just his own. Her family lives in a shabby, old house much like his, but he possesses the skills to maintain his home, and she does not. She has lost her husband in a tragic accident; just as he has lost his own family. Again, he has only himself to care for while she juggles being both mother and father to four little ones. She knows suffering as he does, yet her life has gone on while his has stopped.

Her life may be hard, he thinks, *but the hand dealt me is harder. She is still a mother with children to consider. I'm not a father or a husband, and I have no one.* Trying to rationalize his emptiness is futile. For the past fourteen years, he has surrounded himself with thick walls of self-pity and blame. Now, the tears of this young mother are causing a crack to form. The light shining through that crack is as dim as the light filtering through the dirty basement window—but it was, undeniably, a light.

The soft sobs from upstairs eventually fade into silence. He pictures Janie's mother, just as Liz would have done in desperate times, turning to prayer. Liz would shed her tears, but eventually, she would pray. He remembers walking into their kitchen once and finding Liz at the table, her chin lifted upwards, eyes closed, and her cheeks wet with tears.

"You okay?" he had asked. She opened her eyes and studied him in silence before answering. "I'm fine, but I could be better."

"Tell me what would make you feel better, and your wish will be my command!" he said jokingly.

"My wish is," she hesitated, then continued. "My wish is that you would give God a chance."

"Give Him a chance to do what?" he sighed. This subject always made him feel uneasy.

"A chance to show you He is trustworthy, a chance to show you how much He loves you, a chance to show you how you can depend on Him, a chance…"

He raised his hand, stopping her mid-sentence. "Liz, you know I'm not a man who takes chances. I only act on what I know, and I just don't know for sure about God." He knew his answer was not one she wanted to hear. "But you can keep on praying for me and maybe, someday, I'll give God a chance." He hated to give her false hope, but he would say anything to stop her tears.

"I do pray for you," she calmly replied. "Every day I pray for you, and someday, you will find yourself in a situation where God is the only chance you have. Then my prayers will be answered."

It seemed Liz's prayers were finally being answered.

CHAPTER 6

Monday, January 5, 2009

Monday dawns, his planned day of departure. Before long, the house would empty, everyone off to work or school, leaving him alone in the house. He'd put the finishing touches on the stair railing, then make his exit. The old house clearly needed weeks of work, but there is only so much he can do in the basement. Still, it was a gesture of gratitude to a family unknowingly sheltering a criminal.

The rich aroma of another hearty breakfast soon fills the air, stirring a hunger in him as profound as a bear waking from winter sleep. He is starving, desperate for anything to eat. The thin sheet of plywood separating him from their kitchen drives him crazy, but what can he do? Adding breaking and entering to his charges would only deepen his troubles, but then, did it truly matter anymore?

The front door suddenly slams shut, rattling the walls all the way down to the basement. Car doors close with a bang, and the family auto slowly backs out of the driveway. They are gone, hopefully for the day. Getting up the stairs with a swollen ankle will not be easy, but he is willing to try. Taking the hammer, he carefully hobbles up the steps one by one until he reaches the top landing. Whoever had put up the plywood meant it as only a temporary barrier, at best. Removing it will be easy—just pop out a few nails on one side, pull it back a little, and he can be inside. But he is not a thief. Then again, he never thought of himself as a bank robber either. He stands on the landing debating his predicament for a few minutes, then proceeds to pull out the nails, one by one.

***

Janie's bedroom remains shrouded in darkness as she stirs awake. Monday morning, school day, but her mind is elsewhere, consumed by the scratchy, raw feeling in her throat. Sickness means trouble for Momma. Janie knows her mother's job at the law firm Burgess, Howard & Smith—BHS, as she calls it—does not tolerate too many absences. With four kids, Momma often said she had to "walk a tightrope" between home and work. Truth be told, Janie is eager for school to start again, hoping it will distract her from the worries at home. Hearing her mother cry last night only deepens the shame she feels about her lie. Before, Momma cried because she missed Daddy. Now, her tears are about bills that aren't getting paid. Janie doesn't quite grasp the details, but money worries always make Momma sad. Even when Daddy was alive, Momma fretted about money. They weren't rich like some kids at school, yet they always had what they needed. Janie often heard her mother complain to Daddy. "John, I wish you would show a little more concern about our finances. It seems I do the worrying for both of us! Can't you see that?"

But Daddy would simply hug Momma, offering his usual reply. "Cast all your worries upon God, Bethany, because He cares for you." Hugging was usually followed by tickling, much to Janie's delight, and soon, her mother's frustration would melt away. A wave of sadness washes over her, knowing there is no one left to tickle Momma.

The school day zips by. Afterward, Janie herds her brothers, first and second graders, and her preschool sister into the gym for after-school care. The teachers call her "little momma," a title she secretly cherishes. Every day, as five o'clock approaches, Janie gathers her siblings, helping them with coats and backpacks. The most challenging part is keeping them all corralled until Momma arrives, especially on late days, like today.

By the time they finally reach home, Janie feels worse than she had all day. Her red, watery eyes speak volumes, revealing what her earlier protests had not.

"You, young lady, head straight to bed," her mother orders. "With the way you've been acting lately, I knew you must be getting sick."

"It's not that bad, Momma, just a sore throat," Janie insists, trying to sound reassuring. "You always say a little chicken soup will cure anything."

"A little chicken soup, some medicine, and a good night's sleep do help. Now, head to bed, and I'll bring you a tray with soup."

Feeling "special" is a rare commodity when sharing a bedroom with a younger sister and two brothers. But when sick, each child earns the coveted privilege of a meal tray served right in their room. Sometimes, that tray almost makes being sick worth it.

Most evenings revolve around preparing for the next school day, except on Wednesdays, when Bible Club at church takes precedence. Her father used to say Janie had the memory of an elephant, a truth often proven by the array of patches on her club vest, each one a testament to another memorized Bible verse.

Janie hurries to finish her soup, eager to tackle the week's memory verse before her brothers inevitably burst into the room and make studying impossible. Her fingers quickly find the passage. Interestingly, it is one she has not encountered before: *Hebrews 13:2 Do not neglect to show hospitality to strangers, for by this, some have entertained angels without knowing it.*

Janie loves thinking about angels. After her father died, a sweet elderly lady from church had told her that Daddy was an angel now. But Janie knew that wasn't true. Momma had explained that God created angels separately from people. They had special jobs, like helping people or delivering messages from God. She vividly recalled the story of God sending an angel to Mary and Joseph to announce Jesus's birth, and how angels also told the shepherds.

But this verse says people can entertain angels sometimes and not even know it. *How can this be*, she wonders. *Won't their wings or halos give it away?* She feels sure she would recognize an angel if she saw one, even though it is unlikely she ever would. God certainly doesn't send angels to little girls who lie to their mothers. This is undoubtedly a privilege reserved for only good people, and she doesn't feel like a very good person at this moment.

Time alone in the bedroom quickly ends with the arrival of her brothers and sister. After kisses and prayers, her mother tucks them in bed and turns off the lights. Janie knows she must tell God she is sorry for the lie she told. Slipping out of bed, she kneels and folds her hands. "God, please forgive me for lying to Momma. I know it was wrong, and I don't want to ever lie to her again. Amen. Also, it would be really cool if You would let me see an angel someday. Amen." Tomorrow she will tell her mother the truth about that ripped sleeve.

***

Extreme hunger affects a man in strange ways. For one thing, the ability to reason disappears entirely. What once seemed like a crazy, desperate scheme—prying open a makeshift door and entering a stranger's home uninvited—now feels altogether sensible, even justifiable. He'd be in and out in a flash, just grab a few items, then head back to the basement. No harm done.

He slips the hammer beneath each nail head, prying them up one by one. Carefully, he eases the plywood away from the wall. Beyond it stands a closed door. He hesitates, unsure if it's locked, and reaches for the knob. It turns smoothly beneath his fingers. He pushes the door open, revealing only darkness. Stepping forward, he crosses the threshold—he is in. The home is exactly as he pictured: simply furnished, strewn with toys—clearly a place lovingly lived in. He heads down the short hallway and into the kitchen. Right away, he grabs a mug and pours himself a cup of coffee. "Ahhh... heaven in a cup!" His own voice echoes throughout the tiny kitchen. The coffee is not as hot as he prefers, but even lukewarm coffee is better than no coffee at all.

Luck is on his side; the family had clearly been in a hurry that morning. On the kitchen counter lay the remains of their breakfast. He hastily crams the remnants of uneaten pancakes and bacon in his mouth, savoring each tasty morsel. He feels no guilt—those leftovers were destined for the trash anyway. After washing everything down with a large glass of milk, he rummages through the cabinets, searching for items to take back to the basement. Careful not to take more than the family might miss, he stuffs his pockets with granola bars, some fruit, crackers, nuts, and cheese. Not exactly a feast, but enough to hold him until his escape. A few more sips of coffee, and it is time to hurry back. He rinses the coffee mug and milk glass, then carefully places them back in the cabinet, hoping they will appear untouched.

An odd ease settles over him, an unwelcome guest surprisingly at home. The chilly dampness of the basement recedes, replaced by the comforting warmth of a real home. It is not just physical warmth; it settles deep in his chest, a forgotten comfort echoing the memory of his own home from so long ago.

Unable to resist curiosity, he takes time to explore. The house is even smaller than he had imagined: only a kitchen combined with a dining area, a living room, one bathroom, and two bedrooms. *How is it possible for this family to manage in such a small space,* he asks himself. The four children, it seems, sleep together in one bedroom, brightly decorated with a circus theme. Despite its size, the room is remarkably organized. Each child has a designated spot for their belongings, and a bulletin board proudly displays their accomplishments. Janie's board, he notices, overflows with ribbons and awards from a Bible club.

The mother's room is equally small but tidy and tastefully decorated. On her dresser, several framed photographs offer his first glimpse of the young family. He picks up one of the pictures, recognizing the familiar picnic area his own family had visited near Lake Texoma. The smiling family was gathered together, the mother holding a squirming toddler with one arm and a young boy with the other. Janie stood in front of her father, who held another small boy in his arms. They were a beautiful family.

Hot tears well up in his eyes before he can stop the flood of emotions. He hastily wipes them away with the back of his hand, shaking his head in disgust. *What kind of man cries this easily? Get a grip, dammit!* Returning the photograph to its place, a surge of anger rises within him. *Why did God take this man from his family when they obviously need him? It's not fair when bad things happen to good people. It doesn't make sense, and it never will.* These are the same questions he'd been asking for the past fourteen years, and still, there are no answers. The voice of hopelessness echoes in his head, confirming his long-held belief. "God is not fair nor just. He plays with us like pawns in some great, cruel cosmic game, and we are helpless to do anything." Still wrestling with life's injustices, he hurries out of the bedroom, quickly slipping through the door back to the safety of the basement.

With the plywood securely nailed back in place and his belly pleasantly full, he is more determined than ever to help this forsaken family. Despite his painful ankle, the new, stronger stairway railing is finished in short order. Every piece of lumber, every tool he needed was right there in the stack of building materials. He can only assume the father had planned to replace the old railing himself, hence the supplies. But what other plans did this fellow carpenter have in mind, plans requiring so much lumber and other supplies?

Looking through the numerous cabinets and drawers, he finds the answer. Tucked away in a drawer is a complete set of building plans—meticulously drawn, stamped with a city permit, and ready to build. This father, it seems, had planned to transform a large part of his beloved workshop into a much-needed bedroom for his growing family. Did Janie's mother know? Perhaps it was meant to be a surprise for them all. Regardless, the father's premature death had halted any such dreams in their tracks.

He sinks back onto a chair, his thoughts racing. *What if I finish the basement for them? Everything's here, and I can work while they are gone each day. Plus, I can easily slip in and out for food without being detected. Besides, if they catch me, things can't get any worse than they already are!* He almost slaps himself to snap back to reality, but reality has long since vanished. *It's a crazy idea, but it could work. I need a place to hide until the swelling goes down a little, and Janie's family needs this room. Why can't I build the room her father never had a chance to start?* What began as a far-fetched notion quickly gains traction the more he considers it. *Janie will be preoccupied with school this week, so I doubt she'll have much time to snoop. Come Friday afternoon, I'll be outta here!* It is an irrational plan, but his mind is set, and time is ticking!

After studying the plans, he makes some minor adjustments and then begins to explore the stacked building materials, hoping everything he needs is there. As far as he can tell, it is, along with all the necessary tools, thanks to Janie's father's meticulous attention to detail.

Moving the heavy tools to the far side of the room, a difficult task with his sore ankle, consumes most of the afternoon. The table holding Janie's cradle is the last thing he pushes aside. Examining it more closely, he marvels at the expert craftsmanship. Few could rival his own expertise, yet Janie's father had honed skills even greater than his own. To his discredit, he rarely respected other carpenters, but this craftsman deserved respect. With a single-minded resolution, he sets about snapping the chalk lines for the first wall. God may have forgotten this family, but he will not.

The family returns that evening with the same vibrant energy with which they had left. He had forgotten how raucous small children can be, but the sound of their boisterous activity is unexpectedly comforting. After enjoying an apple and a granola bar from the kitchen, he stretches out on his makeshift bed under the stairs. Funny, but the loneliness that overwhelmed him earlier no longer seems so distressing. He feels different, a strange lightness he cannot quite pinpoint. The few pounds lost due to a lack of food certainly contributed to his physical lightness, but this is a lightness of his heart. The burdens he has carried for fourteen years are still there, yet tonight, they feel less heavy. This puzzles him, considering his circumstances have not changed in the least; in fact, they are worse! His list of crimes has grown—he has stolen money, then food. He broke into a basement, then into their home. Yet, a peace he has not known in years settles over him. Even though the family upstairs does not realize they need him, he knows. He has a job to do, one from which he will not derive a single benefit, except the satisfaction of helping someone else. Sleep comes easily that fourth night in the basement. A warm bed and a full stomach help, but knowing he has a purpose allows him to sleep soundly.

Chapter 7

Tuesday, January 6, 2009

Janie clears her throat several times, but the pain is worse than the night before. Every swallow hurts more than the last. She longs to burrow deeper under the covers, to let Momma bring her more hot soup, but BHS will not like their star secretary taking another day off.

"Janie," her mother calls, "You better get a move on if you want breakfast this morning."

She slides out of bed, dresses for school, and trudges to the kitchen. Head down, she hopes her mother won't notice how truly awful she feels.

"Janie Lynn? Look at me."

Janie lifts her head, offering a weak smile.

Momma's gaze cuts right through her charade. "Does your throat still hurt, honey?"

"Yes, ma'am, but it's not too bad." A tiny, necessary lie.

"Well, I don't think you should go to school today. In fact, I want you back in bed immediately. I'll call the office and then bring you something warm to drink. Maybe I can work from home today."

Her mother disappears into her bedroom with the phone, emerging moments later, a frown etched on her face. As feared, BHS is not happy. A prominent case is nearing trial, and they desperately need their most valued secretary. Seeing her mother's distress, Janie insists she is well enough to go to school.

"No, baby, no job is worth sending you to school this sick. I'll take the kids to school, swing by my office to pick up a few files, and then come home. Do you think you'll be okay by yourself for about an hour?" her mother asks. "Mrs. Beardsley is always home next door if you need anything, and I'll have my cell phone with me."

Janie nods. "I'll be fine, Momma. You don't have to worry."

"Well, lock the doors after we leave, and I'll call you in a little while." With that last instruction, Janie's mother hurries out, the younger children trailing behind her.

Janie had been left alone once before, but only for about thirty minutes. Following her mother's instructions is crucial if she ever wants more responsibility. As soon as the door clicks shut, however, her thoughts turn to the surprise gift in the basement. *Momma said she'd be gone an hour, but is that enough time to get in and out of the basement? What if Momma comes home early?* A shiver runs down her spine at the thought of being caught. Besides, her throat truly aches. It is better to wait for her mother's return, snuggled under a warm blanket. The mystery of her gift will just have to wait another day.

An hour later, the phone rang. "Hi, honey. I'm still at the office and really need to stay until lunchtime. I called Mrs. Beardsley, and she will come over and stay with you until I get home."

This is the opportunity she's been waiting for, but not with Mrs. Beardsley around. Janie quickly replies, "Mrs. Beardsley doesn't need to come over. I'm just going to watch a little TV and work on my memory verses for Bible Club. I'll be okay until you get home." She has lied—again. Her daddy once told her, "Sin begets sin." She did not fully understand it at the time, but she does now.

"Alright, Janie, I trust you will do as I've told you. I'll call Mrs. Beardsley back and ask her to keep an eye on the house. Call my cell if you need me, and I'll see you later this afternoon."

Her mother trusts her. Janie hates the idea of breaking that trust, but her mind is made up. She is finally going to find out what Daddy had left for her in the basement workshop two years ago. With a stomach full of butterflies, she pulls on her pink coat with its mended sleeve and promptly heads out the back door.

***

*D*awn's first light filters through the window, awakening him. Stretching his arms forward to ease the pain in his shoulders, he yawns loudly, forgetting where he is. His hand instinctively reaches for another granola bar, hoping to quiet the gnawing hunger in his stomach. This so-called "bed," though not as comfortable as his old recliner, had granted him a whole night's sleep—a rare luxury.

Eager to dive into the basement renovation, he listens and waits patiently through the usual morning commotion overhead. The family would leave soon, allowing him to finally begin the new project. The familiar sound of car doors slamming, followed by the minivan's whine as it backs down the driveway, signals he is alone at last. Comforted by the thought of a hot cup of coffee, he begins the slow ascent to the top of the stairs. Each day, his ankle feels better, but climbing stairs is still rough. It is throbbing by the time he reaches the landing. Bending over, he gingerly begins to rub his sore ankle, but the unexpected soft pad of feet on the other side of the plywood makes him stand up straight. His eyes widen, and a silent, *Oh crap!* forms on his lips. He freezes, afraid someone has heard him on the stairway, but the footsteps continue past the doorway. Pressing his ear to the plywood, he listens as the back door slowly creaks open, then softly closes.

Not wasting another second, he quickly hops back down the stairs two at a time, ignoring his hurting ankle. Diving under the stairs with only moments to spare, he presses himself as far back into the darkness as possible. From this vantage point, he can clearly see the basement window. He watches anxiously, fearing what is sure to happen next.

***

*J*anie's heart pounds against her chest as she rounds

124

the corner of the house and drops to her hands and knees, crawling under the scraggly bushes. Her plan is simple: unlatch the window, slip into the basement, find her surprise, then get back out as fast as possible. No harm done. Thankfully, Mrs. Beardsley lives on the opposite side of the house. No doubt, their elderly neighbor will be diligently watching their home as promised.

She creeps along on hands and knees under the row of bushes until she reaches the broken basement window. Cautious not to snag her coat again, she slowly inserts her hand through the jagged edges of the glass, searching for the window latch. There it is! The rusty old latch releases easily this time, allowing her to push the window open with little effort. Lying on her stomach, she rests her hands on the window ledge, easing her head into the narrow opening. Rats! Her body completely blocks all daylight. She can't see anything. Maybe if she waits for a moment, her eyes will adjust, but it is of no use.

What choice does she have now but to climb through the window? She must see the gift! Still on her stomach, Janie rotates her body until her legs dangle through the opening. Sliding her body in as far as possible while gripping the window ledge, she takes a deep breath, lets go, and hits the basement floor with a resounding thud.

It has been over two years since Janie set foot in her daddy's workshop. He had never allowed any of the children inside without either him or their mother being present. It was a special place reserved for her father alone. He would spend every spare moment crafting beautiful wooden toys: trucks of every kind, planes with spinning propellers, multi-colored blocks, puzzles in the shape of animals, and doll furniture such as cribs and cradles. Sometimes, his own children were the lucky recipients, but often, the toys went to disadvantaged children around their small town. Janie loved accompanying her father as he visited the women's shelter or the hospital where he distributed toys to the grateful boys and girls. Janie would never forget the pure joy in each child's eyes as they received a special handmade toy. Nor would she ever forget the even greater joy in her father's eyes.

Janie's father had spent his days working as a carpenter, building houses with a framing crew all around Grayson County. Each evening, he would come home smelling of fresh-cut wood, a fine layer of sawdust clinging to his hands and clothes. Janie loved that scent, but Momma often made him shake out his clothes before coming inside, then immediately ushered him off to shower. Daddy's workshop should smell like fresh-cut wood and sawdust—like Daddy once did. But it doesn't. The cold, dark basement now smells musty and stale, no longer a place of warmth and love. Not at all what she had expected.

Janie stands hesitantly to her feet, brushing dust from her pants, relieved that the short fall did not hurt much. She glances sideways, spotting a step stool leaning against the wall. Getting into the basement had been her only focus, but she had not considered how to get back out through the elevated window. She stands quietly, letting her eyes adjust to the dim light. After a few minutes, the familiar outlines of Daddy's tools against the wall and the long wooden table come into focus. How many times had she sat on a barstool at this table, watching her daddy transform a block of wood into a piece of art? Too many to count, she supposes.

Janie feels her way through the murky darkness, resisting the urge to turn on the overhead light. The last thing she needs is for Mrs. Beardsley to come snooping and see her in this forbidden place. Step by step, she slowly inches towards the worktable. The light is faint, but the dark object in the middle must be her birthday gift. She draws close enough to reach out and gently touches it. This is the surprise birthday gift from her daddy, and it is beautiful! Her daddy had made cradles before, but none were as lovely as this one. Eight intricately carved wooden spindles lined each side, each corner spindle topped by a smooth wooden ball finial. Both the headboard and footboard had three cut-out hearts, the middle one larger than the other two on either side. She has never seen anything more wonderful in her young life. She gently rocks the cradle back and forth, feeling the smoothly sanded wood beneath her fingers. Daddy had made this cradle especially for her—no one else. Touching it was like touching Daddy. Warm tears fill her eyes, slowly dripping down her cheeks, forming tiny pools of water on the dusty table.

Lost in thought, Janie stands there, rocking the cradle much longer than she intends. She hates to leave it but knows her gift from Daddy must stay in the musty workshop. Her mother should be told about the gift, but that would involve Janie admitting she had lied about her torn coat and gone into the forbidden basement. Better Momma did not know, for now. With one last loving look at the cradle, she turns towards the window.

Gasping, she clasps her hand over her mouth. A prominent, ghostly figure stands between her and the window! The backlighting from the basement window makes it impossible to see the person's face, but she clearly hears the soft, deep voice of a man.

"Don't be afraid, Janie, I won't harm you." The man pauses, then calmly states again, "Please don't be afraid."

***

From his cramped hiding spot beneath the stairs, the basement window is in clear view. Just as he'd feared, the little girl has returned. He won't be surprised if she does more than just peek this time. But why would her mother leave Janie home alone? She can't be more than nine or ten. Terrified of being seen, he presses himself as far back into the shadows as possible.

No face appears in the window, but the same small, pink-clad arm from before reaches in, this time, successfully unlatching the window. The arm withdraws, then gently pushes the window fully open. Moments later, her head is entirely inside as she peers into the darkness. Luckily, her body blocks what little light comes through the window, keeping him well hidden. But what else might this little girl do? Eventually, she pulls back, turns her body, and slowly slips her legs through the window opening. After dangling for a few seconds, she drops to the floor with a noisy thump.

"Oh my God!" he exclaims under his breath. Was she hurt? He fights the urge to rush to her aid, but she quickly rises and dusts herself off, unharmed. She stands motionless, waiting for her eyes to adjust to the dim light. With her back to the stairs, she begins to look around the room, her gaze settling on the long table. He senses she has found what she is searching for—the wooden doll cradle. Janie carefully feels her way around the tools and cabinets, finally arriving at the worktable. Reaching out, the little girl lovingly runs her hand over the expertly crafted cradle, then begins to gently rock it, lost in thought.

So much for his plans to build the basement bedroom that this family has been desperately needing. The girl's eyes would soon fully adjust to the dim light, making it possible for her to see him. His time as an uninvited guest was coming to a rapid end, and not in the way he'd expected. Of even greater concern is Janie. How can he keep from alarming or scaring this poor child to death? He must make the first move before she sees him.

With her back to him, Janie continues to rock the doll cradle. Silently easing out from under the stairs, he positions himself between her and the window. He desperately hopes she won't panic and run. The thought of her getting hurt while trying to escape is terrifying. His heart beats wildly as he stands motionless, trying to calm his own heavy breathing. Beads of perspiration form on his forehead as doubt creeps into his mind. Maybe he'd made the wrong choice. What if he couldn't calm a hysterical little girl? Maybe...

Before he can further question his actions, Janie turns and gasps. Her eyes wide with fear, she claps a hand to her mouth, staring at him in horror. Frozen in place, tears streaming down her face, she does not scream, only lets out a low moan.

"Don't be afraid, Janie, I won't harm you. Please don't be afraid." The backlight from the basement window keeps her from seeing his face, but his meager words of comfort do little to ease her fright.

"Who...who are you?" Janie stammers, terror etched on her small face. Seeing her fright, he immediately drops to one knee. To hell with her seeing his face! He can only imagine how large and imposing he must seem to this little girl.

"I'm not going to hurt you, honey. I promise." His voice is soft and calm, aiming for reassurance.

Janie's mouth begins to quiver. "Are you going to tell my momma I came into Daddy's workshop?"

"Oh no...no, I wouldn't do that." He gives a short laugh. "Believe me, I don't want you to get in any trouble." Her face relaxes a little, so he continues. "So, this is your Daddy's workshop?"

"Uh-huh," she nods, lowering her head. "My Daddy died before he could give me my birthday gift. I just wanted to see what it was. Momma had Uncle Larry board up the doorway so no one else could get hurt. They forgot to take my present out first." With that, she glances back at the cradle on the table. "Please don't tell...please!"

He cannot help but smile. He understands her fear— the same fear he also feels. "Don't worry, little lady, your secret is safe with me. Do you know how long ago your daddy died?"

"Well, he fell down the stairs on my eighth birthday, and I'm almost ten and a half."

So, a little over two years ago. No wonder the basement is so dusty, and no wonder those crackers had tasted so stale. He points to the basement stairs and the newly rebuilt railing. "Did your Daddy fall down those stairs?"

"Yes," Janie offers hesitantly. "But...but Daddy broke the railing when he fell. Why isn't it still broken?" She pauses, looking perplexed. "Did you fix it?" She holds his gaze, waiting for an answer.

What can he tell her? I'm a bank robber hiding in your basement and just thought I'd do a little repair work to pass the time. The truth is beyond even his own grasp of reality. Before he can think of a reply, Janie offers her own explanation.

"Are you...are you an angel?" she asks shyly.

Surprised by the sound of his own laughter, he quickly replies, "Little lady...the last thing I am is an angel!" Why in the world would she think him an angel? He certainly does not have wings or a halo. Instead, he is probably sporting a tail and horns these days. Her question is truly puzzling. "What makes you think I'm an angel, Janie?"

Sticking out her chin, she answers instantly. "Because Momma told me angels were created by God to give us help when we need it." She continues her discourse on angels. "Sometimes God sends them as messengers, too. Angels told Mary she was going to have baby Jesus, and lots and lots of angels told the shepherds Baby Jesus had been born in a manger."

He knows the stories about Baby Jesus, the shepherds, and the wise men. Mandy had insisted he read the Christmas Story from the Bible every Christmas Eve. But they are just that—stories. Yet, here is a little girl who thinks he, of all people, is an angel. The absurdity of this notion is beyond him.

"So, are you an angel?" she asks again.

He hesitates before answering, bizarre thoughts challenging any rational thinking he still possesses. Suppose he lets her believe he is an angel sent to help her family. Maybe he can convince her to keep quiet long enough for him to finish the "surprise" remodel of the basement. Doing so will also give his ankle enough time to heal and time to make plans about where he will go afterward. This ruse could be the answer to his problems.

Wiping away tears with the back of her hand, Janie continues to look at him with her big brown eyes, waiting for his response.

He takes a deep breath. "If you want to think I am an angel, little lady, then go ahead," he states simply, shrugging his shoulders. He is not sure what she is thinking, but the furrow in her brow shows her doubt.

"Well, you fixed the broken railing, and you know my name, so maybe you are an angel." She pauses hesitantly, then continues her reasoning. "My Bible verse this week said we're to show hospitality to strangers because sometimes they are angels, and we don't even know it!"

Hospitality was a big word for such a little girl, he muses.

"You fix things, you know my name, and you are a stranger, so...so I think you must be an angel." She seems pretty happy with her summation, but her last question catches him off guard. "You know my name, but what's yours?"

Not thinking of the possible ramifications, he gives his real name, "Michael. My name is Michael."

Janie's questioning face breaks into a wide grin. "Yep, I knew it! You are a real angel!"

"So, what convinced you?" Michael asks, genuinely interested in what she has to say.

"I know because there are only two angels in the Bible with names...Michael and Gabriel. And, you said your name is Michael."

Janie is not only a bright little girl, but she also seems to know her Bible. At least, she knows more than he does. Letting Janie believe he is an angel is a gamble, but what other choice does he have? There is no reasonable explanation for a man to be in her basement—not even one a ten-year-old would accept. But she will have to genuinely believe he is an angel for this to work.

"Well, if I were an angel, would you mind if I stayed in your basement a little longer and fixed a few more things around your house?" By now, they are both seated, she on the barstool at her daddy's table and he on the lower step of the stairs. She is clearly no longer afraid, so he presses on. "It will be our little secret. I won't tell your mother you came into the basement looking for your present, and you won't tell anyone you have an angel in your basement."

Janie closes her eyes, pondering his proposition. After a moment, she opens them and looks at him squarely in the face. "Deal!" she states with a single nod of her head.

He feels an instant wave of relief, but the details of their arrangement need further discussion. The last thing he wants is for Janie to feel threatened, but he also has to make sure she understands the consequences if she tells anyone.

"You know, don't you, only you can see me. Right?"

She gazes up at him, eyes wide with wonder. "I hadn't thought about it, but I guess it's true."

He continues. "If you tell anyone you have seen me, then I will have to leave and won't be able to help your family."

She lowers her eyes and says softly, "I don't know why God would let me see an angel, though. I lied to my momma the other day, and now I've sneaked into the basement when I shouldn't have."

Michael is not sure where his response came from; he is even surprised by the words that tumbled out. "God understands we all make mistakes sometimes, little lady. We just have to own up to them when the time is right." He hastily adds, "But the time may not be right…just yet."

She looks up and smiles at him, stirring something in his heart. It has been a long time since a little girl smiled at him with such acceptance and trust. He smiles back, reaching out and touching her arm ever so lightly. "When is your mother going to be home, sweetie?"

"She said she'd be back by lunch." Janie suddenly put a hand to her mouth, trying to stifle a hoarse cough. So that's why she is home from school. Poor little gal is sick.

"Well, little lady, you best get out of here and back in bed before she gets home." She follows obediently as he takes her hand and leads her to the window. Her small hand feels warm and delicate in his big, calloused one. A rush of memories floods his mind, and he struggles to keep his composure.

His own daughter had loved holding his hand. Invariably, her little fingers would find their way over the smooth, nail-less, half-thumb on his left hand.

"Tell me the story again, Daddy, of how you lost your thumb." She would request the story time after time, even though she knew it by heart.

"Well, I was working on a lady's roof one day when I became careless with the circular saw. Before I knew it, I had sawn clean through my thumb, and it was lying there on the ground. Blood was spurting everywhere..."

This was Mandy's cue to scrunch up her face and let out a big, dramatic "Ewww."

"So, I picked up that piece of my thumb and stuck it in a glass of ice water, hoping the doctor would be able to sew it back on. My buddy drove me to the emergency room, but it was too late. All the doc could do was just sew up the end of my poor ol' thumb. He told me I was lucky to have a thumb at all."

With a concerned look on her face, Mandy would then hug his neck while cooing, "Poor Daddy...Poor Daddy."

Trying to rid himself of those memories, Michael drops to his knees in front of Janie once again, looking her in the eye. "We have a deal, right, little lady?"

Janie's small brown head bobs up and down repeatedly. "I won't tell anyone. I promise. Daddy always told me that a person is only as good as their word."

"Well, someone I once knew told me the same thing." He almost adds "as a boy" but catches himself just in time.

Michael steps onto the stool and peeks out the window, ensuring no one else is around. He then hoisted Janie up and out as quickly as she came in. Janie turns around, grinning at him, and asks her final question.

"Do angels eat? Because I can bring you some lunch if you do."

He chuckles. "You can bet this angel eats! Just be careful, Janie. Only bring something if you are sure no one will see."

Her face breaks into a wide, sweet smile. "I'll be careful." With that, she scampers out of the bushes and is gone. He missed her the moment she left.

***

Janie skips with joy! She runs around to the back door, slipping back inside to the safety of her home. She should get back in bed before her mother returns, but first, she needs to make the angel's lunch. A wide grin stretches across Janie's face, the corners of her mouth aching. *Angels eating?* The thought is funny, yet Michael seemed pleased she would bring him food. She must be careful, though, just as Michael had warned. She cannot risk losing this angel—not after God had sent him especially to her family.

She slaps ham and cheese between two slices of bread, grabs a bag of chips, and adds a banana, filling the brown paper sack. There, a proper lunch for the angel. Sack in hand, she moves toward the back door, intent on her mission. Reaching for the doorknob, she suddenly jerks backwards, startled by the intrusive DING-DONG of the doorbell. Her heart thumps wildly. Mrs. Beardsley. It has to be. Should she ignore the bell or answer it? The bell chimes again, insistent. Before Janie can decide, the front door slowly creaks open. How could she have forgotten to lock the door?

"Janie? Oh, Janie? Yoo-hoo? Where are you, honey?" Mrs. Beardsley's voice, shrill yet sweet, echoes through the house.

She has no choice. Mrs. Beardsley will never give up on her promise to make sure Janie is safe. "I'm right here, Mrs. Beardsley," she calls out, rounding the corner from the kitchen. The sack of goodies for Michael dangled forgotten from her hand.

"Oh, there you are. I promised your mother I would check in on you. How are you feeling, dear?" Mrs. Beardsley strides confidently into the living room, ready to stay awhile.

"I'm better," acknowledges Janie. Looking down, she remembers the sack in her hand. "I was just in the kitchen getting a little snack to take back to my room."

She holds up the crumbled sack as proof. Instantly, her heart sinks. Her list of lies is rapidly expanding—not only to her mother but now to Mrs. Beardsley.

"Well, glad you are feeling well enough to eat. Let me help you back to bed." Mrs. Beardsley crosses the small living room, placing her hand on Janie's shoulder and guiding her back to the bedroom. "Honestly, I don't know how your mother does it. Such a small house for all these kids, and your poor father is not here to help." She shakes her head, a heavy sigh escaping her lips. "Lord knows, your dad was a good man, but he sure took his sweet time in getting this old place fixed up, and now your mother is stuck trying to keep a roof over your family's head."

Janie's spine stiffens to a defensive posture. How dare Mrs. Beardsley speak ill of her father! Having been taught to respect her elders, Janie holds her tongue as Mrs. Beardsley continues her idle chatter. Her father's voice echoes in her mind. He had often warned her about the power of the tongue. "Though small, our tongues are the most powerful muscle in our body, Janie. God says our tongue is like the bit in a horse's mouth or the rudder on a great ship. It can steer a course for good or evil. Be careful how you use it." Mrs. Beardsley certainly is not using her tongue wisely. Janie responds by simply nodding her head. The sooner Mrs. Beardsley carries out her caregiving mission, the sooner she can return to Michael.

"Okay, back in bed, young lady. I'll see if I can find a tray for your lunch." Mrs. Beardsley heads back to the kitchen, returning moments later with a TV tray in hand. "I'll just sit here while you eat, and we can continue our chat."

Janie's mind races. Time is short before her mother's return, and the promise to the angel weighs heavily on her. "Well, I was hungry, but now I am feeling sleepy again, so I think I'll just wait and eat later." The excuse is flimsy, but it is all she can manage on such short notice. Mrs. Beardsley lays the back of her hand against Janie's forehead, then her cheeks.

"You don't feel too warm, but sleep is always a good thing. I'll go home now, but you call me the minute you need anything. You have my number, right?"

"I do. But Momma will be home soon, so I'll be fine. Thanks for checking on me." Janie pulls the blanket up to her chin as Mrs. Beardsley backs out of her room.

"Bye-bye, dear. Feel better soon!" She hears the front door open, followed by Mrs. Beardsley's parting instruction. "I'm locking the door behind me. Keep it that way!"

The firm click of the door ensures Mrs. Beardsley will no longer have free access to their house. A sigh of relief escapes Janie, but the clock's steady tick reminds her that time is short. She swings her legs out of bed, scoops up the paper sack, and resumes her mission: delivering hospitality to the basement angel. Once again, she crawls under the bushes, reaching her destination.

"Michael...Michael," she whispers through the hole in the broken window.

"Hey, little lady. You're back!"

"Here's your lunch." She tries to thrust the brown bag through the hole, but it snags. "Oh, better take the banana out," she giggles, pulling the fruit free.

"Thank you, Janie. Now, hurry back to bed and please get well! I don't like the sound of that cough of yours."

"I will, I promise. See you later?" she asks, tentatively. She fears a long wait before revisiting the angel.

"I hope so, little lady, I certainly hope so." With his last statement, the angel fades back into the murky darkness of the basement.

Janie scrambles back inside, the kitchen mess vanishing under her swift hands. She is back in bed just before hearing the front door open and her mother's voice call out. "Hey, baby. I'm home."

"I'm in my room, Momma." Janie pulls the blanket higher, shrinking beneath its thin comfort. A visit to her room is inevitable.

Her mother appears, her cool palm pressing against Janie's forehead. "How are you feeling? You don't seem to have a fever. So, what did you do this morning?"

The dreaded question. Janie tugs the covers up to her chin. "Oh, nothing. Just watched a little television and worked on my memory verse." How easily that lie slides off her tongue. "And Mrs. Beardsley came by to check on me."

"I am so thankful we have such a good neighbor as Mrs. Beardsley. Well, now, why don't you tell me your memory verse? It will be good practice."

"I really don't feel like working right now." Even mentioning the word "angel" around her mother is scary. Her mother has a way of seeing through her, a sixth sense for when things are amiss. She tries changing the subject. "Mrs. Beardsley said Daddy took his time and didn't take care of our house, and now you are stuck with it."

"Oh, she did?" Her mother's brow furrows in a puzzled look. "Well, Mrs. Beardsley didn't know your daddy like we did. Your daddy's priorities were different from most men. He loved to bless others, and numerous people are thankful for his help. But your daddy loved us dearly and always had good intentions to fix up this old house. He just ran out of time. We'll be fine. God is with us, and He will make sure we have all we need."

If only she could reassure her mother—God had indeed provided for them, and in a most wonderfully unique way. Instead, Janie offers a small smile, nodding her head in agreement.

"Now, come on, honey. Tell me your verse. I know you have memorized it already. You always do," her mother coaxes.

Janie sits up, taking a deep breath. No doubt Momma will persist until she repeats the verse. Avoiding her mother's eyes, she begins. "Hebrews 13:2--Do not neglect to show hospitality to strangers, for by this some have entertained angels without knowing it." Fearing her perceptive mother might detect her dishonesty, she keeps her gaze fixed on the blanket.

"That's very good, honey. Do you know what it means?"

"Yes, I think I do," she answers quietly. Oh boy, did she know what it meant!

"It simply means we should be nice to everyone, even strangers. You never know who might be an angel." Her mother winks, a gentle smile playing on her lips.

Once again, the urge to tell her mother about the basement angel swells. The secret feels too big for her small shoulders to bear. But just as she opens her mouth, Michael's words of caution flood her memory.

"You are the only one who can see me. If you tell anyone, then I must leave and won't be able to help your family."

Momma desperately needs help! Convinced God has sent them an angel for this very purpose, Janie keeps the exciting news hidden in her heart. She will tell Momma the truth later—after Michael finishes whatever he intends to do for them.

"Thank you for explaining it to me, Momma. I hope someday I'll get to see a real angel."

"I pray you do, honey. But always look around you. God sends people to our aid all the time who aren't necessarily His angels, but act like angels, nevertheless."

"Like Mrs. Beardsley?" Janie grins. Imagining Mrs. Beardsley as an angel is, indeed, comical.

Her mother laughs. "Yeah, I guess you could say that. She means well, though, and I am thankful she is our neighbor. Now, get some rest. I have a little work to do before picking up the kids from school."

Janie spends the rest of the afternoon in bed, her book open but her gaze unfocused. Every thought drifts back to the basement. She'd always pictured angels with towering wings, glowing halos, and gleaming swords—especially an archangel like Michael—never thinking one might look like an ordinary grandpa. Still, she has no doubt God has sent him for a reason.

Seeing the broken stair railing looking better than new brings a smile to her face. In addition, Momma had remarked how the old wood floors no longer squeaked. Michael must have taken care of that problem, too. Keeping such wonderful secrets from her mother is hard, but necessary. Someday, her mother will understand.

In the confusion of discovering an angel, the beautiful doll cradle had completely slipped her mind. She picks up her doll, trying to imagine herself rocking her baby to sleep in it, but her thoughts keep returning to the angel. If only she knew more about him. Her father always said the Bible was the best place to learn about Biblical things. Remembering how to use a concordance from Bible Club, Janie grabs her Bible. She flips to the back, her finger tracing the words until she finds the sought-after reference: *MICHAEL: Archangel—warrior in angelic realm, protector of Israel.* Several verses from Jude, Daniel, and Revelation are listed below.

Wow! she thinks, *Michael is the archangel and a warrior!* The gentle man in the basement hardly seems like a warrior, but then, she had noticed the missing part of his thumb. Perhaps he lost it in a battle, she muses, picturing him in armor, wielding a sword against the devil and his demons. She will ask him about that next time—if there is a next time. Finding time alone under Momma's watchful eye will be almost impossible.

Meanwhile, she will look up the Bible verses, eager to learn more about the mysterious "basement angel."

Janie glances at the clock on the bedside table. Almost 3:30. Momma will soon leave to pick up the children from school. She is far too excited to sleep, but she can certainly pretend to be. Turning her back to the bedroom door, she squeezes her eyes shut, trying to lie as still as possible, though not an easy task. As if on cue, she hears her mother call." Janie…get your coat on. We need to pick up the kids from school." She does not answer. "Janie?" This time, her mother stands at the doorway.

Janie slowly rolls over, rubbing her eyes. "What?" Attempting to sound sleepy when wide awake is not easy.

"Oh, honey, sorry to wake you, but I need to get the kids. You look sleepy. Are you comfortable staying by yourself again? I'm sure Mrs. Beardsley wouldn't mind running over for a few minutes if you are not."

This is her chance. "I can stay here by myself if it's okay with you. I know Mrs. Beardsley is next door if I need anything."

"It won't take but thirty minutes or so, and then I'll be back. Lock the doors after I leave." Her mother closes the door. Janie springs to the front window, just in time to see her mother's car back out.

Thirty minutes is not much time, but it is enough for a quick trip to see Michael. She darts out the back door, scampers down the steps, and arrives breathlessly at the window.

"Michael! Hey Michael! Are you still there?" She leans close to the hole in the window. Silence. Fearing the angel has left, she calls again, a little louder this time. "Michael! Are you there?"

"Hey, little lady. Sorry, I was just dozing. I wasn't expecting to see you again today." He sounds surprised but pleased.

"Momma left to get the kids from school. I just wanted to see if you need anything else."

Michael pauses, thinking, then pushes the window open a crack. "Yeah, there are a few things I would like. First, could you get me a newspaper? Preferably last Saturday or Sunday's paper?"

"Sure," she replies, "I can get both for you. Momma throws them in the recycle bin, so I know they're still there. Anything else?"

"A bar of soap, a towel, and maybe a spare toothbrush would be great." It was dark inside the basement, but she could see his white teeth gleaming in a smile. It is strange to think of angels needing a bath or brushing their teeth.

"I'll get you some more food, too. I'm sure I'll go back to school tomorrow, so I won't be here to make you a sandwich." What would he do without her?

"That's okay, little lady. I'll be fine. You just run and get what you can for now."

Janie races through the house, gathering the angel's requested items. She finds a leftover chicken breast and a few pieces of pizza, hoping it will be enough to last him through the day tomorrow and that her mother won't notice. Luckily, Saturday's newspaper is still in the recycle bin. Arms full, she dashes back to the window.

"I'm back…with everything…you wanted." Her words come out in gasps, her breath ragged from the mad dash. Michael opens the window entirely, taking each item from Janie's arms: soap, towel, toothbrush, and food.

"You're a sweetheart! Thanks so much. Now remember, not a word to anyone about me, okay?"

Janie nods vigorously. "I already promised I wouldn't tell anyone. You can trust me, Michael."

"I do believe I can!" He gives her a quick wink. "Now, get back in your house before your mother comes home."

The front door opens just as Janie climbs back into her bed. Once again, the quiet house comes alive with the familiar sounds of her family. Keeping secrets from them, especially Momma, feels unnatural and wrong, but she has no choice. She is just showing "hospitality" to this stranger, as the Bible instructed. One significant difference, though, is that she is quite aware that this stranger is an angel.

Sleep does not come easily for Janie that night. Even the soft, rhythmic breathing of her brothers and sister fails to lull her to sleep. Eyes wide open, staring upwards through the darkness, she makes a mental list of questions for the angel: What was God like? Had Michael ever seen her daddy in heaven? Where were his wings and halo? How long would he stay in her basement? Her eyelids grow droopy as sleep begins to take over.

Confident that God must love her and her family very much, she finally surrenders and sleeps soundly.

***

Michael tears into the sandwich Janie had brought, savoring each bite of the meager meal. Putting the re-model plans on hold for another day is disappointing, but there's little he can do about it. Janie's mother would be home all afternoon. Instead, he retreats under the stairs, dozing off and on, as if making up for fourteen years of sleepless nights. When awake, thoughts of Janie cause his stomach to churn with anxiety. *Will she be able to keep their secret? Moreover, maintaining this angelic charade could become difficult if Janie asked too many questions. She is bright, probably knows far more about God and angels than I do.* He grimaces. *If only I'd paid more attention to some of those Sunday School classes Mom forced me to attend as a boy. Angels have names? Who knew?*

Janie's lack of fear amazes him. Such courage can only come from a place of deep belief and faith. How shameful to take advantage of her childlike faith. But it is too late now. Janie believes he was an angel sent to help her family. He must see it through.

Hearing his name calling through the window startles him awake, or is it a dream? He listens carefully, then hears the voice again.

"Michael...Michael, are you there?" A surge of delight makes his heart skip. Janie! Sweet Janie. Her mother had left to pick up the other children from school, and her first thought was of him. He hates to burden her further, but there are a few things that can make life a little more bearable, primarily soap! Angels probably don't need baths, but he certainly does. It has been four days since he'd showered; even a cold rinse beats this grime. And he is desperate to find out what the local paper said about the bank robbery.

Janie takes his order and is back within minutes, arms laden with everything he had requested, including more food. Knowing her mother will soon return, he urges her back inside. He cannot risk her getting caught, not for his sake, but for hers.

With Janie safely back in her house, he unfolds the newspaper. Saturday's headlines, complete with his picture, are the first thing he sees: DENISON POLICE SEEK HELP FINDING BANK ROBBER. He reads the story several times, each word making the whole ordeal more surreal.

> *DENISON—Police appealed for help Saturday in finding a man who stole an undisclosed amount of money Friday afternoon from a bank on W. Main Street. Police released a photograph of the robber from the surveillance camera, hoping someone would recognize him. The robber walked in about 4:45 p.m. Friday, demanding money. He did not show a weapon but indicated he had one in the pocket of his jacket, according to the teller. No injuries were reported. The man left on foot with the cash, police said. Witnesses described him as white, in his late 50s or early 60s, about 6 feet 3 inches tall, and weighing between 180 and 200 pounds. He was wearing a dark knit cap pulled low over his forehead. He also wore a brown leather*

jacket, blue jeans, and dark boots. Anyone with information should call Denison Police at 903-555-2422.

The robber. He is the robber. He closes his eyes, a heavy sigh escaping him. How has he gone from carpenter to robber so quickly? He knows how. A better question might be, why? Why had he done it? "I need to have my head examined," he mumbles, grabbing his head. "People like me don't rob banks." But he had robbed a bank, and now he is trapped in a basement while a little girl thinks he is an angel. Truth, his truth, is indeed stranger than fiction.

He no longer knows what his truth is. Once, he had been a lonely widower, living only for himself, uncaring of the world. Now, he is a bank robber masquerading as an angel. Neither scenario feels right, though, surprisingly, he is starting to prefer the role of a basement angel. Maybe he is crazy, but he has grown attached to the family above him, especially Janie. Who is he kidding? Attachment is not the word. He cares for them—he cares for Janie. The realization sends a jolt through him, his heart thumping, almost as if it has started beating again for the first time in fourteen long years.

The fifth night in the basement begins with familiar routines. Tonight, though, he dines on cold pizza and chicken, followed by an equally frosty sponge bath. Janie had proudly brought him her own personal pink "soap on a rope". The sweet smell instantly transports him back. Mandy. She loved everything pink, especially when combined with sparkles, yet she was no typical "girly girl." One minute, a tiara adorned her head; the next, a baseball cap. A tea party could swiftly transform into a rough-and-tumble football game.

"You know," he'd told Liz, "We are going to be in trouble when Mandy discovers boys."

"I think it will be more trouble when boys discover Mandy," Liz replied with a frown. "You'd better start work on that contract you say boys will have to sign before they date your daughter."

"I decided she's not dating until she's thirty." And he meant it.

Liz lowered her chin, raising her eyebrows in that familiar gesture. "Good luck with that!"

Remembering these exchanges intensifies the familiar ache in his chest. He never would have to deal with boys wanting to date his daughter, nor the angst of raising a teenager. For him, Mandy remained forever four years old, the little girl who loved all things pink and sparkly.

He shivers slightly and rubs his arms, a cold draft from the basement chilling him to the bone. Being somewhat clean with a full belly offers no comfort. The newspaper, still clutched in his hand, is a stark reminder of his predicament. Yet, no feasible escape plan forms in his mind. Remaining in the basement, for now, seems the only logical choice. Building a new room for Janie's family, however, defies logic. Still, he will do it. He owes it to Janie. He will build the basement bedroom and then, only then, figure out when and where to go.

Above him, the house slowly falls silent as the evening wears on. He pictures the children cozily tucked in their beds after their nightly rituals of brushing their teeth and saying prayers. At least, that had been Mandy's nightly routine. Liz usually listened to Mandy's prayers, but every so often, Mandy would demand his presence. He didn't mind listening, but those nights when Mandy asked him to pray were always awkward.

"Okay, Daddy, now you pray," she'd insist, not ask. He was tempted to call for Liz, but Mandy's steely glare left no doubt that she wanted him to pray.

"Uh, thank you God for Mandy, for Mommy, for Nana and Papa. And thank you for a beautiful day. Amen." His half-hearted attempt did not fool Mandy.

"It wasn't a beautiful day, Daddy. It rained all day, and I couldn't go outside." Mandy crossed her arms, a perfect pout forming on her lips.

"Well, if you are a tree or a flower, then it was a beautiful day. If God made the sun shine every day so you could play outside, then we wouldn't have green grass, flowers, and our tall trees to provide shade while you play." His theology was fundamental, but Mandy always seemed satisfied.

Fundamental theology might appease a four-year-old, but how will he answer questions from a precocious ten-year-old like Janie? "If You are up there, God, I think I need some help," he sighs, his eyes closing, his mind surrendering to sleepy emptiness. Michael would not realize it until a few days later, but that was his first genuine prayer.

Chapter 8

Wednesday, January 7, 2009

Wednesday morning breaks bright and sunny, a perfect reflection of Michael's mood. The familiar sound of the car backing out of the driveway signals his freedom. He flicks on the single bare bulb, unrolls the blueprints, and sets off to work. The project is straightforward: frame two walls with a doorway, build a closet, install lighting and a couple of outlets, hang drywall, trim the window and door, add baseboards, and paint. Three long, focused days, if the family keeps to their routine, will see it finished. With any luck, he can slip out of the basement Friday night, while everyone sleeps.

His ankle, a steady throb just days ago, now feels remarkably better, the swelling visibly reduced. Walking will be slow, and crossing the Red River into Oklahoma will take all night. What comes after that, he pushes from his mind. For now, a room awaits his hammer and saw.

Chalk lines snap across the concrete floor in quick succession. The buzz of the saw fills the basement as

Michael cuts the vertical studs, then assembles the two walls. Janie's father, he muses, had been remarkably thoughtful, gathering all the necessary materials before starting the project himself. The new bedroom will halve the workshop's space, but enough room remains for the tools, neatly arranged and familiar.

Walls complete, Michael hoists them into place. He secures the base plates to the concrete floor and fastens the top plates to the overhead floor joists. Next, he frames the closet, then adds all the cross joints between the studs. The space is beginning to resemble a room. He steps back, arms crossed, and a familiar warmth spreads through him—the quiet satisfaction of a job well done.

He does not know who will claim the new bedroom, but the wall directly opposite him seems a perfect spot for Janie's bulletin board. Deciding where anyone sleeps is not his concern; providing more space for this large family, however, is. He presses on.

The afternoon flies by. Michael installs the outlet boxes, drills holes through the studs, and runs electrical wiring throughout the new room. Far from being finished, he quits working by late afternoon. Janie's family will be home soon and time, once again, to retreat to the shadowy recesses under the stairs. He doubts Janie can manage another visit that night, but he really wants to ask her for flashlight batteries. Who is he kidding? More than needing batteries, he wants to see her again! She is the light that dispels the darkness of his basement world.

The family arrives home, but their stay is brief, lasting only about an hour. A flurry of unusual activity fills their short time in the house. Where they have gone is a mystery, but it is his chance. He quickly strips down to his waist and begins splashing freezing water from the sink under his arms, eagerly lathering the soap.

"Michael…Michael…are you still here?" Janie calls him through the window hole.

Wrapping the towel around his shoulders, he walks to the window and eases it open. Janie lies on her stomach, grinning like a Cheshire cat.

"You'll catch a cold dressed like that!" she scolds.

"Well, little lady, I wasn't expecting company this evening. I was about to do a little washing up," he chuckles, feeling a flicker of self-consciousness about his state of undress. "Why aren't you with your family?"

"Momma took my brothers and sister to Bible Club at our church. She wouldn't let me go because she said I looked tired after school today. I hate missing, though, especially since I already have my verses memorized."

"I am sure your momma knows best, Janie. Is your church far from here?"

"She said she would be gone less than twenty minutes, so I don't have much time. I wanted to bring you the peanut butter sandwich I had left from my lunch today." Janie hands a brown paper bag over to Michael, a worried frown on her face." This is all I have for you today."

Michael opens the crumpled bag and peers inside. "I love peanut butter sandwiches. Thanks for thinking of me, Janie." He unwraps the slightly squished sandwich and takes a large bite, a flash of memory transporting him back to another little girl who once loved making peanut butter sandwiches for her daddy. Janie watches him, her smile wide with admiration. He quickly finishes the sandwich, his heart melting a little at the thought that she had selflessly saved her lunch for him. It has been a long time since he has allowed anyone to do something nice for him. He is not sure how to feel.

He hates asking Janie for more, but there are a few things he desperately needs. "You've taken first-rate care of me, Janie, and I appreciate all you've done, but I wonder if you could get a few other things for me?"

"Sure, Michael! I want to help you however I can. What do you need?" she replies. Her eagerness to please him is touching.

"I could use some batteries for my flashlight, as long as your mother wouldn't miss them." He takes a chance and adds, "A book or two would also be great and help me pass the time when I need to be quiet."

"I know we have a box full of batteries. I'll be right back!" She scrambles backward out of the bushes and is gone before he can tell her she didn't need to get the items right at that moment. He would have enjoyed talking to her for a few minutes longer. She returns just as quickly, batteries and a book in hand.

"This is great, Janie. Are you sure your mother won't miss anything?"

Shaking her head, she passes the items through the window, assuring him no one will ever know they are gone.

"What book did you bring me?" he asks.

"It's my Daddy's Bible," she announces proudly. "Momma gave it to me because she knows I love memorizing Scripture the same way he did. I figured you would like to read the Bible since you're an angel."

He tries to hide his disappointment, especially after seeing the look of satisfaction in her eyes. "Thank you, little lady. You're right, the Bible is my favorite book to read. I'll take good care of it." The Bible would not have been his choice of reading material, but he supposes it is better than nothing. "It's getting dark, and your mother will be back soon. Better head back inside, Janie."

She begins to nod but then stops abruptly, her eyes wide as she remembers a crucial piece of news. "Michael, you must be careful. Mrs. Beardsley heard you sawing today, and she asked Momma about it," Janie blurts out.

This is not good. Trying hard to conceal his worry, Michael reassures Janie in a way he knows will bring her comfort. He feels foolish for bringing God into this ridiculous situation, but mentioning God instantly calms Janie's fears. Her sweet smile returns as she tells him goodbye.

"I will try to see you again tomorrow, Michael. By the way, I'm glad you're washing your clothes. They could use it!" she laughs, pinching her nose as she crawls out from under the bush. He can still hear her giggling as she heads back to the warmth of her home. He smiles, shaking his head, closes the window, and goes back to his washing.

Later that evening, in the deep quiet of the house, Michael pulls out the flashlight and opens the Bible Janie had given him. The worn pages, obviously thin and delicate from years of use, are filled with numerous highlighted passages and personal notes scrawled in the margins. He has never seen anyone write in a Bible before, and it feels almost sacrilegious.

Thumbing through the pages, he notices names and dates written beside certain verses. One name catches his eye—Janie: June 6, 1998. Was that her birthday? It is scribbled next to a passage in Psalm 139. He softly reads the words aloud.

"For You created my inmost being; You knit me together in my mother's womb. I praise You because I am fearfully and wonderfully made; Your works are wonderful, I know that full well. My frame was not hidden from You when I was made in the secret place. When I was woven together in the depths of the earth, your eyes saw my unformed body. All the days ordained for me were written in your book before one of them came to be."

A half-smile forms on his lips. Janie's dad had chosen a good verse. That sweet little gal is wonderfully made. But other parts of the passage are confusing. Whoever had written these words had a much more intimate relationship with God than Michael ever thought possible. He glances back at the beginning of the chapter and finds the author is David, the same shepherd boy who killed the giant, Goliath. That story had made quite an impression on him as a young boy in Sunday School. David eventually became a king, but Michael knows very little else about him. With nothing better to do, he begins to read Psalm 139 from the beginning.

"O Lord, you have searched me, and you know me. You know when I sit and when I rise, you perceive my thoughts from afar. You discern my going out and my lying down; you are familiar with all my ways. Before a word is on my tongue, you know it complete, O Lord. You hem me in—behind and before; you have laid your hand upon me. Such knowledge is too wonderful for me, too lofty for me to attain."

A sudden chill snakes down his back, and he rubs his arms. David's words do not line up with his own theology. Having God know—or care this much—is a little too close for comfort. If there really is a God, Michael prefers to think of Him as a distant, grandfatherly figure who only involves Himself in the essential things of life. Being searched and known by God, as David described, is unfathomable. It may be okay for David. He was one of the good guys with nothing to fear from God knowing his thoughts. Michael chuckles to himself. *If God knew all my thoughts, then I should have been struck by lightning long ago!* Intrigued by the passage, he continues to read.

"Where can I go from Your Spirit? Where can I flee from Your presence? If I go up to the heavens, You are there; if I make my bed in the depths, You are there. If I rise on the wings of the dawn, if I settle on the far side of the sea, even there Your hand will guide me, Your right hand will hold me fast. If I say, 'Surely the darkness will hide me and the light become night around me,' even the darkness will not be dark to You; the night will shine like the day, for darkness is as light to You."

Dumbfounded, he leans back against the wall, his eyes darting back and forth, surveying his basement hideout. Darkness. This is where he hides. This is his place of safety. Out of all the passages in the Bible, how eerie to read something so perfectly describing his plight? He is comfortable in the dark just as he has grown comfortable with the darkness of his own soul. Letting light into either place will dispel the darkness and expose the truth of who he is—a bank robber, a thief, and a man consumed with resentment, anger, and bitterness. There can be only one conclusion—darkness is where he lives, and darkness is where he belongs. Any light will only bring more trouble, and he has enough as it is. Maybe he is hemmed in, but it is his own doing, not God's, and he will find a way out. He slams the Bible shut. He should never have opened that book.

***

It is Wednesday, Bible Club Day! Janie still feels far from well, but another sick day home from school guarantees she will miss Bible Club that evening. Her mother half-heartedly protests, but Janie knows staying home is a great burden, and Momma certainly won't let her stay home alone again. Chin up, she forces a smile and climbs into the van with the rest of the kids.

All morning, Janie finds it impossible to concentrate. Staring out the classroom window, lost in thought, she does not hear the teacher call her name.

"Janie," her teacher gently scolds, "You seem to be a million miles away today. Is everything okay? Are you still feeling ill?"

She ducks her head and replies, "No, ma'am. I'm fine. I'll try to pay better attention."

But she cannot. Her mind keeps replaying the encounter with the basement angel. She yearns to tell someone, anyone, about Michael, but her promise holds her silent. Besides, most people wouldn't believe her anyway.

Lunchtime finally arrives, and Janie welcomes the chance to be alone with her thoughts for a few minutes. Momma had packed the usual lunch of a peanut butter and jelly sandwich, an apple, and a granola bar. Though hungry, she chooses to save her sandwich for Michael and eat only the other items. Getting food for him will be tricky, requiring careful planning. She may ask her mother for two sandwiches tomorrow. After all, she is a growing girl.

Her mother picks them up after school, right on time. Janie's red, droopy eyes make it impossible to fool her mother any longer. She speaks hardly a word all the way home.

"You don't look like you feel well, Janie. I don't think you should go to Bible Club tonight, honey. I know you've worked hard to memorize your verses, but you can recite them next week."

Janie frowns, her lips forming a pout.

"Don't worry. You'll remember them. You don't forget things easily." Her mother lays her hands across Janie's forehead. "I don't think you have a fever, but an early night will help you feel better tomorrow."

"But, what about the others? I hate for them to miss Bible Club tonight because of me."

"Well, I can go ahead and take them. But, while I'm gone, I want you to finish your supper and then go straight to bed. I'll be back in about twenty minutes."

Janie's mother ushers the other children out the front door, closing it solidly behind her. Janie runs to the front window. After her mother carefully buckles the last child in, a breathless and slightly red-faced Mrs. Beardsley meets her in the driveway. Janie's stomach twists. Obviously, Mrs. Beardsley has been waiting for the perfect moment to talk to Janie's mother, and that usually means trouble. Janie opens the window slightly to listen.

"Heading out to church with the little ones?" Mrs. Beardsley questions.

"Yes, Janie still isn't feeling well, so she is staying at the house while I run the other children to Bible Club. Thanks so much for taking the time to check on her." Momma seems anxious to be on her way, but Mrs. Beardsley is in no hurry.

"Nice to hear all the sawing and building going on again at your house. I guess you hired a handyman to finish up some of the projects your late husband left behind?"

Janie's mother stares at Mrs. Beardsley, a quizzical look on her face. "I'm not sure I know what you mean. I haven't hired anyone to finish any projects. You must have heard someone working at another neighbor's house."

"No, I'm sure all the commotion was coming from your house," Mrs. Beardsley replies knowingly. "I remember well the sound of your husband working in his shop...often late into the night. I remember because it kept me awake sometimes." Mrs. Beardsley finishes her last statement with a slightly annoyed grin.

"That's odd because no one has even been in the basement since my husband passed. In fact, I had my brother board it up a few days after the funeral just to make sure."

"All I know is what I heard," Mrs. Beardsley states resolutely. "You best get those kiddos on to church now." She turns and begins to stroll back to her house, calling over her shoulder. "Don't worry, I'll keep an eye on Janie for you."

Looking perplexed, Janie's mother stands and stares as Mrs. Beardsley walks away. Finally, she climbs into the car and backs out of the driveway. Janie swiftly shuts the window and sits back on the couch, eyes wide. Mrs. Beardsley could be a big problem for both her and the angel. She must warn Michael right away! Throwing on her coat, she grabs the leftover sandwich out of her backpack and heads out the back door. Darting under the bushes, she calls for Michael through the window. He promptly appears, opening the window with a surprised smile. She notices the towel draping over his shoulder and can't help but laugh. Angels sure seem a lot like regular people.

"Well, little lady, I wasn't expecting company this evening." She likes it when Michael calls her little lady. The tenderness in his voice reminds her of Daddy, who had several pet names for her and the other children. Her favorite was when he called her his "little gift."

"Do you know why we named you Janie?" Her father had said one evening after listening to her prayers.

"I think I do. You and Momma named me after Great-Aunt Jane. Right?"

"Yes, we did, but we also named you after me."

"But your name is John. How can I be named after you, Daddy?"

"Well, Jane is the female version of John. John is a Hebrew name that means 'gift of God.' I took one look at you the night you were born and knew God had given your mother and me the best gift possible. You've always been my little Janie—my gift from God."

She misses her father terribly. She misses his warm smile, his smell of fresh-cut wood, his corny jokes, his loud singing, his big bear hugs, and, more than anything else, his ability to make her feel everything would always be alright. She desperately needs someone to talk with about the angel dilemma, but deep down, she knows what Daddy would say, "Don't talk about your problems. Pray about them!" She will need extra time tonight when saying her prayers.

Forgetting about the warning concerning their snoopy neighbor, Mrs. Beardsley, Janie stares in amazement as Michael eats the sandwich—almost in one big bite! Not since her daddy has she seen someone enjoy their food to that degree.

"You've taken first-rate care of me, Janie, and I appreciate all you've done." Michael wipes the back of his hand across his mouth. "But I wonder if you could get a few other things for me?"

Feeling warm and giddy after Michael's compliment, she is more than happy to bring him a few more items. His list is short, but she must hurry before Momma comes home. Finding batteries will be easy, but she isn't sure what kind of book an angel might want to read. Then it dawns on her. Of course, he will want to read the Bible. After all, he is an angel. Momma might wonder what happened to her own Bible if she gives it to Michael, but her daddy's Bible will not be missed since it is safely tucked away at the top of her closet. She pulls a chair into the closet and climbs up on the seat. Standing on her tiptoes, she can barely reach the shelf holding her most treasured possession. She pulls the box down, lifts the lid, and unwraps the delicate tissue paper. Janie runs her fingers over her daddy's name engraved in gold on the front of the old leather-bound book. Tenderly picking it up, she brings the heavy book to her nose, deeply inhaling the smell of worn leather. Her father had loved his workshop, but even more so, he had loved his old, familiar Bible. Frequently, he would hold it up and tell her, "Don't ever forget, Janie, this is God's Word and the Truth. It is the plumb line by which we measure all else. If what you hear doesn't line up with the plumb line of God's Word, then ignore it." Not too many ten-year-old girls know what a plumb line is, but being the daughter of a carpenter, Janie certainly does.

Time is running short. Janie tucks the Bible under her arm, grabs the batteries, and hurries back to the basement window. The evening has grown darker, but she can still distinguish the outline of the angel waiting at the window. Seeing him smile as she hands over the flashlight batteries and Bible pleases her immensely. If only she could stay and talk with him a while longer. She has so many questions. But Momma will soon be home, and she still has to put the box back up on the closet shelf and get into bed. Michael assures her he will take loving care of her daddy's Bible, but she already knows he will—he is an angel, even if a rather smelly angel. As she is about to leave, she remembers her mother's encounter with Mrs. Beardsley.

"Michael, you must be careful! Mrs. Beardsley heard the saw today, and she asked Momma about it!"

"Mrs. Beardsley? Is that your neighbor?" he asks, raising his eyebrows in question.

Janie nods. "Yes, she is the lady who checks on me when I am home alone. She asked my mom if she had hired a handyman to finish Daddy's projects."

Michael's forehead furrows. "What did your mother say to Mrs. Beardsley?"

By the tone of his question, Janie knows he is worried. "She said she hadn't hired anyone, and no one had been in the basement since Daddy died."

Michael looks past her, the creases on his forehead deepening. After a moment, he looks directly back at Janie. "Thanks for letting me know about Mrs. Beardsley. We won't worry about her for now, as I have a job to do for your family. I think God will help us keep this little secret until I finish." He reaches through the window and pats Janie's hand. "Now run back to bed, little lady, while I get myself and these stinky clothes cleaned up."

Janie backs out from under the bushes and races back inside and to her room. She returns the box to the closet shelf, moves the chair back to its rightful place, then hears her mother return. Another close call. Fearing Momma will want to discuss the mysterious sounds Mrs. Beardsley had heard, Janie jumps into bed and closes her eyes, pretending to be asleep. Her mother cracks open the door and simply says, "Good night, honey. Hope you feel better tomorrow."

Feeling confused, Janie wrestles with her thoughts throughout the long evening. She is fully aware that lying is a sin, and she hates lying to her mother and, now, Mrs. Beardsley. But, if she tells about the angel, then he will have to leave before helping their family, and she knows her mother needs help more than anything else. Michael told her not to worry, so she prays instead—a humble, honest prayer, as only a child can voice, "Lord, I want to do what pleases You. Show me the right path and I will follow it." She hesitates before adding, "whatever that may mean. In Jesus' name I pray, Amen."

Chapter 9

Thursday, January 8, 2009

The slam of car doors jolts Michael awake. He yawns and massages the back of his neck. It had been a long night of fitful sleep, along with anxious wakefulness. No wonder he had slept right through the morning commotions above him. Wrapping a blanket about his shoulders, he limps across the narrow room in search of his clothes. Not sure if they are still damp or simply cold, he puts them on regardless, then rubs a hand over his thickening beard. A shave. A simple luxury, now a forgotten dream.

Six nights he had spent in the basement—almost a week—but the likelihood of a few more is questionable with news of Mrs. Beardsley's suspicions. No doubt the nosey neighbor will be on high alert today, listening for unusual noises to prove her point. A little insulation covered by a piece of plywood over the window might muffle the sound and block prying eyes. He chuckles at the thought. The image of old Mrs. Beardsley on her hands and knees peering into the window is ridiculous. He'd be surprised if she could even stoop that low.

He covers the window, flips on the light, then sets to work hanging the drywall with the practiced efficiency of a master carpenter. Keeping his hands busy might prevent his mind from dwelling on the Bible passage he had read the night before.

Finding those precise verses had been a simple co-incidence, nothing more. At least, that's what he tries to convince himself. Believing in supernatural experiences had been his wife's department, not his. She had attributed everything to God. Laughing to himself, he wonders. What would Liz think of him now? Here he is, an ordinary man unwittingly playing the part of an angel in some strange celestial sitcom. The laugh dies in his throat as his thoughts turn to Janie. He sits down on the cold floor, elbows on knees, burying his face in his hands. How could he have involved this innocent young life in such a horrendous escapade? What if someone had deceived Mandy as he had Janie? Would Janie ever be able to trust anyone again after discovering who he was?

His only hope for redemption is to finish the basement room. Maybe someday, young Janie will be able to forgive him. With renewed determination, he stands up, squares his shoulders, and goes back to work.

The morning passes in a flurry of activity. All the drywall was hung with the joints neatly taped and bedded. The afternoon was for sanding the walls smooth in preparation for primer and paint. But his stomach has other plans. A deep, intense growl rumbles in his stomach, making it impossible to focus. Only one thing will quiet the noise. Food. And there is only one place with food: the kitchen upstairs. Going back into Janie's house is not only risky but invasive. This was their domain, not his. Yet, it is his only option if he wants to finish the basement project.

Prying off the plywood just enough to squeeze through, he slowly opens the door into the now quiet house, making a beeline for the kitchen. He takes a deep breath, inhaling the lingering aroma of the morning's breakfast. Signs of the family's rushed departure are everywhere. Unmade beds. Dirty dishes still in the sink. The remains of hastily-made sack lunches still on the kitchen counter.

Once, a messy kitchen would have sent a wave of anxiety through him. It was a fact Liz never appreciated. Her idea of tidiness and order never matched his, causing friction in their otherwise peaceful home. A flush of embarrassment rises on his cheeks as he remembers a petty argument they had on the subject.

"Michael…Michael? Have you seen my car keys? I left them on the desk and now they aren't there."

"They aren't there because I moved them. All your things are sitting together on the bookcase, so you won't forget them…again." He didn't bother to hide the exasperation in his voice. Liz had the habit of leaving her sunglasses, keys, phone, purse, or whatever was in her hands in various places throughout the house. Leaving for work the following day usually entailed a lengthy hunt for each item, which resulted in her leaving late and his frustration.

"You know, Liz, if you would just…" A sharp look of annoyance immediately stopped him. He tried again. "All I am saying is…"

Liz was quick to interrupt. "I know what you are saying, and I really don't get why you care where I put my things. Finding them is my problem, not yours."

"That's the problem…finding them. I was just trying to help and thought if you had one place to put your things every day…like a tray or basket…then you would save time in the mornings and not be so rushed." He really was trying to help, but the clenching of Liz's jaw told him he'd hit a sore spot.

"Okay then. I'll put my things in one place…on the desk," she said defiantly.

"The desk is where I work, and you know I like it kept clean. The bookshelf makes more sense…to me," he added.

"Right. It makes sense to you, but not to me. When will you realize that just because that makes sense to you doesn't necessarily mean that it makes sense to everyone else? It makes 'sense' to you to fold the laundry as soon as it comes out of the dryer…it makes 'sense' to you to wash and put away the dishes after you use them…it makes 'sense' to you to make the bed as soon as you get out of it every morning, and I could go on and on. I eventually do all those things, but on my own timetable, not yours, and you need to get used to that idea. Just because I'm different than you, doesn't make me wrong!" She ended her tirade with a steely glare he had seldom seen before.

"I was just trying to help." He repeated his earlier plea.

"No," Liz insisted. "You were trying to control me." Her voice softened. "I don't think you realize how controlling you are. You want me to think and act like you, but that is not what God intended. We are two people with two different personalities. Still, together, we make a whole person with strengths and weaknesses that complement each other." She walked across the room and wrapped her arms around his waist. "God accepts us the way we are, and we need to try and accept each other the way God made us."

"I'm sorry, honey. I see your point, and you aren't the first person to accuse me of being controlling. I admit I feel out of control when the house is a mess, but that's my problem."

"There's an easy solution to feeling that way." She grinned.

"What's that?" he asked.

"Clean it!"

Controlling people, controlling situations, and controlling his life are now things of the past. Never has everything been so out of control.

A low rumble from his stomach snaps Michael back to his current mission—food. He rummages through the refrigerator, finds a bunch of grapes, and pops one into his mouth.

DING DONG.

The doorbell's loud chime causes him to drop to the floor, coughing and choking. "What the hell?" he whispers, lying motionless on the cold kitchen tiles.

The doorbell rings a second time, followed by insistent knocking.

"Janie, Janie? Are you there, Janie?" a woman's voice calls out. Then, a little louder, "JA…NIE!"

What if she has a key? What if she finds me? Panic floods his mind. He can't run far with his sore ankle and no shoes, and where would he go? He has no choice but to stay on the kitchen floor. With any luck, she will conclude no one is home and leave.

Finally, silence. He creeps to the kitchen door and peers around the corner into the living room. The large picture window above the couch shows no sign of the woman. He stands up, exhaling with relief. *This is precisely why I should have stayed in the basement. What was I thinking?* Michael turns to go back down the short hallway to the safety of his hideout but freezes mid-step. A shadowy figure appears through the closed blinds of the back door. The hair bristles on his arms. The mysterious figure rattles the doorknob, then tries again, straining to peer through the slats.

"Janie? It's Mrs. Beardsley. Are you home, sweetie?" Even through the door, her voice is shrill.

This woman is relentless. Fearing she might see his shadow, Michael continues to stand motionless, the only movement the quick rise and fall of his chest.

She carries on jiggling the knob as if she can will the locked door to open. After what feels like an eternity, Mrs. Beardsley gives up. With one last call and one final rattle, she backs away from the door and moves off the back porch.

Fearing she will return to the front porch, Michael quickly slips back through the opening to his hiding place. Once inside, he leans against the plywood, breathing heavily. *What a stupid mistake. And even worse, I didn't get any food.*

For the next hour, Michael sits in a tense stillness, afraid even the faint whisper of sandpaper will draw attention to the workshop. As the silence stretches, and with no further sign of Mrs. Beardsley, fragile confidence returns. He picks up the sandpaper and begins to work, the monotonous task a balm to his frazzled nerves. He finishes just as the sound of the family's car fills the driveway. Two more days of hard work are just enough to finish the room to his own demanding standards. But tomorrow is Friday, followed by the weekend. His chances of surviving another weekend hiding, he knows, are slim to none.

***

The final bell of the day is a relief. The afternoon had dragged on; each class since lunch had been a test of Janie's patience. She has saved part of her lunch for Michael but has no idea how or when she will get it to him. As soon as she arrives at the gym for after-school care, Mrs. Hanover pulls her aside.

"We missed you at Bible Club last night, Janie." Mrs. Hanover is one of her Bible Club leaders and the after-school program director.

"I missed everyone, too. I guess you know I was sick the other day. My mother was afraid I would start feeling bad again if I didn't stay home and rest."

"Yes, your mom told me. I was the one who brought your brothers and sister home after Bible Club was over. What did you think about our memory verse this week?" The question sends Janie's heart into a rapid drumbeat against her ribs. She struggles to keep her voice even.

"I guess...I guess I really haven't thought much about it," she stammers. "I do believe in angels, though I don't think I'll ever see one."

"I think I met an angel once," Mrs. Hanover said, her voice surprisingly matter-of-fact. Janie's jaw drops.

"You did? How did you know he was an angel?" The words tumble out, a sense of instant connection blossoming between them.

"Well, first, it was a she... not he. Mr. Hanover and I had taken a trip to Nashville. We were enjoying a lovely dinner aboard the General Jackson Showboat. We were sitting next to another couple, and the woman and I promptly struck up a conversation. She turned out to be a Christian too, so we bonded instantly. Before I knew it, I was telling her all my worries about our upcoming move to Denison. And guess what?" Mrs. Hanover's enthusiasm does not give Janie a chance to answer. "She grew up in Denison! I couldn't believe it. She assured me that Denison was a wonderful town to raise a family and, if she had the choice, she would still live there. She even recommended our church. She said her husband's job had moved them away from Denison, but she went back each chance she had."

"I don't understand," Janie questions, "What does that have to do with her being an angel?"

Mrs. Hanover lowers her voice. "Everything I needed to hear, Janie, she told me... like she was reading my mind. Well, I became suspicious and asked if she was an angel sent by God to help me. She laughed and said she was the last person who would be an angel. I still didn't believe her, so I gave her my email address and told her to email me once she got home. Then I would know for sure. And, do you know what?"

"What?" Janie's eyes grow wide with anticipation.

"Well... I never heard from her. She had given me her name, so I looked all through old school records, newspapers, even old phonebooks, and I never found a trace of her! I tell you, Janie, that woman never existed... she had to be an angel!"

Janie's mind races. Should she tell Mrs. Hanover about her own encounter with an angel? Surely Mrs. Hanover will believe her, but would she keep this all-important secret? Michael's warning was serious, yet the weight of her basement angel secret is becoming more than she can bear.

"Mrs. Hanover, could we go out to the hallway? I need to tell you something."

"Sure, Janie. I'll get Ms. Barrow to keep an eye on things while..." Mrs. Hanover's words are cut short as two boys across the gym begin to scuffle. Seeing the commotion, she forgets all about Janie and runs over to break it up. Janie waits patiently, but Mrs. Hanover never returns.

***

A distant doorbell's faint ringing wakes Michael from a deep sleep. Soft footsteps cross the living room floor, followed by the muffled sound of the front door opening. He instantly dreads the high-pitched excitement in Mrs. Beardsley's voice. Of course, she is here to report something she'd found odd. Only bits and pieces of her conversation with Janie's mother reach him, but what he does hear sends a cold shiver down his spine. The basement window. He had forgotten to uncover the window! The old gal must have been more limber than he thought and tried to look in during one of her earlier trips around the house. Her voice rises in pitch as she tries to convince Janie's mother of what she has seen. Michael sprints across the room, hastily pulling the plywood and insulation from the window. Just as quickly, he dives back under the stairs and pulls a blanket over himself.

Moments later, the front door opens again. The sound of low voices grows louder as Janie's mother and Mrs. Beardsley approach the window. He peeks from beneath the blanket just as the dim glow of a flashlight passes over the glass. Their voices are barely audible, but what he does hear fills him with terror. He sinks deeper under the blanket, hoping it will swallow him whole just as the mythical whale had swallowed Jonah.

"I know I heard someone in your basement today! I knocked on your door, thinking Janie was home again, but no one answered. As I was walking around to your back door, I noticed the broken basement window, but someone had covered it—from the inside! I don't know what is going on here, but I know what I heard." Mrs. Beardsley's voice is unmistakable.

"I don't doubt you heard something, Mrs. Beardsley, but I think I would know if someone was working in my basement!" The flashlight glares brightly through the dirty window, passing back and forth over his hiding place. "I can see the broken glass, but the window doesn't look covered. I'll have someone come out and repair it in the next few days." Janie's mother assures Mrs. Beardsley.

The conversation continues as the women walk back towards the house. Michael lets out a long, low sigh of relief. Mrs. Beardsley is, indeed, trouble, just as Janie had warned. Continuing the project will be impossible, knowing she might be snooping around. The room is not finished, but it is time to leave. An unexplainable sadness fills his heart. There is no rational reason why finishing the room for Janie and her family has become so crucial except that he feels compelled to do so. But, compelled by what or who? The answer no longer matters. The situation is entirely out of his control. The man who once tried to control everything now has control over nothing.

He knows what Liz would do. He'd seen her turn to God countless times when faced with problems, but she had earned that right; she had been a good woman.

Will God listen to a man like him? Things are as bad as they can possibly be, so what harm can a simple prayer do? Falling to his knees, his prayer is simple and straightforward. "I don't know if You will hear this or not, and I'm not sure what to say except I've made a mess of things. I'm not asking anything for myself…I just want to help Janie's family. If you can figure out how to keep Mrs. Beardsley away, then I'll get the room finished and be on my way. Amen."

After Mrs. Beardsley's visit, the family finally settles down and goes to sleep, but sleep does not come easily for Michael. Not only did his empty stomach ache with hunger, but the close call with Janie's mother and the nosy neighbor left him feeling shaken and queasy.

For the last few years, the television had been his constant companion, helping him fall asleep each night. But all he has now is the Bible Janie gave him. Using the flashlight, he thumbs through the worn pages until he finds Psalm 139 again. This time, he reads past the verses Janie's father had marked for her. The last few make him sit up straight.

Search me, O God, and know my heart; test me and know my anxious thoughts. See if there is any offensive way in me and lead me in the way everlasting.

Michael is curious. Why would David ask God to examine him so closely? Was he a fool? Or was he incredibly courageous? Maybe David's life was not full of shame, unlike his own. Whatever the reason, David clearly trusted God would deal fairly with him—no matter what his thoughts or heart revealed. This man, David, fascinated Michael. He knew the Sunday School story about the brave shepherd boy who fought the giant, Goliath, but little else. With the help of notations made by Janie's father, Michael soon finds the book of 1 Samuel. Here, the remarkable story of David unfolds like a good novel. The night hours pass quickly as Michael reads more stories of David's heroic and valiant life. The pattern of David's life becomes obvious with each passage. David was faithful in his obedience to God, and God was faithful to protect him from his enemies.

Growing drowsy, Michael closes the book, leaving David's story unfinished. He has read enough to know his own life pales in comparison to David's. How foolish and impudent to think God will hear a prayer from a man like him. A man whose heart is as dark and murky as the basement where he resides.

From an early age, he was taught to control his emotions, but tonight, grief fills his heart with the sad decision he must make. He will leave the basement tomorrow with the room unfinished. Even worse, his departure will crush Janie's faith and her belief that God had sent her family an angel in their time of need. The outcome of this decision is predictable. After the money runs out, he will be caught, sent to prison, and his life will be just another wasted existence with no purpose. Tears well in his eyes, inching their way down his face. Dark thoughts consume his mind. His fate is inevitable. There is nothing or no one who can change it.

The voice is speaking again. Though barely a whisper, the message of despair is the same as before. He is weary, weak, and helpless to argue, so he reluctantly listens. Pulling the blanket up to his neck, he shivers as the cold darkness of the basement closes in around him. The voice inside his head grows louder, stronger. "No one cares about you. There is no hope. You have no hope. You aren't worth anything. Give up. It's over."

As always, the voice is right. The voice is his truth. He's not an angel but only an old, miserable, lonely hermit whose life no longer matters. He has no purpose for living. Janie will be okay. She has plenty of life ahead, filled with a loving family and a bright future. The sooner he is out of her life, the better. He has hung on to this life long enough. The best thing he can do now is save the taxpayers' money. There's no point wasting good money on housing him for the next twenty years.

At last, the voice falls silent once Michael makes his decision. He knows what he must do. Finding a piece of paper, he hastily scrawls a note to Janie, leaving it on her doll cradle. The plan is simple. He will leave early the next morning with only one item, a rope.

***

Janie's mother is late picking them up from school. "I'm sorry I'm late, kids. Why don't we pick up hamburgers for supper tonight?" her mother asks. The offer of drive-thru hamburgers is a sure sign of her exhaustion. "There just aren't enough hours in the day to get everything done before the trial starts Monday." Her mother releases a drawn-out sigh. "Looks like I will be working this weekend, too. I know the boys have their soccer game in the morning, but I will need to work at the office all afternoon. I hope Mrs. Beardsley will be available to babysit."

This is the opportunity Janie has been waiting for, but convincing Momma to let her baby sit will not be easy. She needs a plan.

The ringing doorbell interrupts their supper of burgers and fries. Janie immediately hops up to answer the door.

"Sit down, Janie. I'll see who it is." Her mother rises from the table and walks towards the door. It is Mrs. Beardsley, and she is plainly agitated. Janie moves closer to the doorway, straining to hear their conversation.

"I'm telling you, Beth, I heard someone working in your basement again today. It wasn't a saw like yesterday, but I know I heard hammering and possibly a drill."

"Mrs. Beardsley, like I told you, no one has been in my basement for the past two and a half years. We live in a large neighborhood. It could have been any house around here, but it wasn't my house you heard the sounds coming from." Her mother stands her ground against their neighbor's insistence.

"Did you recently have someone cover up your basement window?" Mrs. Beardsley's voice grows impatient.

"What do you mean? No one has covered the window as far as I know." At this point, her mother turns her back to Mrs. Beardsley, giving Janie a quick wink. "Janie, get back to the table and make sure the kids finish their burgers." Janie's relief is immense. Her mother is not giving much credence to the accusations.

"You know, after what happened last week," Mrs. Beardsley lowers her voice to a whisper, "with the bank robbery…we just can't be too careful in keeping an eye out for anything suspicious." Janie's mother's annoyance with the disruption of their evening meal is becoming clearly visible.

"Okay, Mrs. Beardsley, let's take a look." Her mother leaves Mrs. Beardsley standing at the door without inviting her inside and walks back to the kitchen. "Janie, run and get a flashlight for me, hon. I need to go outside with Mrs. Beardsley and check our basement window."

"Why? What's going on?" This was the moment Janie had feared. Her mother is about to discover everything—the broken window, the lies, the work Michael had done, and possibly Michael himself. She can only stare at her mother, eyes wide and jaw agape.

"Janie! What's the matter with you? Everything is fine. I just need to satisfy Mrs. Beardsley that no one has been in our basement. I think the flashlight is under the sink, so please run and get it."

Janie retrieves the flashlight. Thankfully, they had two since she had given Michael one the day before.

Her mother puts on her coat and heads out the door with Mrs. Beardsley. "Keep an eye on the kids until I get back," she said, closing the door behind her.

Sick to her stomach, the once delicious burger loses all appeal. This may be for the best. She will certainly sleep better tonight with a full confession of the events of the last few days, even if it means a punishment is sure to follow. Would Michael use his supernatural powers and just disappear when her mother looked in the basement window? It's heartbreaking to think Michael's project will never be completed. Her thoughts race until she hears footsteps on the porch announcing her mother's return. Janie holds her breath as her mother enters the room alone and takes off her coat. This is it!

"Well, I see why you had a scared look on your face, Janie. What do you know about that broken basement window?"

"I knew there was a hole, but I don't know how it happened." This much is true. She honestly did not know how or by whom the window had been broken. "I guess I should have told you."

"Yes. You should have told me. Does that broken window have anything to do with your torn jacket?"

Time to come clean—at least about this part of the story. "Yes, ma'am," she replies, her eyes cast downward. "I'm sorry, Momma. I was crawling under the bushes and snagged my sleeve. I should have told you the truth when it happened." It's not the whole truth, but it's a start.

Her mother sighs heavily. "You need to stay out from under those bushes until we get the window repaired. You're lucky your coat protected you from being cut. I'll have to cover it this weekend until I can afford to have a glass company come out. We certainly don't need any critters making a home in our basement."

"I thought Mrs. Beardsley said the window had been covered." Janie asks, a hint of confusion in her voice.

Her mother chuckles. "I'm not sure what Mrs. Beardsley saw. I looked as best I could, and everything looked normal except for the hole. Bless her heart, I suppose she doesn't have anything else to do except keep tabs on our house." The ringing of the phone interrupts her mother. "Hello again, Mrs. Beardsley." Her mother is silent for several minutes. "Please don't worry about it. You've been so kind to help with the children. I hope you know how much I appreciate it." More silence. "Well, have a safe trip, and please give Janet our love. I'll be praying for her."

Janie's mother hangs up the phone, shaking her head. "It seems we have a slight problem. Mrs. Beardsley just got a call from her daughter down in Fort Worth, who is having emergency surgery tomorrow. She must leave first thing in the morning and will be gone for at least a week. I had asked her to babysit you kids tomorrow afternoon while I go to the office. Now, it's too late to call anyone tonight. I guess I'll find someone tomorrow."

Janie tries to contain her immense relief, but she cannot help but smile.

"What are you smiling about, young lady?" asks her mother.

Janie must think fast, "I guess Mrs. Beardsley has something to do now and won't be keeping tabs on our house for a while."

"No, I guess not." Her mother gives her a short laugh. "But, I'm not sure that is a good thing."

Oh, it is a good thing, Janie thinks to herself. *A very, very good thing.*

Chapter 10

Friday, January 9, 2009

"Thump!" The dull thud shatters the silence, pulling Michael from a deep sleep. The night had been long, reminiscent of sleepless nights in his old recliner. He often woke more tired than rested. Only a week has passed since he'd known the comfort of his own bed, but it feels like years. Rising from his pallet, he glances at the window, barely visible in the breaking dawn. The thump had come from that direction. Pulling the thin blanket tight around his shoulders, he shuffles over to the window, his sprained ankle protesting with each painful step. There, directly below the pane, is the source of the noise—a crumpled brown paper bag. He picks it up without examining the contents. Clearly, sweet little Janie has taken care of him again.

"Oh, Janie," he groans, tossing the bag aside. "Just one more reason I must soon leave. You can't continue to risk getting caught for my sake." He is hungry, but he has no desire to eat. He whispers into the darkness,

"Thanks for thinking of me, little lady. Nice to know someone does."

He is angry with himself. He had intended to leave before the first hint of light, but now it is too late. The family will stir soon, and he can't risk exposure, especially by the meddling Mrs. Beardsley. His only option is to stay hidden, wait for the house to empty, then be on his way. With his scraggly beard and filthy clothes, it will be easy to blend in like another homeless person. If his boot does not fit over his swollen ankle, all the better. Dirty, unkempt, and shoeless—no one will suspect he is the infamous Denison bank robber from last week. His plans are simple. The money, of no use to him now, would be left for Janie's mother to discover. She would do the right thing and return it to the bank; she was that kind of woman. He has no will, so he hastily writes a few instructions on a piece of paper:

I don't have much, but what I do have needs to be sold by my sister-in-law, Leslie Graham, with the money distributed among those who need it the most. You vultures can fight it out for all I care.

The neatly coiled sisal rope, waiting patiently under the workshop table, catches his eye. He reaches for it, his fingers tracing the course strands, the rough texture a stark reminder of his intent. "Sorry, little lady," he whispers into the quiet. "Wish I could've been a real angel for you. Hope you don't let this ruin your faith. You, of all people, don't deserve this." Michael pulls the blanket even tighter around his shoulders and hobbles back to his bed to wait for the family's departure.

***

$\mathcal{J}$anie's watch alarm went off, jolting her awake. The watch, a treasured gift on her tenth birthday, rested snugly on her wrist, a symbol of newfound maturity. "You're old enough for a real watch now, Janie," her mother had announced, her voice full of pride. "I need you to help me remember all our schedules. You can use the alarm to help us count down the time until we leave for school, or you can use it to regulate how you spend your time in the evenings. You're a smart girl, and I am confident you will find other ways to use this watch."

It certainly came in handy this morning. Careful not to wake her sleeping sister, Janie slips out of bed, pulling on her robe and slippers, their thin fabric doing little to fend off the bedroom's chill. She tiptoes into the kitchen, grateful Michael had taken care of the creaky wooden floors. Inside the refrigerator, the extra lunch she had made for Michael is waiting. Each evening, it is her job to assemble the lunches, making it easy to hide the angel's meal among the others. The sudden surge of bright light from the open refrigerator floods the kitchen. She hastily pulls out the sack, stuffs a note inside, and tucks it under her robe. Cautiously, she waits one or two minutes, hoping no one has been roused by the sudden light. The house is still dark and silent. The coast is clear. Taking small, soft steps, she creeps down the hallway, eases open the back door, and steps out into the pre-dawn cold. The sun has not yet risen, but the eastern sky is already growing lighter.

Her breath frosts in the cold air as she makes her way around the back of the house.

A nagging worry had gnawed at her all night. Had Mrs. Beardsley's unexpected visit sent Michael fleeing back to heaven? Surely, God had other urgent assignments awaiting His angel. But if he is still in the basement, her note holds crucial reassurance that Mrs. Beardsley will no longer be a problem, leaving him plenty of time to finish the project.

Crawling under the bushes, she presses her ear to the small hole in the window. A wide grin spreads across her face. Muffled snoring means Michael is still here. Wasting no time, she pushes the sack through the window hole, backs out of the bushes, and rushes back inside to the warmth of her bed. Moments later, her mother's alarm sounds, and the day begins.

"Up and at 'em, sleepyheads!" her mother sings out, her head popping into Janie's room.

"I'm already awake," Janie answers, a surge of triumph mingling with her relief. She made it back in time.

"This room is freezing! Here, I'll get your robe for you, hon." Her mother reaches for the robe hanging on the back of the door and tosses it across the bed. Janie's heart sinks. Two distinct splotches of mud are clearly visible on the front of her once-clean robe. "Good grief, Janie. What in the world do you have all over your robe?" Her mother eyes her suspiciously. "Is that mud?"

Now what? Janie's mind races for a reasonable explanation. She can only stare back at her mother, horror written on her face.

"When did you go outside in your robe?" her mother presses. "And why would you get mud on it?"

"I… I don't remember," Janie stammers, stalling for time. Her mother runs a hand over the muddy spots.

"Well, it couldn't have been too long ago because this mud seems fresh. What's going on, Janie? What have you been up to?" Knowing her mother will persist, Janie decides it is time for another partial truth.

"I crawled under the bushes to see the hole in the basement window." The words tumble out, another sliver of the actual truth finally surfacing.

"I don't understand your fascination with that hole, but you stay out from under those bushes and away from that window. The last thing we need is for you to cut yourself on broken glass. I plan to cover the hole this weekend, but, in the meantime, I'd better not catch you near that broken window again."

Janie ducks her head. Her face flushes with heat. "Yes, ma'am," she replies softly.

Fortunately, her mother doesn't press her further about her early morning excursion. She hates being scolded, but she knows, deep down, she deserves it. Her mother, however, deserves the whole truth. Her eyes burn with unshed tears, thinking how disappointed Daddy would be and, even more importantly, how disappointed God must be. The thought is unbearable.

***

The family's departure is a relief. The engine's sound dwindles, swallowed by the sudden quiet that feels almost too heavy for the morning air. Michael feels a strange calm. Ending his life is not a decision he has ever consciously contemplated, though perhaps he should have long ago. But now, it is the right thing to do. The voice inside him whispers that it is best for everyone. Fourteen years of loneliness and isolation have convinced him that his existence serves no purpose. A strange sense of peace settles over him, knowing the unrelenting pain will soon end. He pictures himself in a burning building, flames at his back, no escape. Death is inevitable. He can either be consumed by the fire or take control and choose his own demise. Only the thought of Janie gives him pause, but the voice reminds him, again, that this decision is best for her, too.

The boot slips over his tender ankle without a problem. He takes a few tentative steps. The pain is still there, but manageable. A city park with large oak trees is less than a mile away—the same park where he had once taken Mandy for ice cream after his failed attempt to educate her on local history. A park bench, a local newspaper, Janie's carefully packed lunch—just the right props to create the illusion of normalcy, a man enjoying a peaceful break in the afternoon sun. The early darkness of a winter night would provide the cover he needed to "jump" out of the burning building.

Climbing out of the basement window with the aid of the step stool is easy. He crouches behind the bushes, waiting for his eyes to adjust to the bright sunshine. It had been a long week in the dark, and the sun is blinding. His eyes dart back and forth, watching the street. Most people have gone off to work or school, and it is too early for the mail carrier. Shielding his eyes, Michael steps out from behind the bushes and rounds the corner of Janie's house, head bowed, quickening his steps as he passes Mrs. Bearsley's manicured lawn. A sigh of relief escapes his lips when no shrill voice calls after him. The street ahead is deserted. He zips his jacket higher, pulling his cap down over his ears, in a futile attempt to ward off the encroaching chill that seeps into his bones. The small toolbox he carries holds the tools of his escape: the newspaper, Janie's lunch, and the sisal rope. He almost looks normal, albeit a bit grubby. But what does normal mean anymore?

Leaving the basement behind is strange, the familiar and safe darkness replaced by dangerous exposure to the stark sunlight. The biting cold keeps most indoors, yet a young woman and an elderly gentleman emerge from a nearby house, the woman's arm supporting the man as he struggles into the passenger seat of a car. Typically, a helping hand would have been an automatic reflex, but today, he can only offer a forced smile and a whispered "Good morning," his gaze darting away. It is a gamble, a chance he cannot take, the risk of a stranger's recognition from the photo in the paper, a haunting image of a man who no longer feels he deserves a place among the living.

Jones Park is much farther than he remembers, each step increasing the dull throb in his ankle. He finally reaches it. The park is mostly deserted except for a mother watching her two children on the swings, their laughter a bright contrast to the gloom clinging to him. He finds a bench at a distance and sits down, grateful to be off his foot. The morning sun, warm on his shoulders, offers a momentary illusion of peace, a fleeting thought that perhaps, just for a moment, he could be one of them, a man enjoying a beautiful day. But the persistent whisper, the voice within, piercing the calm, a cruel reminder of his purpose, pulling him back to the edge. Michael turns away, but their laughter, light and innocent, is inescapable. A few minutes later, a softball rolls to a stop by his feet, followed by the crunch of small shoes on the grass.

"That's my ball," a shy voice announces. The boy, no older than five or six, waits patiently.

"Here ya go, buddy." Michael picks up the ball and tosses it back.

The boy immediately throws it back. "Catch!" he grins widely. Michael, caught off guard, catches the ball with ease.

"Nice throw. Do you play on a team?"

"Not yet," the boy said. "But I'm gonna play T-ball this year. My daddy's the coach."

"Well, good for you. Okay, now you catch the ball." Michael tosses the ball gently, but the boy fumbles, dropping it. Before he can think, Michael is on his feet, kneeling beside the child. "Here now, don't hold yourself so stiff. You should have a little give in your arms. Keep your elbows bent and pull them into your body when you catch the ball. Let's try again." Michael throws the ball once more, and this time, the boy catches it without a problem.

"I did it!" the boy exclaims. "Hey, Mom, I caught the ball!" Michael turns to see the boy's mother standing behind him, cautiously watching the impromptu lesson

"Oh, I'm sorry," he said, a flush creeping up his neck. "Can't help myself. I'm an old baseball coach from way back."

The mother offers a small smile, a hint of unease in her eyes. "Well, thank you for helping him, but we need to leave now." She turns to her son. "Come on, Joey. Time to go."

As she leads her son away, Michael knows the young boy is in for a stern lecture about the dangers of talking to strangers. And he should. Strangers are not always who they appear to be.

The park remains empty for the next hour, but the interaction with the little boy lingers with Michael. He begins to rethink his plan to use a tree in the park. Too many young families use this park. What if a child were to find his body? The poor child would be traumatized forever. Maybe he should continue walking, heading for the open country. The only question is his ankle. He is not sure how far he can travel with the pain. His plan had been poorly thought out, but there was no other recourse. The relentless voice within hammers him with the same message.

"No hope, no choice, no one cares. No Hope, No Choice, No One Cares. NO HOPE, NO CHOICE, NO...ONE...CARES!"

The sun is high in the sky as noon approaches. Michael sees a patrol car slowly circling the park. On its second pass, he knows he is being watched, and a jolt of panic seizes him. Thank goodness for his props. Reaching for the toolbox, Michael pulls out the newspaper, pretending to be engrossed, his hand shaking slightly as he pulls out the small apple Janie had packed. He takes a bite, forcing a casual air. Out of the corner of his eye, he sees the patrol car pulling into the parking lot. Resisting panic, he calmly continues to eat the apple. Beads of sweat begin to form on his upper lip despite the chilly air. Reaching up, he pulls off his cap, exposing his face, a desperate attempt to appear unconcerned. He swallows hard. The apple, a lump in his throat, refuses to go down. The urge to run is strong, but that would be foolish; his ankle would never allow it.

The police officer sits in the car for several minutes before opening the door and getting out. Not daring to turn his head, Michael continues to munch on the apple. The officer strolls slowly across the field toward Michael, his right hand resting on his holster, a casual but unsettling gesture.

"Good afternoon, sir," the officer's voice, polite but firm, cuts through the quiet. "Wonderful day to be outside enjoying the sun for a change."

"Yes, sir. We don't get too many days like this in January. I thought I would take a break and enjoy my lunch here in the park," Michael manages to reply. The words catch in his throat, his trembling hands betraying the calm he tries so desperately to project. He forces another bite of the apple; the act is a struggle.

"You work around here?" the officer asks, his gaze unwavering.

"Yeah," answers Michael. "I'm doing a remodel project a few streets over. I keep seeing this park on my way to work, so I decided to stop by today."

"Oh, really?" The patrolman eyes him suspiciously. "Where's your vehicle?"

"My truck's over at the job site," answers Michael. "It's such a beautiful day, I walked over." Heat rises to Michael's face, a telltale blush, and he hopes his scraggly beard offers some concealment. "Care to sit down and join me, officer?" Michael moves to one side, secretly hoping the officer will not take him up on the offer.

"Thanks, but I've got to get back to my rounds." The officer turns to leave, but turns back around, looking Michael directly in the eye, and adds, "Don't know if you've heard, but we've had some trouble in the area recently. You haven't seen anyone suspicious around here, have you?"

"Not at all. A mom and her kids just left, and other than that, there hasn't been a soul in sight," Michael replies, trying to sound as relaxed as possible, despite the apple still caught in his throat.

The officer removes his hand from his holster while looking around. "Okay, well, keep an eye out if you don't mind. Let us know if you see anything out of the ordinary." A curt nod, a touch to the brim of his hat, then, "Enjoy your lunch, sir." He turns to leave, striding only a few steps before, once more, turning back around. "Where did you say your job site was?"

"Well, I didn't say, but it's just a few blocks south of here. Over on Hull Street." The words taste bitter. Hull Street. It seemed a lifetime ago he had driven that street, looking for a woman who needed a bid. If she had offered him the job, perhaps none of this mess would be happening.

"Hull Street? I'm surprised anyone would spend the money to remodel a house in that area, especially in this economy." The officer's eyes narrow, suspicion returning.

Michael reaches into the paper sack, pulls out the sandwich, and begins to unwrap it, forcing a laugh that was a bit too loud, a bit too strained. "Peanut butter... again. My little girl makes my lunch every day, but variety is not her forte." Still smiling, he holds up the note written on pink paper, which had been stuck to the sandwich wrapping. "At least she always remembers to send her daddy love notes."

The officer's face softens, suspicion replaced by a wistful smile. "You are a lucky man! My girls are grown and gone now," he said. "I sure miss those little love notes." Touching his hand to his hat for a second time, he adds, "I'll let you get back to your lunch. Have a nice day, sir."

Michael holds his breath as the officer turns and, this time, heads back to the patrol car. With one last wave, the officer disappears down the street, leaving Michael gulping for air. He must move on. No doubt the officer is headed to Hull Street to look for his truck. Michael shoves the half-eaten sandwich back into the paper sack but holds on to the note from Janie. Carefully unfolding it, he reads the message, then rereads it.

Dear Michael,

I Hope you are okay. I am sorry I did not get food for you yesterday. I no you like penut butter so I made you anuther sandwich. Mrs. Beardsley is leaving tomorrow morning to go to fort Worth to take care of her dauter. She will be gone all week so don't worry about making noise. Momma wants to cover the hole in the window this week end. She hates crawling under bushes so I will do it. But please be carefull and hide. Everything will be okay.

Love, Janie

P.S. My brothers have a soccor game on Saturday so we will be gone all morning.

At once, he remembers the words from his prayer the night before, a desperate plea for a miracle. *If you can figure out how to keep Mrs. Beardsley away, then I'll get the room finished and be on my way.*

It is too much. A coincidence, a cruel twist of fate, nothing more. It must be a coincidence. Why would God listen to him? Liz once told him there was no such thing as "coincidence." She said there were only "God-cidences." He shakes his head hard and reads Janie's note a third time. This is crazy. If it had not been for the officer, he would not have even known about the note. He lifts his eyes toward the sky, silently pleading. *Is this really Your doing, God? My mom used to say You work in mysterious ways. Well, if this is You, then it is certainly mysterious.*

He braces himself for the familiar voice, the one that had been his constant companion for the past few days, if not years, whispering promises of doom and despair. But the voice is silent. Instead, a new voice begins to fill the quiet spaces of his mind, a gentle whisper that resonates deep within his heart. "Don't be afraid, Michael. I'll be with you. Do not be afraid."

He can't explain the new voice or the sudden sense of peace that washes over him, chasing away the shadows of despair. Coincidence, or God's intervention, he does not care. School will be out soon, and he must be back before the sidewalks are filled with children. He sets a determined pace, ignoring the sharp protests from his injured ankle. The pain, once an agonizing burden, now feels manageable, almost an afterthought. Mrs. Beardsley is gone, and he has a promise to keep.

The trip back feels shorter, the steps lighter. The sidewalks remain empty, a silent passage back to the dark confines of the basement. He had entered it last, feeling trapped, a prisoner of circumstances. Now, he chooses to return, a strange sense of belonging settling over him, as though he is coming home.

***

On Fridays, Janie's mother usually collected them from school early, a welcome break in their routine. Given the upcoming trial, Janie half-expects a delay, but her mother is on time, and they are home by 4:30. The ride home is unusually quiet, a silence that leaves Janie wondering if something is wrong, if her fragile hopes for the weekend will be shattered. After the children and backpacks get out of the car, Janie's mother calls her into the bedroom, her voice weary.

"What is it, Momma?" Janie asks.

"I don't know what I'm going to do about tomorrow," she replies, the sigh deeper this time. "I've spent all afternoon calling everyone I can think of, but no one is available to watch you kids tomorrow afternoon while I work. Even Uncle Larry and Aunt Rhonda are out of town. This is not good timing for Mrs. Beardsley to be gone as well."

"I can watch the kids!" Janie blurts out, her voice a little too eager, hoping her over-exuberance has gone unnoticed.

"Not all three of them. That would be too much. But maybe..."

Janie can see her mother thinking.

"Maybe... the boys could play over at one of their friends' homes. I think it would be okay to leave Hannah in your charge. More than likely, she will spend most of the afternoon napping. Let me make a few more calls."

Janie can barely contain her excitement. The prospect of spending more time with Michael over the weekend is coming much more easily than she expected. It will not be until Sunday before her mother tries to cover the window, giving Michael time to finish the project and be gone. Soon, she will no longer have to keep secrets. It is not long before Janie's mother comes out of the bedroom, a smile on her face, a burden lifted.

"Good news! The boys can go home with Jimmy after the soccer game tomorrow morning. Jimmy's mom said you and Hannah are welcome to come as well."

"I'll just stay here. Hannah needs her nap. You know what a grouch she can be if she doesn't get one."

Janie's mother nods in agreement. "Yes, I do! Hopefully, I'll only have to work a couple of hours. If I time it just right, Hannah will never know I left. Okay, it's settled." Lifting her eyes upwards, Janie's mother said, "Thank you, Lord." Then, grinning at Janie, she adds, "Now, let's order pizza!"

***

The family comes home a little earlier than usual, but Michael is ready for them. He closes the paint can, puts the brushes to soak in turpentine, and then, with a sigh that carries the exhaustion of the day, slides into his makeshift bed beneath the stairs. The sounds of busy feet and laughter filter down, filling the basement with warmth despite the damp chill. Just a week, yet the family's nightly ritual was etched into his memory. He imagines Janie's mother, a bit more lenient on Friday nights, allowing the children to stretch bedtime a little. He is right. It is ten o'clock before the noisy house settles into a peaceful slumber.

The day's events leave Michael tired and confused, but with an entirely different frame of mind than the night before. Question after question swirls through his mind, with no practical answers. Elizabeth would have immediately attributed everything to God's plan, but Michael wrestles with the idea of a God so intimately involved in his own bewildering chaos.

On one occasion, Liz didn't have an answer right away. They had given Mandy a kitten for her third birthday, even though he was allergic to cats. She adored

200

that cat, and it loved her—as much as a cat can love a person. They had returned home from an outing to find Bailey, Mandy's beloved kitten, a small, lifeless bundle on the asphalt just past their driveway.

"Why is Bailey sleeping in the road?" Mandy innocently asked.

He knew immediately. Bailey was not sleeping. "I don't know, honey. You and Mommy go in the house, and I'll check on her."

Liz, her face pale, quickly steered Mandy into the house while he retrieved the small body with a shovel and a bag. Mandy's wails were inescapable as he walked back toward the house. He took his time before coming in, grateful that Liz, with her intuitive understanding, would be the one to comfort their daughter. She always found the right words when his mind went blank. This time, though, Liz's own face was etched with a raw grief that spoke of her helplessness. Holding her daughter tightly, Liz let Mandy cry until exhaustion and sleep took over. He would never forget seeing her little face wet with tears or the heart-wrenching sound of her whimpering with grief. Liz carefully placed their daughter in bed before picking up her Bible.

"I've got to find something to comfort her when she wakes up. Right now, I'm at a loss for words. How do you explain this kind of loss to a child?"

"Well, I sure don't know what to say," his voice brusque, uncomfortable with the display of raw emotion. "But she'll get over it. Death is a part of life. Besides, it's just a cat."

Liz frowned. His lack of sympathy obviously frustrated her. "Maybe just a cat to you, but Bailey was everything to her. I don't want Mandy's faith to be shaken, but rather, strengthened through this tragedy." Liz turned from him and marched into their bedroom, shutting the door behind her.

"Good luck," he called after her, still glad it wasn't up to him to handle the situation.

Mandy slept for a couple of hours but woke up crying for her kitten. Liz scooped her up, and they settled on the couch. This time, he knew from the look on Liz's face that she was prepared with words of comfort for their hurting daughter. Michael, despite himself, leaned in, eager to hear what wisdom Liz had discovered.

"I know your heart hurts, honey. So do mine and Daddy's. We all loved Bailey, but you loved her most of all."

"She was my best friend, Mommy!" Mandy's voice quivered, fresh tears welling up in her big brown eyes.

"I know, and she was a wonderful best friend to you. God knew how much you wanted a cat, so He picked Bailey especially for you. God also knew Bailey would only have a short time on Earth, so He wanted her to have the best home ever with a little girl who loved her so very much."

"But why didn't God let Bailey live a long time with me? I took really good care of her." Mandy's question seemed plausible to Michael. Why didn't He?

"Of course! You took excellent care of Bailey. I don't know why God didn't let her live longer, but we must trust that God allows everything for a reason—whether we understand or not. He is the One who created Bailey, and He is the One who decides when she is to come back to Him."

"So, is Bailey Jesus's cat now?" Mandy asked, wiping her cheeks with the back of her hand. A slight sniffle escaped.

"Why, yes, she is! And Jesus will take very good care of her, too," Liz replied, her voice soft with reassurance.

A wave of compassion washed over Michael, an unexpected surge of emotion. He moved to the couch, wrapping his arms around both his girls, pulling them close. "Mommy's right, Mandy. God loved Bailey so much that He wouldn't let just anyone take care of His kitty. Only a special little girl like you gets to do that. Bailey's in heaven and will be waiting for you to come up there someday so you can be best friends again."

"Can I go to 'hea-ben' tomorrow and see her?" Mandy asked, her voice hopeful.

Liz chuckled softly. "Probably not tomorrow, but someday. Right now, God has given you to Daddy and me to take care of, just like He gave Bailey to you. But we know you really belong to God and, someday, He will take you back. Until then, God wants us to love each other and trust Him in all things."

They spent the rest of the afternoon preparing a special box for Bailey's remains. They buried her beneath the sprawling oak tree in the backyard. Mandy, comforted by the thought of her kitty with Jesus, found a fragile contentment in the promise of their eventual reunion.

How easily he could slip back in time, the details as vivid as if they had just happened. Funny, Michael had not thought of that conversation in years, yet Liz's words of wisdom echoed in his mind, clear and sharp as the day he first heard them. For a moment, he allows himself to feel the raw, aching agony of his own loss.

"You trusted me to care for Liz and Mandy, didn't you, God? But I just don't understand why You had to take them back so soon." Michael begins to softly weep. "How can I ever trust you like Liz and Mandy did? Oh God," he cries, the words torn from his chest, "I desperately need that same comfort and contentment that You gave Mandy. Please, God, please." Michael prays once again, but this time with the hope that maybe, just maybe, God is listening.

CHAPTER 11

Saturday, January 10, 2009

The day dawns, not with the usual laziness of a Saturday, but with Janie's eyes snapping open as the first rays of light filter through her curtains. She lies in bed, replaying the events of the past week: the broken window, lying to her mother, finding her cradle, discovering an angel living in her basement, the close calls with Mrs. Beardsley, and, today, the chance to see Michael again. Excitement outweighs her fear of disobeying her mother's orders to stay away from the broken window. In the end, her mother will understand when she sees how God has sent them an angel to finish her daddy's project. She pictures Michael reading the note, the one that held the welcome news of Mrs. Beardsley's unexpected departure. Her smile fades, replaced by a wave of unexpected remorse. No, she did not want anything bad to happen to her neighbor's daughter. She prays a quick prayer for Mrs. Beardsley's daughter to feel better soon — but not too soon.

After a breakfast of pancakes and sausage, Janie's family piled into the car, prepared to spend the morning watching her brothers play soccer. A beautiful, sunny day warms up nicely, thanks to a slight southerly breeze. Usually, the roar of the crowd and the thrill of the soccer games captivate her, but today, Janie's thoughts constantly circle back to the afternoon, to Michael, and the promise of their reunion.

"Hannah better take a long nap today," Janie murmurs, surprised by the sound of her own voice.

"What's that, Janie?" her mother asks.

"I didn't say anything," Janie replies, her voice a little too bright.

"I thought I heard you say something about Hannah's nap. If you're worried, then we can make other plans. Jimmy's mother is happy for you and the boys to join them after the game."

"I'm not worried. Really, I'm not, Momma. I can read books to Hannah to help her fall asleep. Don't worry about us. We'll be fine."

"Honestly, Janie, I don't know what I would do without you. You are way too young to carry such a heavy load of responsibility." Putting her arm around Janie's shoulders and pulling her close, her mother continues. "You never complain, and you do everything with a smile. I don't tell you enough how much I appreciate you. There is a reason your daddy named you Janie. You are, truly, my gift from God! I love you, honey."

Janie feels the familiar lump of regret in her throat. Her mother's words, meant to affirm and soothe, instead twist with the bitter taste of guilt. She has lied repeatedly, and the only reason she has offered to care for Hannah is to see Michael again. After today, she promises herself that, once she has warned Michael, she will tell her mother everything.

***

Just as Janie said in her note, the family leaves early for the boys' soccer game, giving Michael much-needed time to work on the room. He cut the trim pieces, each with a carefully mitered corner, a testament to his father's lessons. Priming the wood is next, followed by installing the window seal, and then the trim around the closet doors.

All plans halt to a quick stop with the slam of a car door in the driveway. What time is it? Absorbed in his work, he completely forgot to watch the time. He lowers his paintbrush, then silently crawls back to his place under the stairs. A gnawing emptiness in his stomach reminds him of the half-eaten sandwich from his "park lunch", still waiting in the brown paper sack. He pulls it out, the bread now dry and crusty, but he eats it anyway.

The usual ruckus from two energetic boys is noticeably absent, yet soft footsteps still sound from above his head. A long afternoon looms, frustrating his schedule. No more work on the room until tomorrow, church morning. But if all goes as planned, he will finish the room then and be on his way Monday morning. The only snag is the possibility that Janie's mother might crawl under the bushes and fix the window herself.

Janie has promised to handle it, but can he really trust a ten-year-old? He is as good as gone if her momma looks inside.

The familiar groan of the family car backing out of the driveway drifts down to the basement, an unexpected but pleasing sound. The house is still, a quiet that promises uninterrupted work, or so he hopes. He walks to the basement window, but a sudden shadow blocking the sunshine sends him instinctively ducking out of sight.

"Hey, Michael. It's me, Janie," a sweet voice whispers. His face breaks into a genuine smile. Trusting she is alone, he lifts the window.

"Well, hello, little lady. What are you doing here today? I thought everyone had left the house."

"I brought you some food. I bet you're hungry!" She shoves a sack full of food through the window. "Momma left me home to watch my sister while she goes to work. Hannah's taking a nap, so I came out to see you." Evident from the grin on her face, she is happy to see him, too.

"Are you sure your sister is asleep?" he asks, the image of another little girl discovering him momentarily overshadows the joy of seeing Janie.

"Yep, she is. I made sure before I came out. She fell asleep on the way home from the boys' soccer game, so Momma put her to bed before she left. Momma said Hannah will probably sleep for a couple of hours. So... so I was wondering..." Janie's voice trails off.

"Spit it out, little lady. What do you wonder?" He saw the hesitation in her eyes, the worry etched on her brow.

"I was wondering...Can I come inside the basement?" she asks timidly.

His mind races. Talking through the window was one thing, but allowing her back inside? "I don't know if that is such a good idea. Are you sure Mrs. Beardsley is gone?" he asks. It seems impossible that Janie's mother would leave her alone, unprotected by the vigilant Mrs. Beardsley next door.

"Yep, she's gone. She won't be back 'til later this week." Janie peers around Michael's head. "I was hoping I could see what you've been working on."

More than anything, he wants to show her the new room, a tangible representation of her father's love and his plans for his family. He wants Janie to understand the depth of his own unexpected affection for her and her family. And, most surprisingly, he wants her to know that God has not forgotten them, that he, a man who claimed no angelic title, had been sent to fulfill her father's dream. These thoughts churn within him as Janie waits, her anticipation a palpable presence in the air between them.

"All right, little lady, come have a look," he said quietly. Reaching through the window, he lifts Janie by her shoulders and gently lowers her to the basement floor. "Well, what do you think?"

***

Janie blinks, surprised by Michael's quick agreement, expecting a much longer debate. Her eyes struggle to adjust to the muted light of the basement, which now smells of clean-cut wood and fresh paint. This comforting scent evokes vivid memories of her daddy. As her vision clears, she gasps. She is standing in a real room, complete with four freshly painted walls and a small closet.

"Now, mind you, it's not finished yet," Michael said, grinning broadly. He gestures around the room, pointing out what is missing. "I still need to add the closet doors, hang the light fixture, and then paint it all. Your mom will need to get someone to lay the carpet, but you can get a pretty good idea of what it will look like in a couple of days."

"It's... it's beautiful. How..." she stammers. "Where... how did you get all the things to build the room?" Her eyes dart around, convinced they are playing tricks on her.

"It was all right here. Your daddy bought everything needed. He even had a permit from the city. This was all his doing, not mine. I am just the lucky guy, I mean, angel who got to do it."

"But what happened to all of my daddy's tools?" she asks.

"Come on. I'll show you." Michael takes her hand, leading her out of the room and around the corner. He flips a switch, lighting the once-dark area. "See? Your daddy's workshop's still here."

Her father's heavy worktable, scarred from years of use, had been pushed against the wall, next to the sink, with all the tools carefully placed on it. On the opposite wall were the drill press and saws, all ready for action, as if her daddy had just momentarily stepped away.

"It looks just like it did before. Just a little smaller," Janie observes with wonder. "I can't believe there is still enough room for a bedroom." She steps back into the newly framed bedroom, her gaze lingering on every detail. "Daddy always said that someday he would build a room for him and Momma in the basement, but I never thought it would happen. Never ever!"

Michael's eyes soften. "Well, two bedrooms aren't enough for four kids. Maybe this new room will help ease the crowding a little. I thought your mom might take this room, leaving a room for your brothers and one for you and your sister."

"But, Michael, how will Momma get down here?" She points to the plywood at the top of the staircase. "The door's covered up!"

A reassuring smile forms on Michael's lips. "Don't worry, little lady. I'll take care of everything, including removing the plywood so the door can be used again."

"But how can you do that without Momma seeing you? Are you going to let Momma see you?" Before Michael can answer, Janie continues, her voice trembling. "I hope you are, because I need to tell Momma the truth. I need to tell her I lied." Tears well in her eyes, hot and insistent, spilling down her cheeks as her confession pours forth. "I don't understand why God would let me see you. I haven't been a good girl like

Momma thinks. I've sinned against Momma, but my daddy always said we sin against God first."

Janie crumbles to the floor, burying her face in her hands, her shoulders shaking with sobs. Shame washes over her, a heavy blanket. How can she, a sinner, stand before an angel? What must Michael think? More terrifying still, what must God think of her?

Before long, she feels Michael's strong arms around her shoulders. He kneels beside her, gently uncovering her face, and places a hand under her chin, lifting her gaze to meet his.

"Hey, little lady," he said. The tenderness of his voice only brings more tears to Janie's eyes. "Aw, don't cry, honey. You aren't perfect, and God doesn't expect you to be perfect. He knows we all sin now and then..."

Janie interrupts him. Her voice is thick with emotion. "You're an angel. You don't sin!"

A faint smile, quickly suppressed, plays on Michael's lips. "Did you know angels have a choice whether to sin or not?" Janie shakes her head. Michael continues. "That old devil was once a beautiful angel, but he chose to disobey God. He never admitted he was wrong, so God threw him out of heaven—along with all his friends who believed the same thing."

"I know about that," said Janie, wiping tears away with the back of her hand. "The devil thought he was perfect like God. But no one is perfect—only God."

"You're right. So, even angels aren't perfect, and neither are you. The important thing is admitting when you do mess up and asking God to forgive you and help you to not mess up like that again."

Janie smiles back at Michael. "You sound a lot like my daddy."

"I know you must miss your daddy very much, and I think that's why God had me come build your momma a new bedroom. Maybe God just wants to remind all of you how much He loves you." Michael's eyes glisten, looking as though he might join Janie in her tears.

"Momma said we may never understand why God took Daddy to Heaven, but we can always trust that God will take care of us. She said Daddy's purpose was to love his family and to love others, and he did both extremely well—so well that he got a promotion to Heaven! I'm just glad I'll get to see him again someday when I get to Heaven." Janie pauses, then asks the question she most wants to ask Michael. "Have you ever seen my daddy in Heaven?"

Michael seems surprised. A flicker of uncertainty crosses his features. "Uh, no. No, I've never seen your father before."

Janie's face falls, hope draining from her expression. This is not the answer she longs to hear. "Oh, well, I just thought maybe you could tell me how he was doing."

Michael hugs her. "Oh, sweet little Janie. I may not have seen your father, but, looking at you, I feel like I have! Rest assured, little lady, your daddy is happily living in Heaven now, and I know you will see him again."

Comparing her to her father is the best thing Janie has heard from Michael. She has a few more questions, but a loud thump from upstairs cuts her short.

"Oh no, Hannah's awake! I have to go." She ran to the basement window, and Michael swiftly lifted her out.

"Michael," she exclaims, breathlessly, before leaving, "It's time. I want to tell Momma the truth. When will the room be ready?"

He does not answer right away but just stares off in the distance for a moment. "Tell her Monday," he finally said, a slight pause before continuing, "but not until after you get home from school. The room will be finished. I promise." He offers her one last smile, then closes the window.

"Sissy! Sissy, where are you?" Hannah's voice carries from the back door, and Janie sees her rounding the corner of the house.

"I'm here, Hannah. I'm right here." Janie tries, unsuccessfully, to hide her frustration. Hannah had certainly put a damper on her plans to spend more time with Michael.

"Why were you under the bushes, Sissy?" The innocent question hangs in the air, and Janie feels a surge of panic. Her face, she fears, betrays her. The last thing she needs is for Hannah to recount her adventures under the bushes to their mother.

"Oh, just checking on that old broken window that Momma wants me to fix." Janie forces a calming breath, takes Hannah by the hand, and leads her back into the house. "Come on, Hannah, I'll get you a snack." She can only pray that Hannah's memory will fade before her mother returns home. Monday, she realizes, cannot come quickly enough.

***

$\mathcal{M}$ichael closes the window and walks back to his bed, grateful Janie's little sister had put an end to the visit. While he cherishes his time with Janie, her earnest questions about angels and Heaven caught him off guard, forcing him to dredge up long-forgotten snippets from Sunday School lessons. He hopes the answers he came up with are accurate. He is genuinely mystified—even impressed—with his own memory. He glances upward. Had someone given him a little help? Janie seems satisfied for now, but he knows she might think differently upon further reflection. Only time will truly tell.

Pushing his worries aside, he tears open the sack of food left by Janie. The familiar peanut butter sandwiches and fruit are there, but to his delight, a few more slices of cold pizza and carrot sticks are also included. He washes it all down with a juice box, then pats his belly, amused by Janie's "kid food" selections. Truthfully, at this point, he will eat anything and be grateful for it.

The house above remains quiet for the afternoon, except for the occasional patter of footsteps. He immerses himself in painting the new room, yet his conversation with Janie keeps circling back to his thoughts. To be compared to her father is a high compliment, but he is the opposite of her father. Her dad had been a good man, but Michael feels a stark emptiness within himself, a lack of that very goodness.

The insidious whispers of hopelessness, which had haunted him the day before, begin to loom, threatening to engulf him. Just as the shadows deepen, the new voice, the voice of hope, resonates within him, clear and steady. "Don't be afraid. You are not alone, for I am with you. Keep your promise, and everything will be okay. Don't be afraid. I am with you, and I will never leave or forsake you." Learning to listen to this new voice and trust its guidance will take time.

Janie's mother and brothers return late in the afternoon, forcing Michael to stop painting. The smell of fresh paint seeping through the old floorboards worries him, but the kitchen commotion of preparing supper offers reassurance. The smells of supper would soon overpower any telltale paint fumes. After supper, he hears the low hum of the television as the family settles in for a movie before bed. Another long, solitary evening stretches before him, and he yearns for anything to occupy his mind.

The old Bible Janie had loaned him lies open where he had left it the night before. Still curious about the story of King David, Michael picks up the book, flipping through the pages once more. He reads late into the night, fascinated by the complexity of David's relationship with God. David's loneliness and despair while hiding in cold, damp caves, fearing for his life, are reminiscent of his own plight. Except, unlike himself, David was not there by his own doing. Janie's father had carefully marked passages from the Psalms in the margins of 2 Samuel, highlighting David's raw vulnerability during this time of trial. David's desperate plea for deliverance in Psalm 142 strikes a chord with Michael:

I cry aloud to the Lord; I lift up my voice to the Lord for mercy. I pour out before Him my complaint; before Him I tell my trouble. When my spirit grows faint within me, it is You who watches over my way. In the path where I walk, people have hidden a snare for me. Look and see, there is no one at my right hand; no one is concerned for me. I have no refuge; no one cares for my life. I cry to You, Lord; I say, "You are my refuge, my portion in the land of the living." Listen to my cry, for I am in desperate need; rescue me from those who pursue me, for they are too strong for me. Set me free from my prison, that I may praise Your name. Then the righteous will gather about me because of Your goodness to me.

He rereads the last two sentences, the words echoing in the stillness of the basement.

Set me free from my prison, that I may praise Your name. Then the righteous will gather about me because of Your goodness to me.

Did I dare utter such a request to God? Michael laughs. *Even the Almighty God Himself,* he thinks, *would have a tough time setting me free from the tangled mess I've created.* The last sentence of the passage is confusing. David, despite his struggles, had clung to God's presence, a stark contrast to Michael's own descent into despair. God, it seemed, was preparing David for a purpose far grander than he could ever envision. What kind of purpose could God possibly have for him with all that had happened?

Michael's mind drifts back to the time he and Elizabeth had lost Mandy at the mall—or perhaps, Mandy had lost them. She loved to walk just ahead of them, although her mother repeatedly warned her not to get too far. Sure enough, Mandy went to the left around a kiosk while they went right, and she was nowhere to be found when they emerged on the other side. She was gone. A frantic search yielded nothing. Mandy had been schooled on what to do should she ever be separated from them: go into a store, talk to someone behind the counter, and stay put until they find her. It seemed like an eternity, but the call they hoped for finally came over the loudspeaker. Michael's immediate instinct was to rush to Mandy's side, but Elizabeth, always wiser, suggested they observe her from a distance for a few minutes, allowing the gravity of her premature independence to fully sink in.

His heart ached at the sight of Mandy sitting on a stool behind the counter, the busy clerks oblivious to her distress. Big crocodile tears streamed down her face as she anxiously watched the entrance for the first sign of a familiar face. Liz held onto Michael's arm.

"Just a few more minutes. I know she is scared and lonely, but she needs to learn we have reasons for asking her to obey." Liz grinned and whispered, "She's so much like you in that respect—independent to a fault. It's our job to keep her independence as an asset without letting it become a liability—called pride."

"Are you insinuating I am prideful?" he asked, unsure whether she was joking or serious.

"Well, if I were—it wouldn't be the first time," she said with a knowing smile. "But, at the moment, we're talking about Mandy. I have no doubt God has big plans for our little girl, and this little incident is just a part of her training in righteousness. She's learning to trust and obey us now so that trusting and obeying the Lord will come easier someday. Lessons in humility are always painful, but it's one she won't repeat again." After a few minutes, Liz whispered, "Now, let's go get our girl."

Mandy burst into fresh tears the moment her eyes met theirs. Michael scooped her into his arms, letting her sob quietly into his shoulder.

"Daddy's here, honey, Daddy's here," he said soothingly, pushing the damp curls from her tear-streaked face.

"I was scared, Daddy, but I knew you would come," she said, finally catching her breath. "I did what you said, Mommy. I went to the store and told the lady that I couldn't find you. She told me to sit and not move, and you would come. I don't think those ladies cared about me because they forgot me." She hugged Michael even tighter. "But I always know you care about me and will never forget me."

"You're right, Mandy, but you were wrong not to listen to Mommy and Daddy. We have rules to keep you safe, not to keep you from having fun. What were you thinking about while you waited for us to come?" he asked, his voice gentle but firm.

"Well, I was thinking I probably won't get an ice cream cone now since I disobeyed you." The honesty of a four-year-old warmed Michael's heart, and he could not help but smile.

"No, no, you won't be getting an ice cream cone today, honey. Did you think about anything else?"

"Yes," she answered slowly. "I thought—I will never, ever disobey you again."

Michael knew Mandy was completely sincere, but he was not naive enough to believe this was the last time she would disobey. Liz was right, Mandy learned best through experience—much like he had learned—much like he still was learning.

If David could sit alone in a cold, dark, desolate cave with no escape and no hope and wait for God's deliverance, then maybe—just maybe—he could, too. Perhaps God had brought him to this place to reroute his life, not to end it. Maybe things were finally falling into place rather than falling apart. Maybe God did care about him after all. Maybe, just maybe, God had a plan for his life, too.

Michael folds his hands while lifting his eyes upward. "I'm not a good man like Your servant David, Lord, but if You will free me from this prison…" He hesitates before continuing. He is not a man of empty words or promises. "If You will free me from this mess, I will praise Your name. I pray that Your goodness to me will somehow draw others to You. Amen."

Now what? he asks himself. *Now what?*

CHAPTER 12

Sunday, January 11, 2009

Just like the previous Sunday, the young family rises early and heads to church. Michael stands beneath the exposed ceiling beams, eyes on the basement door above. He has not meant to stay this long, but somehow, two Sundays have come and gone, and here he remains, but not for much longer. He has promised Janie she can tell her mother everything on Monday afternoon, and he is a man who keeps his promises. Where he will go on Monday is still a mystery, but after his prayer the night before, he feels confident God will show him the next step. First things first. He has a room to finish and very little time to do so.

He reaches for the baseboard trim leaning against the wall, drops to his knees, and begins nailing it in place, one piece at a time. He measures the closet opening, then swings the bi-fold doors into place. They click into their tracks neatly, folding as they should. Stepping back, he admires his work. The room is beginning to look like a bedroom.

Janie's father had bought precisely what was needed to finish the room: door hardware, plug covers, light switches, and even a light fixture. Everything down to the last hinge was there. This was a man after his own heart, thorough and exact.

Michael picks up the paintbrush, dips it in the tray, and begins to edge the trim. But the steady rhythm does not come. Not this time. His strokes grow uneven, dragging too long, lifting too soon. His thoughts keep catching on one word: Monday. By then, Janie would have told her mother. He can only imagine the panic her mother would feel, fear creeping into every room in her home. A man had been living in her basement, and only her daughter had known. A man who dared to let a little girl believe he was an angel. The brush slips from his hands and clatters against the tray. Michael leans against the wall, breathing heavily. Worrisome thoughts run rampant. He pictures the ugly scene in his mind—sirens in the distance, police officers knocking on the door, flashlights sweeping the basement like he was some kind of monster. The connection between the phony angel and the bank robber at large would soon be made. His stomach turns. He can see Janie standing there—eyes wide, heart broken, trust shattered, scarred for life, unable to forgive. He drops to his knees. What if it had been Mandy? If someone had tricked her the way he'd let Janie believe…he cannot stand the thought. Suffering the consequences of his mistakes is one thing, but having innocent people suffer because of him is unbearable.

"Oh God." The word cracks in his throat. "I don't know what I was thinking. I thought I was helping her. I wasn't. I was…" his voice falters, "…I was helping myself." He presses his forehead to the floor. "I'm not good. I'm not safe. I'm just…broken." Tears come hot and fast. Quiet at first, then louder, until sobs wrack his chest and spill onto the cold floor. "Kill me and be done with it," he whispers. "Just…just don't let me hurt anyone else. Not Janie. Not her family." His shoulders shake. "I blamed you for everything. For Liz. For Mandy. For not stopping it." He swallows hard. "But You tried. I didn't listen."

Silence falls again, heavy and still. His tears slow, but something else is leaving with them. All the grief, pain, guilt, and bitterness from fourteen years is peeling away, one painful layer at a time, leaving something fresh and raw. Something he has never felt before.

Then, without sound, the new voice comes again. Only a whisper…it is different this time. No longer the voice that fed his shame, but, instead, soft words of compassion, love, and forgiveness.

"Michael, my son…you just took the first step to freedom."

Michael does not move. He can't. He now recognizes this new voice, the voice of The Lord.

***

"Hey, Janie! How come you didn't come to Bible Club last week?" Ashley rushes over the minute Janie walks through the Sunday school door.

Janie, caught off guard, simply shrugs and makes her way to take a seat.

"Were you sick or something?" Ashley follows her to the chairs.

"Yeah, I was sick", Janie mutters, not in the mood for her friend's usual barrage of questions. "But I'm fine now," she added, hoping that would be the end of their conversation.

"Well," Ashley said, a proud smirk on her face, "You didn't get to say your verse, and now I'm ahead of you in the book!" To Ashley, Bible Club was a competition, and she was clearly winning. "Were you too sick to memorize your verse? It was about entertaining angels without even knowing it. Wouldn't that be crazy...to see an angel? I think I would know the difference between an angel and a regular human being. Mrs. Hanover said she saw an angel once. Can you believe that?" Ashley hardly takes a breath between sentences.

"Yes, I can believe that," Janie calmly replies, but Ashley is not ready to drop the subject.

"I'm not sure I believe in real angels," Ashley continues. "I guess if someone believes in angels, then they might as well believe in unicorns or fairies, too."

Janie's voice is quiet but steady. "The Bible says there are angels. So, like my daddy always said, 'If the Bible says so, then I believe it.'"

Ashley shrugs, "Maybe."

Something twists in Janie's stomach. The words slip out before she can stop them. "Besides, maybe I've seen an angel, too." Too late to take it back.

Ashley blinks, then leans in with a dramatic gasp. "Oh, really, Janie? Somehow, I doubt that!"

Janie swallows hard, trying to rein in the heat rising to her cheeks. Daddy always said to hold her tongue—but her jaw tightens instead. "You can believe what you like, Ashley, but that will all change this week," she said, folding her arms across her chest. "Be at Bible Club on Wednesday. I'll have a story you'll want to hear."

Ashley arches a brow, lips curled into a smug grin. "What kind of story? One about Janie and her invisible angel? I'll be there, but I bet you won't have a story!"

Ashley's taunts threaten Janie's usual sweet disposition, but she breaks into a sly smile, knowing the truth is on her side. "I guess we'll see on Wednesday," she said, shrugging her shoulders.

Before Ashley can answer, the teacher's voice rings out above the chatter, calling everyone to attention. Janie pulls out her Bible, but her mind is not on the verses. Her stomach drops. A sudden, terrible thought hits her. *Once Momma finds out about my lies, I could be grounded from Bible Club. I could be grounded for the rest of my life!* It might be a long time before she can tell Ashley the story of the basement angel.

***

*C*ar doors slam shut, sending Michael back to reality. His cheek, damp against the concrete floor, reminds him he's been curled there a long while. He pushes up to his knees and slides up the wall. Soundlessly, he moves to his place beneath the stairs. *One more night,* he thinks to himself. *One more night, then this nightmare will be over.*

Seeing Janie again before his departure tomorrow morning seems unlikely. Anyway, what can he possibly say that will help her in the days to come? Be strong and brave; never stop believing and trusting; remain humble and kind; be like her daddy and not like him. She might listen to him today, but tomorrow, she will forget all he said. He will instantly go from angel to criminal in her eyes. Indeed, her mother will never allow her to believe anything good about him, even if it is true.

"Write her a letter." It is a simple commandment from the new voice in his head, from The Lord.

"I don't know what to say," he argues.

"Just write and I'll tell you as you go." The voice insists.

He finds the pen and paper Janie had brought him earlier. "Okay, Lord, how do I start a letter to someone who will probably hate me? 'Dear Janie' seems so shallow."

"Just write," the voice whispers.

With pen in hand, he writes. The words begin to flow naturally with ease, and an hour later, he is finished. It is no masterpiece, but it is heartfelt and, he supposes, what God wants Janie and her mother to hear. But where to leave the note? Knowing her father's Bible will, more than likely, be the first item retrieved from the basement, Michael leaves the letter tucked carefully among the pages of Psalm 139—at the same place where Janie's father had written her birth date. It might take some time for her to find it there, but he has to trust God will direct her to see it at the right time, before hatred has a chance to grow in her young heart.

The afternoon dips into evening, casting long shadows on the basement floor. Still no sign of Janie. The upper house is quiet, except for the occasional bump from one of the kids. Sunday afternoons were always a peaceful time with Liz and Mandy. After lunch, Liz would send Mandy to her room to rest while he and Liz would lie together on the couch, discussing their upcoming week. He clearly remembers one such discussion.

"There is a seminar at church this week you might be interested in." Liz turned over and rested her chin on his chest.

"Hmmm, I doubt that. A seminar on what?" Michael asked.

"Heaven and hell."

"Angels and demons, huh?" He couldn't resist the urge to tease her.

"You might say that, but I think it's more about what the Bible says about Heaven and hell," she replied.

"I can tell you what you need to know about Heaven and hell. St. Peter is sitting at the pearly gates, checking off who comes and goes. If you are good, then you get to walk the streets of gold. If you are bad, then you head down to fire and brimstone, where the devil resides with a pitchfork in his hand. Seems pretty straightforward to me." He was ready to end the discussion, but Liz wasn't.

"How good is good enough and how bad is bad enough to send someone to hell?"

He hated it when she asked those kinds of questions because he knew his answer would not be what she was looking for. He gave an exasperated sigh, looked up to the ceiling, and then back at Liz. "I don't know Liz. We know good people and we know bad people. I suppose good people treat other people with kindness and bad people don't."

"So, good is always treating people with kindness, or just sometimes treating them with kindness." She pressed him further. "Are you kind to people who mistreat you or your family?"

"Don't back me into a corner, Liz," he warned. "I doubt I would treat someone kindly who tried to harm me or my family, so, in answer to your question, goodness is treating people with kindness most of the time."

"So, it depends on their behavior as to whether they should be treated with kindness?"

"If you say so, yeah. Can we end this discussion now?" He was growing weary of the topic.

"It's not what I said. It's what you said," she responded. "I kind of feel sorry for old St. Pete up there making all those decisions about where someone spends eternity. I hope he believes that all the times I treated people unkindly were justifiable. That entire process seems a bit arbitrary."

"Okay, you made your point, Lizzie. I'm unsure about the process for determining who goes to Heaven or hell, or if there's a true Heaven or hell. I admit I'm not sure what 'good enough' or 'bad enough' implies. I guess we can all just hope we get to Heaven someday."

Liz stared at him squarely in the eye. "Michael, we don't have to simply hope; we can know if we are going to heaven. God told us exactly how good we must be to go to heaven."

"And just how good must we be?" he asked.

"Perfect. Perfect in every thought, action, and manner," she replied.

"Good luck with that!" he said with a hint of sarcasm. "Lizzie, you are as perfect as any person I've known, but even you aren't perfect all the time. I remember a few of those stories from when you were a little vixen teenager." He gave her a short laugh. "Wish I had known you back then."

"You, of all people, know I'm not perfect. No one is perfect, and according to God, we all deserve separation from His holiness. We all deserve eternity in hell."

"I guess that makes St. Peter's job pretty easy then. We can all just go to hell!" He grinned, but Liz ignored his feeble attempt at a joke and continued.

"I know I am going to spend eternity with The Lord because He died for me on the cross. I believe He took the punishment for my sins, thereby giving me entrance into Heaven to walk those streets of gold, as you said. St. Peter doesn't make that decision. I made it when I accepted Him as my Savior. God no longer sees my imperfection. He only sees me as washed clean and pure because of the shed blood of Christ."

"That appears a little too simple and doesn't leave much responsibility on our part." Now he was completely ready to end this talk.

"It *is* simple! God says it only requires a child-like faith to accept His grace." Her eyes implored him to accept what she was saying.

"That's fine for you, Liz, but I'm just not there. I need time to process what you've been telling me." He picked up the Sunday paper, indicating the discussion was over.

She smiled and kissed him on the cheek. "Take all the time you need. God's timing is always perfect."

Funny how he remembers every word of their conversation as if it had just happened last week. Elizabeth had been a good person, especially compared to him. He is confident she is in Heaven along with their precious daughter. But, according to her, goodness is subjective. The more he contemplates their discussion, the more he begins to understand her point. Liz didn't believe she could ever be good enough to get into Heaven. She seemed to think she deserved punishment for her sins, but she also believed Christ had taken that punishment when He died on the cross. Maybe Christ died for her sins because they were few, but what about his sins? They were huge in comparison.

"Lord, help me to believe," he quietly prays. "Help me to believe I am someone worth dying for."

Michael's thoughts are broken by the slight creak of the basement window being pushed open. He freezes, not daring to even blink. Was this Janie's mother coming to fix the broken window? He waits silently, not knowing what to expect. A tiny pink arm slips through the gap, drops a small package to the floor, then carefully withdraws. That precious little arm was the last part of Janie he would ever see.

***

Home from church, Janie and her siblings trail their mother up the porch steps and into the house. Her mother gives them a weary smile before disappearing into her bedroom, one hand on the doorknob, the other rubbing her temple.

"I'm just gonna close this door for a bit while I nap," she said.

Janie blinks at the closed door. *That's rare*, she thinks. *Momma never closes her door—not unless she is really tired.*

A slow smile spreads across Janie's face. Two more days. Just two, and Momma will be enjoying her new bedroom. Michael had promised to finish today. And tomorrow, she will finally be able to tell her mother about the basement angel. No more lies, no more secrets. The weight on her shoulders is already beginning to lift.

Her mother has no plans to leave the house today, so finding a way to get food for Michael will not be easy. Janie dares not risk getting caught anywhere near the broken window. Her mother would say she was "skatin' on thin ice" as it was. But, with her mother and Hannah napping and her brothers watching cartoons, she might be able to sneak out to him unnoticed. Only if she is careful.

In the kitchen, she pulls out the sack from the drawer and starts filling it—a ham and cheese sandwich, a banana, chips, and a folded napkin with a tiny heart drawn in red pen. She rolls the top tight, just as the floor creaks behind her.

"Janie?" her mother calls.

She jumps and spins around, hands behind her back. "In the kitchen, Momma."

The bedroom door opens again, her mother's hair slightly mussed.

"I forgot we were going to look at doing something about that broken basement window. Remind me after my nap. Okay, sweetie?"

"Sure, Momma." Janie nods quickly. "But don't worry about it now. Just get some rest. I'll keep the kids quiet."

Her mother gives her a soft smile. "Thanks, honey. I know I can trust you to watch out for them. Wake me if you need anything." The door clicks shut again.

Janie slowly exhales. She slides the paper sack into the cabinet below the sink and eases the door closed. The clock on the microwave blinks 1:30. If she is lucky, she has an hour. But her luck did not last long. Hannah's door creaks open next, her tousled hair spilling over her face.

"Juice?" she mumbles, rubbing one eye.

Janie nods. "Shhh. Come on. Let's go get some." She hands her a sippy cup.

For the next hour, she shuffles snacks, settles fights over the remote, and hushes her brothers. There is no chance of sneaking out now. Not with three pairs of eyes tracking her every move.

She scribbles a quick note to Michael, folds it in half, and tucks it into the sack with the sandwich. Michael will understand. He has to.

The afternoon light fades with no sign of her mother. Finally, the door cracks open again. "Oh goodness, Janie." Her mother stretches and yawns. "Why did you let me sleep so long? It's too dark to mess with that window now."

Janie seizes the moment. "Why don't I cut a piece of cardboard and tape it over the window? That should last until we get someone out to repair it." Janie is quite proud of herself for this solution. She can easily drop the sack of food in the window and then cover it. Tomorrow, this charade will all be over anyway.

Her mother raises an eyebrow, considering. "I guess that is as good as we can do this evening." Her mother yawns again. "Okay, grab that old box from under my bed and we'll get to work before it gets any darker."

Together, they bent over the cardboard, making rough measurements and cutting it with scissors. They line the edges with duct tape and press them down tight. When it is done, Janie slips her jacket on, the paper sack concealed beneath.

Outside, the cold air bites at her cheeks. She crouches low under the bushes, the route to the window now familiar. With one quick glance over her shoulder, she slides the sack through the window, then quickly seals the cardboard over the hole. She runs her palm over it once, smoothing it down. Just one more night. Then, no more secrets. No more hiding angels in the basement.

***

From under the stairs, Michael waits, motionless, as Janie tapes the cardboard in place. Then silence. He exhales heavily. Smart girl. Clever, really. Somehow, she has managed to patch the broken window herself, saving her mother the trouble and him the risk of being discovered.

Cautiously, he steps out into the dimly lit basement, the concrete floor cool beneath his feet. The paper sack lay just beneath the window, untouched since it had fallen. He picks it up and carries it over to the small workbench where the flashlight flickers. Ham and cheese today, along with a banana and chips. His stomach grumbles in gratitude. He eats slowly, savoring each bite, washing it down with another juice box. The napkin with the small heart drawn on it is touching. He opens the sack again, hoping for something sweet this time. Instead, he finds a folded pink paper note from Janie. He opens it carefully.

> *Dear Michael,*
> *I am sorry I could not tell you good bye in person but my momma was home all day so I could not come out to see you. Thank you for everything you have done for my family. I no my momma will love her knew bedroom. You are a very specil angel to me. Please tell my daddy I said I love him when you get back to heaven. Also, tell God that I love him to. I am glad I can tell my Momma the truth about you tomorow.*
> *Your friend, Janie*
> *P.S. I love you too*

Michael folds the paper and stuffs it into his pocket. Tears flooded his eyes for the second time that day. God had used two little girls to change his life. One buried, one still full of life. Both had loved him, not for who he pretended to be, but despite who he was or what he had done. If these two little girls could love him, then maybe God could love him as well.

"I loved you enough to pursue you, Michael." Was this his voice or the Lord's?

"I loved you enough to pursue you," the voice repeats. Those words were not his own.

His lips parted. "Why?" he whispered. "Why would you love me, Lord?" His voice cracks in the quiet. "Who am I that You would love me?" There is no answer from the shadows of the room, only silence from the darkness that envelopes him.

His hand moves to the Bible—Janie's father's old, leather-bound one, resting on his bed of quilts. The flashlight battery is low but still gives enough light for reading. He is curious to find out more about God's mighty warrior, David. He thumbs through 2 Samuel until he comes to chapter 11, simply titled "Adultery." The story of David and Bathsheba's affair and the later killing of her husband, Uriah, dumbfounds him. His brow furrows. *This was the same David? The one they call a man after God's own heart? He has an affair and murders her husband? And, still, God loved him?* He reads on, eyes scanning fast now, heart pounding. He can undoubtedly relate to this story. How did he think he could rob a bank and get away with it? How did he think he could fool a little girl into thinking he was an angel and get away with it?

He turns the page to chapter 12. God's love for David becomes a little more understandable. David had done something horrible, but when confronted by Nathan the Prophet, David admitted his sin—not just against Bathsheba and Uriah—but against the very God who had anointed him as King of Israel. Michael swallows hard. The weight of it hits him. He leans over the Bible, flipping to the Psalm marked in the margin—Psalm 51, David's confession.

Be gracious to me, O God, according to Your loving-kindness; According to the greatness of Your compassion blot out my transgressions. Wash me thoroughly from my iniquity and cleanse me from my sin. For I know my transgressions, and my sin is ever before me. Against You, You only, I have sinned and done what is evil in Your sight, So that You are justified when You speak and blameless when You judge.

The words sear through Michael like fire on ice. All these years, he has been angry—angry at the world, at Liz, at God. He has worn his grief like a chain, wrapped tight around his neck, blaming the only One who can truly free him. His fingers tighten around the old Bible. Tears soak the pages. Barely able to see the remainder of the passage, he reads on:

Create in me a clean heart, O God, and renew a steadfast spirit within me. Do not cast me away from Your presence and do not take Your Holy Spirit from me.

Restore to me the joy of Your salvation and sustain me with a willing spirit. Then I will teach transgressors Your ways, and sinners will be converted to You. Deliver me from blood-guiltiness, O God, the God of my salvation; Then my tongue will joyfully sing of Your righteousness. O Lord, open my lips, that my mouth may declare Your praise. For You do not delight in sacrifice, otherwise I would give it; You are not pleased with burnt offering. The sacrifices of God are a broken spirit; A broken and a contrite heart, O God, You will not despise.

Michael's knees hit the basement floor. "I get it now," his voice trembling. "It wasn't just that David was sorry. It was that he was broken. That's all You wanted." He raises his hands towards heaven, tears streaming down his face. "Give me a clean heart, O God, give me a new spirit! I want You to see me the way You saw Elizabeth—washed clean by the blood of Jesus Christ." His shoulders shake. "You loved David despite his sin, and I know you love me the same way because You have pursued me all the way to this basement. I thought this was my prison, but the real prison was the life I lived, rejecting Your love." He lifts his face, eyes shining through tears. "Set me free from this prison I've created for myself, and I will serve You all the days of my life. Give me a purpose in Your kingdom for the rest of my life and, like David, my tongue will joyfully sing of Your righteousness, and my mouth will declare Your praise!"

At that exact moment, love breaks through the darkness of the cold basement, and Michael believes.

Years of self-pity, blame, and hatred slide off his back like a child removing their school backpack. And, to his amazement, the lonely emptiness of the past fourteen years has vanished entirely. For the first time in his life, Michael knows, without a doubt, he is free! And just as suddenly, he knows what tomorrow will bring. He knows exactly where to go. And exactly what he must do.

Chapter 13

Monday, January 12, 2009

A small cry from Hannah cuts through the quiet. Janie's eyes snap open. For a moment, she lies still, blinking into the half-dark room, her thoughts foggy. *Sunday?* No…her breath catches. *It is Monday. This is the day. Today, she can tell the world about Michael. Today, she can confess her sins to her mother. Today, Momma will get a brand-new bedroom. Today, the basement door will finally be open. But today is also the day Michael will leave.* Her joy quickly turns to sadness. After this day, she will never see him again.

Hannah stirs, murmurs, then settles again. Janie carefully pulls back the blanket and eases out of bed. The wood floors beneath her feet are cold, but she does not flinch. She silently tiptoes across the bedroom, thankful Michael has fixed all the creaks in the old floor. The ticking clock on the wall reads 5:30—a full hour before the rest of the house will begin to wake. She creeps down the hall, holding her breath with each careful step. Passing the boarded stairway, she pauses, peeking into her mother's room. A steady, soft snore rises and falls in the dark. Good. Everyone is fast asleep.

She slips out the front door and into the frosty air. The stars still shine brightly, but the faint glow of morning is on the horizon. She carefully eases behind the big bush and kneels before the basement window. Her fingers find the edge of the cardboard covering, which she has taped in place herself. She tugs. Nothing. Another pull and still nothing. Little puffs of frozen breath escape her lips, quickly dissipating in the frigid air.

"Geez," she grumbles. "I stuck this cardboard on better than I thought." Her fingers stiffen, feeling the effects of a wintry morning. She yanks again, harder this time, and the patch finally gives way. She leans close, squinting through the jagged hole. The window is locked.

"Michael," she whispers. "Hey, Michael." Dark silence is her only answer. "Michael, are you there?" She tries, once again, to peer through the hole but only sees darkness. "Michael, please, are you there?" Again, no response. She was about to call a little louder when the front porch light blinked on, flooding the yard with sudden brightness. Janie shoots out from under the bush and runs around the corner of the house. Her mother stands in the front doorway, her robe wrapped tight, hair wild from sleep.

"What on earth are you doing out here in the cold, Janie?"

Janie, eyes wide and non-blinking, opens her mouth, but no words come.

"Janie," she repeats, a little sharper this time. "I'm talking to you. What are you doing out here this time of the morning?" Silence stretches between them. Her throat tightens.

"Momma, may I please tell you later today why I'm out here?" Her voice comes out small.

Her mother steps forward. "Why can't you tell me now? What's going on, Janie? Are you okay?"

"I'm fine. I just need you to trust me and let me tell you later today." Janie blinks quickly, her eyes beginning to tear.

Her mother studies her for a moment, then opens the door a little wider. "Come inside, honey, so we can talk. It's freezing out here." The warmth of the house hits her like a wave as the door closes behind them. "I'm not going to pretend to understand what you are up to, but something's not right." Not wanting to wake the children, her mother's voice is quiet and low. "I suspect you were doing something you shouldn't. Am I right?"

Janie stares at the floor. Her voice barely rose above a whisper. "Everything is fine, Momma. Today is a special day, but I can't tell you why. What I can tell you is…" Janie pauses. She needs to tell her mother something to ease her worries. "What I can tell you is God has done something wonderful for our family!"

Her mother's brow arches. "Is that so?"

"It is," Janie said, firmer now. "God did something. You'll see."

Her mother shakes her head slowly. "Okay, Janie. After school, I expect answers. All of them. Got it?"

Janie nods in agreement. "Yes, ma'am. I promise."

"Alright then, it's time to get the others up for school. Go wake your brothers and sister—gently please."

Janie runs to the bedroom, glancing at the sealed basement doorway as she passes. *Momma will forgive everything once she sees the new room,* she thinks to herself. *Today is the day!*

***

The basement clings to the last shadows of night. Michael blinks towards the window, the soft morning light barely penetrating the gloom. Course whispers escape his lips, "I'm here, Mandy. I'm here." Groggy with sleep, he pushes himself up on one arm and listens. The voice is faint, but it is not Mandy calling him. It's Janie.

"I'm here, Janie," he calls, his voice still raspy. "I'm here." But she is gone, leaving him with only faint memories of a dream. A dream of little girls, ribbons in hair, offering him peanut butter sandwiches with outstretched arms. Mandy. Or maybe…Janie. The image quickly breaks apart as footsteps thump softly above his head.

The familiar sounds of the family upstairs fill the quiet basement. The aroma of frying bacon drifts down, a comforting contrast to the musky basement air. After breakfast, the children would cram into their tiny bathroom. Then, the muffled arguments over toothpaste would begin, a daily ritual that had, in just ten days, carved a space in Michael's heart. He has grown fond of the subtle rhythms of their lives—the small moments of their everyday routine—and will miss them greatly. He knows their names: Janie, Hannah, Benjamin, and Caleb, even their father, John. Their mother remains a nameless presence, referred to only as Momma by the children. In contrast, they are entirely unaware of his existence, a hidden observer in their lives. All except Janie.

The slam of a car door jars him from his thoughts. Time to open the doorway. His mind floods with memories of the last time he had entered through that doorway. Only a week ago, he had been a different man, fueled by self-righteous anger over Janie's father's death, but that indignant anger has dissolved, replaced by a profound realization. Their material possessions might be humble, but their father had given them a far richer inheritance—the love of God.

At that moment, the blinders fell from Michael's eyes. Lizzie and Mandy, his own lost loves, had left him the same legacy. Their physical presence was gone, yet God's love remained, ever present. He falls to his knees in gratitude, tears streaming down his face. "Thank You, Lord," he whispers, his voice thick with emotion. "Thank you for forgiving me. I'm so sorry I didn't see Your hand of love in my life during the years You gave me with Liz and Mandy. I've wasted too many years, but that's over now. I want to honor the rich inheritance You have given me. What remaining life I have, I will spend loving and serving You, O Lord, alone." Remorse turns to joy, and he continues his task.

For the final time, Michael pries the nails from the plywood barricading the basement door. He opens the door, the old rusty hinges squeaking loudly, disrupting the quiet stillness of the house. Back downstairs, he retrieves a small oil can from the workshop. "A few drops and she's good as new," he murmurs, swinging the door open and closed several times, testing its newfound smoothness. He surveys his handiwork from the top of the stairs. The repaired railing, the new bedroom, the condensed workshop—all finished and ready to be enjoyed. He sighs, his words a silent prayer. *Well, Lord, no use hanging around here any longer, I guess it's time to go.*

He descends the stairs one last time, then sinks onto his makeshift bed, his gaze resting upon the worn work boot he had arrived in. He slips it on, his ankle only slightly swollen from the injury that had led him to this unexpected place. He rises, testing his weight on his foot. "I probably can't go too far, but I can make it far enough," he concedes, a faint smile playing on his lips. He gathers his few belongings—his jacket, knit cap, and the $3000.00, pressed flat and wrapped in rubber bands. He holds on to it for a moment, then tucks it deep into his coat pocket. He yearns to give the money to Janie's mother, but that is not the Lord's plan. *There's got to be another way to help them. Just show me, Lord,* he silently prays. *Your will is my will.*

The morning sun shines brightly as he climbs out of the window for the last time. He stands for a moment, blinking at the unexpected brightness, the world outside sharp and vivid after the dark confines of the basement. Exhaling heavily, Michael looks upwards and whispers, "Okay, Lord, here we go. Lead me on the path to freedom."

***

The sharp clang of the final school bell makes Janie jump, the sound echoing through the emptying hallways. She flinches, a tremor running through her shoulders. Beside her, Emma turns, a furrow forming between her eyebrows. "Janie, what's wrong with you? You've been acting weird all day."

Emma's stare locks on Janie, her brow creases. Had it been so obvious?

"Did I?" Janie manages, her voice barely audible.

Emma's expression softens, concern replacing her annoyance. "Yeah, you haven't said much, and you barely touched your lunch. Are you sick again?"

Janie shakes her head, gathering her books. "No, just a lot on my mind." They join the crowd heading toward after-school care.

Emma's eyes twinkle, a playful smirk on her lips. "Like what?" she nudges Janie's arm. "What could be on your mind besides, maybe, Daniel?"

Janie glances at Daniel across the hallway as he stands with a group of boys. The sight does not lift her spirits. "I'm not the one who likes Daniel—you do." She points across the room. "Why don't you go talk to him?"

Emma's eyes widened, a blush rising. She mumbles, "Maybe I will," and, to Janie's relief, hurries towards Daniel.

Mrs. Hanover's voice stops Janie outside the gym. "Janie, your mom called and said she's picking you and your siblings up early. Gather them and their things and go to the front. She should be there soon. Oh, and I hope to see you at Bible Club this Wednesday."

A nervous ache starts in Janie's stomach. "Oh great," she thinks, her heart beats frantically. "I bet I know why Momma's picking us up early."

She moves through the gym, driven by a frantic energy that urges her onward. Soon, Hannah, Benjamin, and Caleb are ready, clutching their belongings. They march to the front of the school, the crisp winter air doing little to calm Janie's racing heart.

Her mother's blue minivan gleams in the afternoon sun. Her mother offers quick greetings, her gaze immediately on Janie. "Are you ready to talk now?"

"Yes, Momma," Janie replies, her voice gaining steadiness. "I told you I would, but can we wait until we get home? I want to show you something."

Her mother's eyebrows arch, a faint frown wrinkling her forehead. "I've had a long day, so I hope this is something good."

Janie's heart flutters. "It is something very good and I know you will be happy!" The drive home feels endless. The butterflies in her stomach multiply with each block. As they turn into their driveway, she can feel them practically dancing. "I'll go in first and make sure the surprise is ready."

"Make it quick, Janie, while I get the kids out of the car."

Janie burst through the door, heading straight for the narrow hallway to the basement. The door! Does it open, just as Michael promised? She reaches out, fingers trembling, and wraps them around the doorknob.

The door swings inward, revealing the faint glow from the basement window, illuminating the new stair railing and Momma's new bedroom. A gasp escapes her. She quickly pulls the door shut, a wide grin spreading as she turns to face her mother, who is entering the living room.

"That is an awfully big grin on your face," Her mother exclaims, a hint of exasperation in her tone. "Okay, now tell me what is going on."

Janie bounces closer, her excitement bubbling over. "Look, Momma. Open the basement door."

Her mother walks past Janie, her gaze drawn to the door. Her hand flies to her mouth, a sharp gasp escaping her lips as she slowly opens the door. "How in the world…who…how did…who took down the plywood? Has your Uncle Larry been here? Did you tell him to open the doorway?"

"No, it wasn't Uncle Larry, it was…" Janie hesitates, the words catching in her throat. Saying his name out loud to her mother suddenly feels like a secret whispered into a hurricane.

"If it wasn't Uncle Larry, then who did this? Who has been in our house, Janie?" Her mother's voice, laced with a growing note of irritation, sharpens with each word.

Janie remains frozen, wide-eyed, the words tumbling out of her in a rush, a dam breaking under the pressure of a week's worth of secrets. "God sent us an angel! Just as it says in Hebrews, we can sometimes entertain angels without even realizing it. I found him in our basement while looking for what Daddy was working on for my birthday. His name is Michael—he is an archangel! He used all the building materials Daddy left to build you a new bedroom. He even fixed the stairs and opened the doorway—all for us, Momma. He's not there anymore because he had to leave today. I guess he went back to Heaven. I'm sorry I lied to you, but Michael said you wouldn't understand, and I needed to keep it secret until he left."

Her mother's eyes widened, a panicked gasp escaping her lips. "Oh my gosh, Janie! What do you mean, there was a man in our basement? Tell me this is just one of your stories!" She reaches for the doorknob, her hand shaking. "You are scaring me, Janie!"

A soft whimper escapes Hannah's lips as Janie's mother fully pushes the door open, revealing the newly transformed basement. Her mother's face turns instantly ashen, a sickly pallor replacing the usual warmth of her skin. All four children peer around their mother's legs, their small faces mirroring her growing alarm.

"See, Momma. This is your new bedroom," Janie said, her voice surprisingly weak, the earlier confidence draining from her with each beat of her mother's increasingly frantic heart. She can see the fear etched on her mother's face, a fear that is quickly eclipsing the surprise and delight she'd hoped for. "It's okay. Michael did this for our family…for you."

Her mother takes a cautious step down, her gaze sweeping across the repaired railing, the fresh paint, the neatness of the room. "Who fixed this railing? Who did this?" she asks again, her voice a thin, reedy sound, panic now unmistakable.

"It was the angel, Michael, like I told you," Janie repeats, trying to infuse her voice with a conviction she no longer feels. "Michael did this."

"No, Janie. That man was not an angel. I…I don't know who he was or is, but this was no angel. Oh God, Janie, why didn't you tell me what was going on? Back up the stairs, everyone!" Her mother's voice rises to a shrill shout, the sound echoing through the small house. "I'm calling the police!"

***

The January sun beats down, warming Michael's face as he walks along the sidewalk. A dull ache throbs in his ankle, a constant companion since the ill-fated attempt to escape Janie's home. He'd done his best to appear respectable, scrubbing the dirt from his hands and clothes, knowing most people would assume he was just another homeless person. Still, a genuine smile lights his face, a radiant beam that seems to defy his circumstance. He cannot help himself. "Good morning! Beautiful day we're havin'," he calls to everyone he passes.

Most people offer a polite nod, but one lady, pushing a baby stroller, stops. "Good morning to you! You're right, it is a beautiful day!"

The little boy in the stroller, barely more than a year old and bundled from head to toe, looks up at Michael with wide, curious eyes.

"Zachery, can you say hello to the nice man?"

The little boy gives him a shy smile. "Hey-wo," he replies, burying his face in the blanket tucked neatly around him.

"Good to be out and about after all that nasty weather last week," said Michael, his voice surprisingly bright.

"Yeah, it's also good to be out again after the recent bank robbery. Hard to believe something like that could happen…right here in Denison! I'm sure you heard how awful it was. That poor bank teller, Mrs. Porter, was unable to sleep for a week. I was afraid to go outside for a while myself, but decided I wasn't going to be held captive in my own home. Let's just hope that horrid man is long gone by now."

Michael's smile vanishes. He has not considered the ripple effect of his actions beyond Janie and her family. The thought of anyone living in fear because of him only adds to his guilt and shame. The image of Mrs. Porter's terror-stricken face flashes in his mind, sharp and clear.

Heat rises to his face, a flush that he feels certain is visible. He clears his throat, trying to sound casual. "Well, I'm sure he is gone by now as well."

"Denison is such a sleepy small town. Hard to imagine someone could rob a bank and get away with it. Oh well, things seem back to normal now. Guess we'd better get on with our shopping. Wave 'bye-bye' Zachery."

The little boy, with a look of serious concentration, holds up his chubby hand and makes a tiny, fluttering motion. "Buh-bye.'"

"Bye-bye," said Michael, holding the door open for them as they entered the store, his cheerful façade shattered.

The words of Psalm 51 come to mind as he continues down the sidewalk, the weight of his actions heavy on his shoulders.

"'Restore to me the joy of Your salvation, and sustain me with a willing spirit,'" he whispers. "'Then I will teach transgressors Your ways, and sinners will be converted to You. Deliver me from blood-guiltiness, O God, the God of my salvation; then my tongue will joyfully sing of Your righteousness'…Amen."

With each step, the feeling of freedom grows once again, a tangible lightness settling in his heart. More determined than ever, he marches on.

The building stands before him, unassuming and unremarkable. Functional is the word that comes to mind. He stops across the street, watching the ebb and flow of people entering and leaving its doors. He has no idea how long he stands there, lost in thought. He glances upward. The sun is directly overhead now, leaving him to guess it is getting close to noon. "Better get this over with." He speaks in a whisper, barely audible. He crosses the street with deliberate slowness, each step a conscious act, then climbs the steps to the door. The sign on the glass simply reads "City of Denison Police Department." He pushes the door open, takes a deep breath, and steps inside.

The uniformed officer behind the information desk does not look up, engrossed in something on the screen before him. Michael stands, waiting. He clears his throat.

"Yes, sir. What can I help you with, sir?" said the officer, still not looking at him.

Michael hesitates. Did he really want to do this? Had he truly heard from God? His palms begin to sweat, his heart beating rapidly. He can turn and walk away… right now. "God give me strength to do what You ask," he prays silently, a desperate plea.

"I believe you might be looking for me," Michael finally answers, his voice quiet, almost lost in the hum of the room.

The officer's head snaps up, his gaze finally meeting Michael's. "And who might we be looking for?"

"My name is Michael. Michael…" He stops speaking, closing his eyes. A strange irony washes over him. His last name. It had not occurred to him until this moment. "Oh God," he thought, "You have such a sense of humor." The words of Psalm 139, the scripture Janie's father had earmarked for her birth, come to mind.

For You created my inmost being; You knit me together in my mother's womb. I praise You because I am fearfully and wonderfully made; Your works are wonderful, I know that full well. My frame was not hidden from You when I was made in the secret place. When I was woven together in the depths of the earth, your eyes saw my unformed body. All the days ordained for me were written in your book before one of them came to be.

Lord, You knew me before I was even born, and You knew the name my precious mother would give me, and You knew what it would take for me to give my life to You. Now, I know you are with me, and You will never leave me. Okay, Lord, here I am, he continues his soundless prayer. *Do with me as You will.*

The officer's impatience is evident in the subtle drumming of his fingers on the desk. "So, your name is Michael. Michael who and why are we looking for you, sir?"

Michael opens his eyes and smiles politely. "DeAngelo. My name is Michael DeAngelo."

The officer smiles sarcastically, rolling his eyes. "Okay. So, you are 'Mike the Angel'. But you still haven't told me why we are looking for you."

Michael hesitates, not from fear, but from a profound sense of peace. All fear has vanished, replaced by a deep, unwavering calm unlike anything he has ever experienced. A peace that can only have come from God.

He inhales deeply, then, quietly, he speaks. "I'm Michael DeAngelo...the man who robbed the bank."

CHAPTER 14

The sun streams through Janie's bedroom on Tuesday, a sharp contrast to the grey uncertainty that has filled their home since the previous night. Neither Janie nor her mother slept much. Janie doesn't go to school on Tuesday, and her mother doesn't go to work. By the time the police left the night before, it was late, and her mother had a headache. Uncle Larry brought them hamburgers, but her mother was too upset to eat.

"Don't worry, Janie, your mom will be fine by morning." Uncle Larry's voice was a soft comfort, his hand gently patting her shoulder. "You can help by getting your brothers and sister to bed this evening. I'll come by tomorrow and pick them up for school, but your mom wants you to stay home with her."

Confusion swirls within Janie. She overheard the policemen talking to her mother about the man who had turned himself in to the police station earlier that day.

"Ma'am, you don't need to worry. You're safe now. This guy turned himself in and admitted everything.

He's locked up and not going anywhere." The officer's words, meant to comfort her mother, deepened Janie's bewilderment.

Were they talking about Michael? The thought sent a jolt through her. *Why would he turn himself in to the police? He hadn't done anything wrong.*

Her mother had offered little explanation before retreating to her bedroom, the new basement door remaining tightly shut. "We will talk about all this in the morning, honey. Right now, we both need to get some sleep."

Janie desperately wanted to calm her mother's fears. *If only Momma could see what Michael did for our family,* she thought, *then she wouldn't be so scared and upset.* Her only solace was the promise of a new day, a fresh opportunity to tell her family more about their angel, Michael.

The next morning, Janie has her siblings ready for school just as Uncle Larry's car pulls into the driveway. She waves goodbye, a slight pang of loneliness in her chest as they drive off, then walks back inside. Her mother is standing in the living room, still dressed in her robe.

"Let's sit down, honey." Her mother pats the sofa beside her. Janie obediently sits, her gaze fixed on her mother's drawn face. "First, I am not angry with you. I'm just glad you are safe." She pulls Janie into a tight embrace, a wave of relief washing over Janie. "I don't think you have any idea how dangerous this man was. Janie, he robbed a bank! Remember when the police officer came by the night we got home from Grandmother's house?"

Janie nods, a knot tightening in her stomach.

"It was to warn us that a man had robbed a bank on Main Street, but the police were unable to find him." Janie gulps as her mother continues. "He saw we weren't home and broke into the basement to hide out."

Janie's eyes widen, and she inhales sharply.

"You found him and, I guess, he pretended to be an angel so you wouldn't tell anybody."

"But Momma," Janie interrupts, her voice a desperate plea, "his name was Michael—just like the archangel in the Bible. He was really nice, and he never did anything to make me feel afraid. He wanted to help our family, not harm us!"

"Did this man actually say he was an angel?" Her mother's gaze was sharp, unwavering.

Janie pauses, searching her memory. "No, he didn't say anything like that. I just guessed that's who he was."

"Oh, honey, he took advantage of you being a child. I don't think that makes him a nice person. In fact, it makes him a very bad person."

"But he read the Bible while he stayed in the basement. I gave him Daddy's Bible to read." Janie continues her argument for Michael. "He…"

"You did what?" Her mother inhales sharply. "You gave him your father's Bible? Oh, Janie, how could you?" She jumps up, her eyes wide with alarm, and runs to the basement door. She turns, a worried glance darting towards Janie. "Daddy's Bible is precious to me. If he took that…"

She flings open the basement door and sprints down the stairs, Janie scrambling behind her. Her mother stops abruptly at the foot of the stairs, her breath catching in her throat. She stands in silence for several minutes, her gaze sweeping across the transformed room, her eyes wide with a mixture of disbelief and awe.

"Oh, Janie. What did this man do?" Her voice is barely a whisper, a soft sob escaping her lips as she slowly steps down. "What did he do?"

"I tried to tell you, Momma. He built a bedroom for you. Look, he also fixed the railing where Daddy broke it. And look over here." Janie runs ahead of her mother, her voice fills with excitement, her earlier dejection fading with each step she takes. "He kept Daddy's workshop even though it's a little smaller now." Janie can't help but grin. "Michael told me he fixed our old squeaky floors, too."

Her mother continues to stare in amazement at the revamped old basement. "This room…this bedroom… it's beautiful. I had no idea…no idea, Janie. How did he do this? Why did he do this for us?"

"Because God sent him to help us. Isn't that what angels do?" Janie smiles, pointing under the stairs. "Look, Momma, there's Daddy's Bible!" Tucked neatly away among the blankets is the familiar leather-bound book. "I knew Michael would leave it here for us."

Janie reaches under the stairs and lovingly picks up her father's old Bible. As she hands it to her mother, a folded piece of paper falls out, gently floating to the basement floor. Janie instinctively bends down and picks it up. The note is addressed simply *To Sweet Janie*. Before she can read a word, her mother's hand reaches out.

"Give it to me, Janie." Her mother's voice is firm, commanding.

"But it's for me, Momma," she pleads, clutching the note tightly. "I think it's from Michael."

"All the more reason why I need to see it. Now, young lady!" The sharpness in her mother's voice leaves no room for arguing. Reluctantly, Janie hands the note over. Never taking her eyes off Janie, her mother slowly unfolds the crumbled paper, then she begins to read silently. Though the time is brief, the change in her mother's expression is undeniable. The worried lines etched on her forehead soften, her frown fades, replaced by a softer, more thoughtful expression. Janie holds her breath, praying her mother will let her read the note as well. After a few minutes, her mother folds the note and hands it back to Janie.

"You're right, Janie. Michael left this letter for you. After you read it, come upstairs again so we can talk."

Her heart beats fast as she takes the letter, her fingers trembling. Carefully unfolding it, she begins to read.

> *Hey Little Lady,*
>
> *I know you are probably feeling pretty bad right now, and I don't blame you. As it turns out, I am not who you thought I was, and I hate knowing I disappointed you. All I can ask is that you don't let what happened this past week ruin your trust in God, your family or anyone else. People may tell you I am a bad person, but I'm not. What I did was bad, for sure, but I am not a bad person. I made a huge mistake, but I know God has forgiven me.*

I also know He has forgiven you for any lies you told on my behalf.

Janie, I want you to know that God allowed me to make all these mistakes because He wanted me to hit rock bottom so He could lift me up. He has set me free in more ways than one. Thank you for bringing me your Daddy's Bible. I read it almost every night and God showed me His love for me through His Holy scripture. God also showed me His love by letting me meet such a precious young lady as yourself. I don't quite know what will happen to me in the future, but please know that I intend to do what God wants from here on out. I am through running from the law and, more importantly, running from God. I hope you can find it in your heart to forgive me someday. Janie, this is what I truly know—you, little lady, are the angel!

Love always,
Michael DeAngelo
P.S. Thanks for all the peanut butter sandwiches.

Janie tenderly folds the letter, tears blurring her vision. She closes her eyes, the tears spilling freely from beneath her dark eyelashes. It does not matter what anyone else thinks of Michael. She knows the truth. "I forgive you, Michael, I forgive you," she softly whispers. "You will always be an angel to me."

EPILOGUE

Monday, November 23, 2009

Michael stares at the bank statement, his brow furrowed. Thirty thousand dollars. He had expected only a small amount, barely enough to clear his name. Instead, a substantial sum remained even after the lien on the house, the realtor's cut, and his lawyer's fees had been deducted. He presses his lips together, letting a silent whistle escape his throat. "Not bad," he murmurs, a slow smile spreading across his face.

He remembers Liz's favorite phrase, "a God thing," and for the first time, he truly understands it. Who else could deliver a cash buyer for a house that was falling apart, a house sold "as-is"? The thought brings warmth to his chest. He glances at the narrow slits high on the cell wall, reflecting. *Bars on the windows, but my heart feels free.* He exhales deeply, whispering, "Thank you, Lord."

The money, he knows, is not meant for him. It is a gift, a tool in God's hands. He grabs a pen and a sheet of paper. Phones and the internet are luxuries no longer available to him, so he needs to write to Joe, his lawyer.

Dear Joe,

My sincerest thanks for handling the sale of the house and for settling my debts. The remaining balance of $30,000 is to be deposited directly into your employee, Bethany McCuistion's, bank account, as we discussed. Please let me know when this has been completed.

Sincerely,

Michael D'Angelo

He rereads the letter before adding it, along with those from his fellow inmates, to the outgoing mail. Leaning against the concrete wall with his arms folded behind his head, a genuine smile appears. Thanksgiving, the day of gratitude, he thinks, is going to be great this year. It is all just a matter of perspective.